WITNESS
THE

Luke 1:37
For Nothing will be
Im Possible with God!
Acts 1:8
GAl. 2:20
Rev. 12:11

The Witness is a powerful story of God's love, and His willingness to rescue, redeem, and restore even the worst of sinners. Pastor Robert's story is a great example of God's mercy, grace, and love that will encourage your faith and show the hope of Christ even in the darkest of times.

Justin Murff
International Grants & Foundations Manager
Christian Broadcasting Network

This riveting and amazing story...is akin to a James Bond movie. Robert gets in some major scrapes and you are wondering how or if he will survive, but somehow he does. Once you start the book, it's hard to lay it down.

Bill and Ellie Dooner
Entrepreneurs

Robert is as unlikely an evangelist as Paul was an apostle... His simple culminating statement is, "If God can save me, he can save anyone."

Brian Swiggart
The Community at Lake Ridge

Robert's testimony will help those who struggle with forgiveness, feel unworthy of God's grace, and inspire others to move forward in finding their ministries.

Paul Mints
Lead Pastor, The Community at Lake Ridge

WITNESS
THE

A tale of the Life and Death
of a
MAFIA MADMAN

ROBERT BORELLI
and H. Scott Hunt

The Witness

by Robert Borelli and H. Scott Hunt
Copyright © 2014, 2022 Back To Acts Ministries, Inc.
All rights reserved
Available from Amazon.com and other retail outlets

Third printing, 2023

ISBN: 978-1499108521

Connect with Robert

www.robertborelli.com
www.facebook.com/thewitnessbook

This book is dedicated to
Mary, Robert's mother, and
to all praying mothers who
never give up on a wayward
child.

PROLOGUE

Summer of 2010
Age 55

Robert sat on the living room sofa, nurturing his fourth cup of coffee, dressed but not quite ready to leave for his valet job at the airport. He wore his usual black slacks and yellow polo shirt with the logo of the valet company printed across the left breast—the only other uniform he ever wore besides prison jumpers.

It was June, but way too hot, even by Texas standards. Just the thought of working in the summer heat, running after cars and dealing with terse, non-tipping customers, drained him.

He stared at his cup for a while, weighing all the thoughts on his mind: lots of bills and not enough money to pay them, packing a lunch, letting the dogs out, and mundane exercises meant to maintain the appearance of a normal life.

Normal?

The thought bordered on incredulous, sending him back to a time when he was about six years old. It was Christmas. All the family on his mother's side gathered at his Aunt Rosie's house for the big dinner and festivities. The kids were running around the house, getting yelled at when something crashed or someone got hurt. The women were in the kitchen, cooking fish, shrimp, and pasta. Pies and cakes waited patiently on a side table. The men gathered around his grandfather in the living room, drinking various libations, telling jokes, and grabbing at the kids as they ran by. Uncle Barry was blinding everyone with the light from his 8mm video camera as he recorded the event. Later on, Santa

Claus came with a bag and handed out presents to everyone. There was dancing and lots of drinking.

The pleasantness of Robert's early childhood was a dream, an ideal normal for a child, but it wouldn't last for long. Shortly, Robert began a migration to a very dark place where eventually *normal* included pounding a guy's face until he was unconscious, or shooting a friend in the head because he thought he was stealing from him. *Normal* was extinguishing portions of his memory by binging on drugs for days at a time or gambling away thousands of dollars that weren't even his. Distrust, paranoia, hatred, arrogance, greed, deviance, womanizing, addiction—these were some of the elements that represented his *normal* for a long time.

Who was that guy?

He's dead, Robert reminded himself.

Shaking the thoughts of his past, he returned his focus to what was really pressing him, what he had been avoiding, glaring at him from across the room—the opened package sitting next to the TV.

His feelings toward the package were bittersweet. He knew its contents were precious, but his memory chose to punish him by hovering above the shadowy realm that used to be his world, forcing him to look into his past, seeing the many times and many ways he had messed up. Unworthiness laced with remorse had overwhelmed him, so he set the opened package next to the TV.

Two days later, his feelings were the same, and he doubted they were on the verge of changing soon.

No more stalling.

He set his coffee down, went to the bulky manila envelope, and removed its contents.

In his hand were three DVDs. He slipped the first disc into the DVD player and eased into the sofa again, holding his coffee in both hands. After a few seconds, the screen popped up on the TV, and he clicked the remote to choose the first selection. As Maurice Chevalier began to sing "Thank Heaven for Little Girls," photos of his daughter Briana flashed across the TV screen. He looked into the big brown eyes of the precious child, watching frame-by-frame as she grew up. By the time he got to the end of the DVD, his stomach was in knots. The many images of his daughter transforming into a young lady didn't include a single picture of him.

While he watched the slideshows on the first two discs, he recalled his daughter as a baby—just seven weeks old. He had an argument with her mom. He couldn't remember what the argument was about—maybe his drug or alcohol abuse, or his lack of an active role in his new daughter's life. Whatever the reason, he chose to walk away instead of staying and working things out. Within an hour, he was high on crack, and his role as an absentee dad began.

Several years later, he had a conversation with her, which had played in his head ten thousand times since then. At the time, he was locked up at Rikers Island, awaiting trial for crimes that could put him behind bars for a very long time. His daughter wasn't old enough to realize how bad a father he was. He had done nothing to protect her, provide for her, or any of those things a good father does. As her fourth birthday neared, Robert phoned her. During the conversation, Robert heard the distress in her voice. Soon, she was crying.

"Sweetheart," Robert said. "What's wrong?"

She sobbed, not saying anything. Finally, she settled down enough to speak. "Daddy, why don't you come see me?"

Her words were torpedoes, slamming into his heart and sinking him into the dark depths of shame. He wanted to respond, but how could he? How could he explain selfish decisions that had driven him farther away from her, landing him where he could no longer see her?

Now, after years in prison and hiding out as a government witness, he watched the special moments in her life, which he had missed. There was the picture of her holding an *Elmo* book on the set of *Sesame Street* and one where she was wearing a Dalmatian puppy costume and didn't seem happy about it. In one picture, she was waiting to take communion for the first time, dressed in a white dress, looking like a miniature bride. Several photos were with father figures. A bunch showed friends he had never met and boyfriends he never got to shake down. As each photo flipped to the next, his choices in the early part of his daughter's life haunted him. Her little voice bounced around in his head, saying, "Daddy, why don't you come see me?"

The third DVD was a video of her Sweet Sixteen party, held at Villa Russo, an upscale restaurant in Queens. Briana arrives at the restaurant in a limousine, wearing an elegant pink gown and tiara. Inside the restaurant, she, family, and friends are dancing, eating, and drinking. Near the end of the video, Briana, gracefully basks in the attention as she lights seventeen candles. Sixteen represent the important persons in her life. The seventeenth was in memoriam for those she loved who had died. She starts the dedication by lighting candle number one with her mother, Lauren, the one person who had always been there for her. She dedicates the second candle to her aunt. The third goes to a boy she said was like a little brother to her. One by one, she dedicates candles to relatives and friends, both living and deceased. Robert never expected one of those candles to be dedicated to him, but he held on to a glimmer of hope that she might mention him, or at least his mother. For whatever reason—fear of someone making a connection between the two of them or just the sobering fact that she had no emotional attachment to him—his name never came up.

Robert was crushed, knowing he was getting what he deserved. He pressed the power-off button and set his empty coffee cup on the table. For the next fifteen minutes, he cried nonstop—tears of regret and anger. Not a single tear belonged to him. They were all shed for his daughter, a belated birthday gift.

His hope was for a fresh start with this beautiful girl, who deserved the best a father could give, but he knew that was impossible. No, it had to start where it was, with no roots, in the shadow of the ugliness and pain, fighting to prove he was more than the less-than-stellar reputation preceding him.

As his habit had been for the past twelve years, he bowed his head and referenced the source of his strength. "Father God," he said, "protect her. Help me restore the relationship with her like you did with me. Show me once again that it's never too late."

Robert wiped his face with the back of his hand and walked to the sink, where he rinsed his coffee cup. He grabbed his car keys off the kitchen countertop and left for his job, parking cars in the searing Texas summer heat.

PART I

A LITTLE RASCAL

ONE

August 1963
Age 8

F rankie, come this way," Robert yelled.

"Shh!" Frankie caught up to Robert and thumped him on the arm. "Shut up, or they'll hear us."

It was the summer of 1963. While soothing a country still coping with the fallout from the missile crisis, President Kennedy was bumping chests with Cuban dictator Fidel Castro. On the other side of the world, the United States' involvement in another country threatened by communism—Vietnam—was creating tremendous tension, with the uncertainty of war looming.

Robert and his brother were not aware of the volatile situation of the world in which they lived, nor were they concerned. To them, their world consisted of a small Italian neighborhood in Brooklyn, centered on Fulton Street and Rockaway Avenue and extending a few blocks in every direction from their home. They had no time to worry about wars or rumors of wars with other countries. Where they were, they had plenty of their own battles to deal with. Summer vacation was in session, which was more important—a time when kids had no agenda, no schoolwork, and nothing on their minds except having fun. With summer coming to an end, they wanted as much play time as possible.

From the other side of the apartment building to the elementary school PS 155, all they were interested in was the sneak attack they were about to unleash on unsuspecting victims.

Even though most of the kids in the neighborhood attended the Catholic school several blocks over, in another neighborhood, Public School 155 was where they all liked to hang out during the summer. It was similar to most of the other buildings in the area: four stories high, arched windows with no ledges, and little architectural details. But its appeal was more than its façade. To the teenage girls, it was a place away from home where they could talk about crushes and the latest trends without parents or younger siblings listening in on their conversations. For the teenage boys, it was where the girls were. For the younger kids, it was the ideal site for a game of hide-and-seek.

Robert was eight, and Frankie was a year older. They had an idea what was happening in the outside stairwell of the school, so as they got closer, they quit talking and snuck up along the wall. They heard voices. One stood out from the rest. Robert and Frankie both tipped their heads up and sniffed the air like hound dogs and smiled, their suspicions now verified. They crept a little closer, until they were right next to the stairwell but still out of sight. As they heard the screech and roar of the elevated train nearby, Robert and Frankie nodded to each other, jumped out, and yelled.

All the girls hanging out in the stairwell screamed—except their sister Betty. After the noise of the train had subsided, she said, "Frankie! Robert! What are you doing here?"

The two boys laughed, slapping each other on the back for successfully scaring Betty's friends.

"That's funny," Robert said, knowing they had caught her doing something she wasn't supposed to be doing. "We were about to ask you the same thing."

"None of your business."

"Maybe not, but it *is* Mommy's business."

Their mother was the backbone of the family. Despite the small budget she had to deal with, she kept all five of her kids well-fed and clothed. She was also the disciplinarian and never hesitated to keep her kids in line.

Betty brought out the cigarette hidden behind her back, stared at Robert and Frankie for a second, and took a long drag.

Man, she is cool, Robert thought. He remembered the commercials on TV of good-looking girls and well-built guys running around the beaches, enjoying the sun and surf, smoking Bellaire cigarettes.

"I'm almost fifteen." Betty blew out a stream of smoke that curled back on itself and then dissipated into the brightness of the sun. "I can smoke if I want."

"Okay." Robert shrugged. "Come on, Frankie."

They headed toward their apartment building.

"Wait!" Betty stepped down from the stairs, crossing her arms as she planted herself in front of them. With squinted eyes and a smirk, she said, "What do you want?"

The brothers turned and walked back. "Teach us how to smoke. Like *you* do."

"What? Like I do?"

"Yeah, you know. Cool like."

Betty was tough—not just tough for a girl, but tough by any standard. Up until she was about fourteen, she was a tomboy who loved to play sports. She had a temper. All the kids in the neighborhood had either seen its fury or experienced its wrath. Even the boys were afraid to fight her.

Robert was known as "Betty's little brother." Even though he never let her know it, he was okay with that. He knew he could count on her to look after him, despite his pesky, little-brother ways. When the neighborhood kids played punch ball, Betty would always pick Robert when she was captain, despite his being the smallest kid on the block and unable to play very well. Now, even though she was more into flirting with boys than fighting them, everybody still respected her. More than anything, Robert wanted respect. In a way, he wanted to be like her, which meant learning how to smoke like she did. With that in mind, he had devised the blackmail scheme and included his brother in his plans.

Betty looked around and uncrossed her arms, the cigarette dangling between her fingers. "So that's it? That's all you want?"

Robert and Frankie nodded.

She scoffed and shook her head. "Mommy'll kill me if she finds out I let you two smoke."

"She'll kill you if you don't," Frankie said.

Betty's friends stood nearby, taking in the scene, wondering its outcome. Her best friend, Rosalie, said, "Just do it, Betty. Give the little jerks what they want so they'll leave us alone."

Betty looked at Rosalie, then turned to the boys. "You're little brats. You know that?"

Frankie laughed and nudged Robert.

"After you smoke, you're outta here. Got it?"

"We got it."

Betty reached down to the step, picked up her cigarette pack and shook two of them out.

Robert took one, and Frankie took the other. Robert put his between his lips while Frankie looked his over.

Betty popped Frankie on the shoulder. "What? You the health inspector or something? Put the thing in your mouth already." From the book of matches in her back pocket, she tore out one and lit the cigarettes.

Robert was apprehensive. As he sucked in, he didn't draw the smoke into his lungs. Apparently his brother did. Frankie started gasping and choking.

Robert and Betty laughed.

"Not such a tough guy anymore, are ya?" With the two fingers holding her cigarette, Betty pointed at Robert. "And you? You look like a fish blowing bubbles."

Robert stopped laughing.

Rosalie threw down her cigarette and squished it into the pavement. "I'm glad they're your brothers and not mine. Listen, I gotta go anyways. Genie's coming over." She was referring to Gene Gotti, her boyfriend and one of Robert's heroes.

"I saw him yesterday," Robert said.

Rosalie glared at him. "And?"

"I don't know. I just saw him, that's all."

After Rosalie and the rest of the girls were gone, Robert and Frankie finished their cigarettes. Frankie didn't look too good, and Robert felt just as bad as Frankie looked.

Betty noticed. She reached into her jeans pocket, pulled out some coins and handed them to Robert. "Here, go get yourselves a Coke. It'll make you feel better. Get some breath mints too."

Robert took the coins and slowly walked with Frankie to Jerry's, a neighborhood candy store. His head felt light, but not in a good way. To avoid getting too dizzy, he found it was best to keep his head down.

Halfway there, Frankie stopped in the middle of the road. "Robert, I'm gonna—" Before the sentence was complete, he made a deposit on the street in three equal installments.

Robert's stomach churned as he stood to the side, trying not to do the same. "Come on, Frankie. You gonna let one little cigarette make you do all that?"

"Shut up." Frankie straightened, his face drained as he wiped his mouth with his T-shirt.

When they got to Jerry's, Robert bought two Cokes and some breath mints. He handed a Coke to Frankie. As they sat in the shade of the store's overhang, they both downed their drinks without saying anything. The nausea soon subsided, and they headed back to their home on Fulton Street.

Robert handed Frankie one of the mints. "Here, suck on one of these."

Frankie popped the mint into his mouth, and Robert did the same. As they turned onto Fulton Street, red lights were flashing, and a crowd had gathered out in front of their apartment building. Robert ran the rest of the way, anxious to see what was going on, Frankie not far behind. The ambulance and police were there, and people were coming in and out of the building. Robert pressed through the crowd and went inside. Part of the stairwell banister leading to the second floor was broken and lying on the first floor. His grandfather, who was living with his family at the time, was leaning against the wall at the landing between the first and second floor, wheezing. The medics were trying to help him.

Robert's grandfather was very special to him. He and his family had moved into his grandfather's neighborhood when he was five, after the death of his grandmother. Soon after that, his grandfather moved in with them. He was an old-fashioned Italian, only speaking in his native tongue. Robert didn't know if he even knew English. He liked his beer, and with every meal, he had to have his wine. He laughed when he said his favorite Italian phrase to little Robert, which meant *Do you smell or do you stink?*

His grandfather had a regular routine. After pulling a chair up to the apartment window, he propped his arm on a pillow on the windowsill, sipping a beer, just so he could watch Robert and his friends play ball out in the street.

Robert felt good knowing his grandfather was watching, so he tried his best to impress his grandfather, who was the first to introduce him to alcohol. One holiday, while Robert sat hidden under the table, he gave him some wine. Robert got so drunk that he kept banging his head against the legs of the table. Robert felt like he was one of his grandfather's favorites and loved him a lot.

Now, seeing his grandfather lying helpless in the stairwell was devastating. "Grandpa!" he yelled, trying to get to him.

Before he could get up the stairs, a police officer stopped him. "Hold on a second."

"That's my grandpa!"

"I understand." The officer walked toward the front door with Robert in tow. "Just wait out here so we can help him out." He opened the door, gave Robert a gentle push outside, and ordered everyone else to leave.

Robert looked around for any of his family. His mother was holding his baby brother Richard in her arms. For a moment, jealousy replaced the urgency of his grandfather's demise, present ever since the baby was born. Next to them were Frankie and his other sister, Anna. He pushed through the crowd to reach them. His mother was crying, dabbing at her nose and eyes with a handkerchief.

"Ma! What happened?"

"I don't know. I was inside the apartment when I heard your grandfather's footsteps coming up the stairs. Then a bunch of noise. I came out and found him." She started crying again.

A few minutes later, the medics brought his grandfather out on a gurney and eased him into the back of the ambulance.

Robert's father had arrived from his job and started up the family car. Betty came up behind Robert and Frankie, just in time for their mother to hand Richard off to her.

"Me and your father are going to the hospital," his mother said. "All of you, stay close to home."

"But Ma, I want to go too."

Robert's protest fell on deaf ears as his mother went around to the other side of the car, following the ambulance out of the neighborhood, its lights flashing and siren blaring.

Later that evening, Betty called Robert at their aunt's house, a few doors down. Her voice was trembling. "You and Frankie need to get down here."

When they arrived, Rosalie and Doreen—another friend of Betty's—were coming out of the building, crying.

"What's wrong?" Robert said to Rosalie.

"Just go on inside." She and Doreen left.

As Robert walked in, many of his aunts, uncles, and cousins were there, all with mournful expressions or wet eyes. From the living room, he saw his weeping mother in the kitchen, clinging to Richard as if someone had just tried to steal him. Both Robert and Frankie ran to her. She unlatched one arm from the baby and wrapped it around both the boys. Robert savored his mother's attention, a rare commodity since the arrival of Richard.

Robert looked up to her. "Is Grandpa dead?"

His mother tightened her lips, her face unable to hide the anguish, as she weakly nodded. She explained that their grandfather was climbing the stairs to their apartment and was a little tipsy from drinking too much. He made it to the top but lost his balance. To keep himself from falling. Apparently, the banister was as old as he was and gave way to the stress, sending Grandpa tumbling down to the landing. The fall broke a rib and punctured his lung. He died at the hospital.

The rosary was held at a nearby funeral home for three days. Robert's parents didn't allow him to go. On the third day, Robert was sitting on the stoop outside his apartment.

His Uncle Barry walked up. "Have you seen your Grandpa yet?"

Robert shook his head.

"Do you wanna see him?"

Robert nodded.

Uncle Barry looked around, then whispered, "No one's in the parlor right now. How about I sneak you in?"

Robert's face lit up.

"Okay. Come on."

Robert closely followed his uncle. Across the room was a coffin, something Robert had never seen before. His breaths became shallow, since he had never seen a dead person before. He looked up at Uncle Barry, hesitant.

"It's okay." He gave Robert a little nudge. "Go ahead."

Robert made the short walk to the coffin as long as possible. He wasn't tall enough to see the body from the other side of the room. As he approached, his grandfather began to appear—first his hands, then his chest. Finally, standing next to the coffin, he saw his grandfather's familiar face. His eyes were closed, just like the many times he had seen him sleeping.

"You need to say something to him?" Uncle Barry's voice startled Robert. "Go ahead. Tell him what you want to tell him."

Tears never start in the eyes. They come from some place deep within. As they form, the entire body trembles, like a volcano on the brink of eruption.

As Robert stood there, gathering his thoughts, he felt the birth pains of his tears, parented by Sadness and Anger and fueled by Uncertainty. "I love you, Grandpa," he said, his tears falling on the satiny material draping the coffin.

He had a brief conversation with his grandfather, occasionally interrupted by sniffles and swipes by his forearm. But the words he really wanted to express formed questions never asked: *Who's gonna watch me play punch ball now? Why did you have to get drunk and fall? When I'm hurting so bad, why does Richard get all of Mommy's attention?*

When he was finished and this tears had transformed into salty rivulets streaking down his face, he went back to the stoop. The one person who consistently showed him attention was now gone. He felt very much alone.

"Hey, Little Robert, sorry about your grandfather."

Robert hadn't realized that Alberto Devacio had approached him. He didn't know much about Mr. Devacio, except that he owned a couple of businesses in the neighborhood and drove a really nice car.

"Listen." Devacio leaned over and placed a hand on Robert's shoulder. "If you or your family need anything, just ask me. I'll see to it that you're taken care of. Okay?"

"Okay," Robert whispered. He watched as Devacio walked down the street, greeting admirers as he went to his Cadillac and drove away.

TWO

July 1965
Age 10

R obert ran out of his apartment building, jumped off the stoop, raced down to Van Sinderan Avenue, and turned right. The clear skies had graduated from a dark blue in the west to pitch black in the east.

Since he and his brother Frankie attended Our Lady of Lourdes Catholic School from September through May, he rarely saw many of his non-Catholic friends who attended PS 155. Weather and shorter days restricted the amount of time outdoors, which left the brothers inside the apartment. As with most siblings, this resulted in either playing or fighting.

Summers, on the other hand, were a completely different scenario. From the time their feet hit the floor to the moment their heads returned to their pillows, Robert and Frankie's days were completely occupied by activities with their buddies, the entire neighborhood serving as their playground. Whether it was playing on the monkey bars at Callahan Kelly Park, battling with rocks and empty beer bottles at an abandoned warehouse, or playing punch ball out in the street, Robert and Frankie never had a lackluster moment during summer vacation.

Robert's friends were all older, and they formed a gang called the Fulton and Rockaway (F&R), made up of Italian boys who mimicked the popular street gangs on TV, such as the Dead End Kids or the Little Rascals. Like the TV gangs, the F&R was always getting into mischief or causing trouble. Stealing from the fruit stand outside the produce store, fighting with rival gangs, and playing jokes on one another were just a few ways the crew entertained themselves.

Robert looked up to these guys. They were tough and brave, whereas he was small and not very gutsy. Frankie said he was afraid of his own shadow, which incited Robert into a shoving match, but he knew Frankie was telling the truth. His size made him easy prey for most kids, even the ones he regarded as friends. He was especially afraid of the Bushwick Boys, a gang of African-American boys who resided just a few blocks over, on Bushwick Street. On the way with Frankie to and from school, his stomach twisted into knots as he anticipated the gang members' taunts and threats.

At the end of Van Sinderan, he slowed his pace. He saw the familiar parapet that surrounded the stairs leading down to a tunnel belonging to the Long Island Railroad. Leaning against the parapet were the members of the F&R gang—Joey Iacocca and his older brother Marty, Vinny Gotti, Alley Boy Octavio, James Augustus, and the newest member, Robert's brother Frankie. The only member not there was Jamesy Reed. The Iacocca brothers' cigarette embers brightened in the dense darkness as they inhaled.

"Who did your dad say got mugged?" Alley Boy asked as Robert approached.

"Mr. Luciano," James said.

"The old man at the deli?"

"Yep. Said a black man hit him in the head and took his wallet while he was in the middle of the tunnel, trying to get home."

Robert began gnawing his index fingernail.

"And he was just sitting down there waiting for him?"

"Maybe," James said. "Or he just waited to hear footsteps from the other end of the tunnel. I heard there's lots of bums down there, all black and strung out. Any one of em could rob you blind. Or worse."

Robert knew about bums. They littered the stairwell of his apartment building, especially in cold weather. He often had to step over one who was sleeping, and he was always afraid someone would grab his leg.

Joey was looking at him, wearing a sly grin. "Does that scare you, Little Robert?"

At twelve years old, Joey wasn't the oldest of the bunch, but he was their leader and the one Robert looked up to the most.

"No!" Robert said, his chest rising. One look down the stairs into the ominous entrance to the tunnel caused him to reconsider his answer. During daylight hours, he had been in the tunnel many times and never saw strung out black men. Who knew what happened at night?

"Then I guess you wouldn't have a problem goin to the other end."

"What? Right now?"

The boys laughed.

"Yeah, right now."

"Ain't nobody here brave enough to go in there," Robert said. "I'd rather spend the night in a haunted house."

"Marty did it when he joined the F&R."

Robert looked at Marty. "Is that true?"

"Yeah, I did that." Marty blew out a stream of smoke, looking to the sky at nothing specific.

"Tell you what," Joey said. "If you go into the tunnel, me and the boys here will let you be a member of the gang."

Just the thought of doing what Joey proposed caused the same stomach tension incited by the Bushwick Boys. Robert knew that dares proposed by the F&R could be dangerous. A month before, while he was tagging along with his brother and the gang, he was challenged to touch the third rail—the source of electricity that powers the Long Island Railroad trains. Despite knowing that he could easily get hurt, he succumbed to the desire to show he was tough. He touched the rail … and nothing happened. He was then challenged to touch it with a wet finger. Still nothing. One foot in the air. Nothing. No matter how Robert touched the track or with whatever appendage, he never got electrocuted. Another friend wasn't so lucky. He suffered third degree electrical burns and was in the hospital for a couple of weeks. And he didn't even touch the rail. He threw a piece of metal that exploded when it hit it.

Robert looked down to the tunnel again. "Just go in there?"

"And go all the way to the other side," Joey said.

Robert hesitated. It was one thing going in there for thirty or forty feet and come back. But to go all the way to the stairs and out the other side—a good two hundred feet away? He might as well kiss the rest of his life goodbye. There were no lights in the tunnel, so by now it had to be pitch black most of the way. If someone was in there waiting for a victim, he'd be dead meat. "I can't see down there."

"Here." Joey handed him a lighter. "Now you got a torch." He put his arm around Robert's shoulders. "So you gonna do this?"

Robert stared at the lighter in his hand. The desire to be accepted into the gang outweighed the risk. He nodded.

"Okay." Joey patted his back. "When you get to the other side, just give us a wave with the lighter." A few of the boys snickered. and a couple of others cheered. His brother Frankie just grinned.

Robert slowly crept down a couple of the steps and turned around.

Joey shooed Robert toward the entrance. "Go ahead."

Despite a sudden urge to run away and live with the humiliation of being known as a coward, Robert descended the rest of the steps and entered the tunnel. As he moved deeper into the tunnel, his heart found its way to his throat. His footsteps echoed off the concrete walls and the flat roof. The darkness smelled of urine and oldness, and a few other distinct odors he couldn't quite make out. He opened Joey's lighter. The light helped him see a few feet ahead, but it also created looming shadows that made Robert even more nervous.

He was moving much slower than he'd anticipated, only because he couldn't see very far in front of him. As he moved along, the tunnel appeared to get smaller. From the other end of the tunnel, he heard the familiar screech of the train as it approached the stop. But coupled with the darkness and the possibility of danger, the train sounded creepy, even foreboding. He picked up his pace, wanting to get out of the tunnel as fast as possible.

Seconds later, he heard a noise, which was still echoing when he stopped. Goose bumps shot up his spine, raising the hair on his neck. He froze, his shadow trembling as the flame from the lighter gave it life. Even though it was a warm evening, Robert felt cold chills, shaking and wanting to turn back. But if he did, he could never face the F&R again. He could never be a member of the gang. The sound was gone, and he wasn't hearing any other noises, so he started moving again, only to stop when he heard a whisper.

He turned around. "Frankie? Joey?"

It was a single voice, very low, its words unintelligible. Footsteps followed him, then stopped.

It's just somebody getting off the train and heading to the other side.

He breathed the vile odor of the tunnel and continued walking toward the other side. *You gotta do this, Robert,* he told himself. To drown out any further noises, he sang—or hummed when he didn't know the words. Fear had him so focused on surroundings that he didn't sense how hot the lighter was until it was too late. He juggled it from one hand to the other, only to drop it, sending him into utter darkness. He swore as he turned around and squatted, placing his hand on the ground to brace himself. Unfortunately his hand landed in a puddle of unknown origin. He immediately jerked back and fell on his butt. In a panic, he groped the ground in the darkness, solely dependent upon his sense of touch, careful to avoid anything wet. After what seemed like forever, his fingers finally located the lighter. Just as he tried to relight it, he heard whispering again, much closer this time.

"Frankie?"

Frantically, he spun the thumbwheel, trying to spark a flame. As the fumes from the lighter ignited and lit up the surrounding area. His eyes adjusted to the brightness.

Another whisper, but this time, distinct. "Roberrrrt." On the edge of the lighted area, something moved.

Robert screamed, and without concern for anything but his life, he turned and ran, keeping the lighter out in front of him. One thing he had going for him: he was a fast runner. It didn't take long for him to reach the steps leading back to ground level, where he was greeted by a chorus of laughter.

"Somebody's in there!" He pointed toward the tunnel, trying to regain his breath.

This only made the boys laugh even harder.

"I'm not lyin'!"

He heard his name echo out from the tunnel. "Roberrrrt."

"Did you hear that?"

By this time, Alley Boy was rolling on the ground in hysterics, and Joey and Vinny were crying on each other's shoulders.

"He's coming. We gotta get outta here." Robert grabbed Frankie's sleeve and tugged.

Frankie pointed toward the tunnel entrance. "Look!"

At first, all Robert could see was the silhouette of a person, much smaller than the person he had imagined. As that person came into the glow of a nearby streetlight, he saw the missing gang member.

"Roberrrrt," Jamesy Reed whispered with the same chill as he used inside the tunnel. He climbed the steps, holding his arms in the air like a ghoul.

"Hey!" Even though Robert realized he was no longer in danger, his heart still pounded.

Robert loved pranks. Once, he nearly gave his mother a heart attack when he painted his shirt in ketchup and came tumbling out of his and Frankie's room, claiming Frankie had stabbed him. Being the joker was one thing. Being the butt of a joke was completely different. He didn't like it, especially since it negated the chance of him becoming an F&R member.

"Jamesy!" Robert walked over and pushed him.

"Easy, easy." Joey threw an arm around Robert's shoulder.

"That's not fair! He—"

"It's okay," Joey said, still chuckling and wiping his eyes.

Robert felt like shedding tears but knew that would just bring on more teasing and taunting. "But I didn't make it to the other side."

"You know what?" Joey said, moving Robert in front of him. "I think just you going in there proved you're pretty brave. What about youse guys?" He looked at the rest of the crew.

Even though they were still shaking from laughter, all the boys either said yes or nodded.

"You see?"

"So does that mean—?"

"Yep. You're now an official member of the F&R."

THREE

November 1968
Age 13

The dimly lit hallway leading from the classrooms to the offices of Our Lady of Lourdes Catholic School was filled only with the echoing muffles of teachers drilling their students on various subjects. On the way to the office of Miss Howell, the social worker assigned to him, Robert dragged his hand along the locker bank and counted the glossy vinyl tiles on the floor, not in any hurry to get there. At the end of the hallway, right before turning the corner to the main corridor, he crept up to the classroom door on the left and peeked in. His best friend, Angelo Sali, was on the third row, fourth seat back. Robert made enough motion with his hand to get Angelo's attention. Fortunately, no one else saw him, especially the teacher, Miss Ann.

Robert had a special dislike for Miss Ann. She was his teacher in third grade, where he quickly earned the reputation as the troublemaker who did just about anything to draw attention to himself—writing on the chalkboard when she stepped out, shooting spit balls, making noises with various parts of his body. There was nothing he wouldn't do for a laugh, and Miss Ann was determined to punish him for every instance. For the most part, he had accepted the punishment as the price he had to pay for being the class clown and harbored no hard feelings toward her. That changed halfway through that school year. An hour after lunch, Miss Ann was in the middle of teaching a multiplication lesson to the class when Robert raised his hand and asked permission to go to the restroom. He had drunk not only his thermos full of Kool-Aid but Angelo's chocolate milk as well. When they went back to class, they had an opportunity to use the restroom, but Robert didn't need to go. Now, his bladder felt like it would burst, and he was squirming like a worm.

"No," Miss Ann said. "You'll just have to wait until we all go as a class."

"But I have to go really bad," Robert said.

"That's enough. Let's continue with the lesson. No more interruptions."

Robert tried to ignore his discomfort. He crossed his legs, pressed down with his hand, tried to think of something else, but it was no use. Like a flood, the warm urine created a puddle beneath him that spread quickly, filling his seat and flowing down the sides to the floor below.

A couple of kids next to him noticed the pee and screamed as they pointed. "Ew! Robert peed his pants," they yelled, bringing all eyes in the classroom on Robert.

He loved to have everyone's attention, but this was not the kind he wanted. This was humiliating and made him want to hide. As the laughter and exclamations of disgust continued, Miss Ann walked up to Robert's desk, her hands on her hips, nostrils flaring. "You did this on purpose, didn't you?"

"No, Miss Ann, I—"

"You'll just have to clean it up." She pointed to the narrow cabinet built into one of the walls. "Get the paper towels in there. Grab the trash can too."

"But Miss Ann, I'm all wet." Robert tried to fight back the tears.

"Now, young man, or you'll be making a trip to Principal Aquinas's office."

Robert was well aware of the bare-bottom paddling administered by the principal and wanted nothing of it. So he got up and did as Miss Ann said. The squishy squeak coming from his shoes brought more laughter from his classmates, which transformed his humiliation into anger.

"Shut up!" he yelled as the threat of tears shook his words, effectively quieting his tormentors.

From that day forward, he never rid himself of the bitterness he had for Miss Ann, especially since she continued her campaign against him in grades four and five. Many times when he didn't know the answer to a problem, she rapped his knuckles with a drumstick. Once, he was caught combing his hair. She forced him to wear a bow and sent him to the girl's class, where he had to parade around for a while. Then she sent him to Principal Aquinas for a bare-bottom paddling.

Now, as he stood outside her door making faces at his friend Angelo, mocking Miss Ann as she taught the class, he felt the satisfaction of a little revenge, though it was far from complete. As one last strike before he continued to his social worker's office, he wiggled the handle of the door and took off running.

When he got inside the main office, he walked straight back to where Miss Howell's office was, straightening his shirt and slicking back his hair. Every week, Robert looked forward to his visit with his social worker. Besides getting out of class, he got to spend time with a very pretty woman on whom he happened to have a crush. Her door was open, so Robert peeked in.

She was sitting at her desk, scribbling on a piece of notebook paper. She looked up from the papers splayed across her desk. "Come on in, Robert."

He eased inside and slid into the single wooden chair in front of her desk. The office was small—not much bigger than the janitor's closet. Besides the desk and two chairs, the only other furniture was a bookshelf filled with texts on psychology and child behavior. Like the rest of the school, the walls were painted drab gray. A print of Mary, the mother of Jesus, hung on the wall behind her. To her right was a calendar.

In direct contrast to the office's dull features, Miss Howell's puffy black hair shimmered, and her sparkling blue eyes were just as radiant. What warmed Robert the most was her smile with which she greeted him. And he didn't have to tell a joke or make a funny noise to get her to do it. He was so enraptured by her beauty that he didn't realize she had been speaking to him.

"Robert, did you hear me?"

He straightened. "Uh, no, Miss Howell. I didn't."

"I said I was just looking over your grades from the last six weeks."

"Yeah. They stunk."

Miss Howell nodded. "I have to agree, but you're a bright young man."

Robert sat up. *She thinks I'm a man.*

"There's no reason you should be making these kinds of grades. So tell me, Robert, what's going on?"

Robert shrugged. "I don't know."

"I disagree. I think you do know."

He shrugged again. "Maybe I'm just bored."

"When you're bored, you do whatever entertains you. That gets you into trouble. So what we need to do is figure out how you can continue to participate in class without getting into trouble."

She kept talking about his behavior, about half of which he never heard. The conversation went right up until lunch, at which time Miss Howell said he could rejoin her class.

He found his buddy Angelo near the end of the lunch line in the cafeteria and jumped in front of him. Behind Angelo was Matthew Boccio, who started to protest. Sensing his objection, Robert turned and glared at him. The mouth that had opened to complain slowly shut without a single word escaping.

There was a good reason for Matthew's retraction. Within five years of the incident in Miss Ann's classroom, Robert's reputation went from the small, cowardly kid who peed his pants to one of the toughest street fighters in the neighborhood.

The latest incident that added to his new status occurred at the first part of the school year, while he was walking his brother Richard home from school. It was Richard's first year at Our Lady of Lourdes, and their mother counted on Robert to walk him home and protect him. This annoyed Robert at first. Richard had not only taken the attention once reserved for him by his mother, but now he was also responsible for his safety.

There were only two ways to school—through the Puerto Rican neighborhood down Eastern Parkway or the Black neighborhood down Stone Avenue. Every day, while they went to Catholic school, Robert and his kid brother crossed paths with the Blacks and Puerto Ricans of rival gangs going to the public school. For the most part, they just stared one another down or made snide remarks, making sure the other side knew the hatred was real.

Two weeks into the school year, Robert and Richard were walking down Stone Avenue, headed home. Three of the Bushwick Boys—a black gang that staked a claim to the neighborhood adjacent to Robert's—followed them. All of them were bigger than Robert, and the tallest of the three carried a stick. Robert and the rest of F&R had dealt with these guys before, clashing in gang fights throughout the summer. But facing them without his buddies was a completely different scenario for Robert, especially since he was lugging his little brother like a ball and chain.

"Give us your money," one of the boys said, giving Robert a shove.

Both angry and afraid, Robert cursed them and said, "I ain't got no money."

"You're not so tough without your friends, are you?"

Apparently, they recognized Robert as one of the F&R gang members. They kept pushing him and calling him names. But by the time they got to the corner of Truxton Street and Stone Avenue, Robert's anger and fear had morphed into rage. They continued to taunt him.

He rushed his brother Richard over to the median. "Stay here."

The three Bushwick Boys were surprised when Robert turned and charged after them. The tall guy swung his stick, but Robert blocked it with his arms. The impact caused the guy to lose his grip, and the stick fell to the ground. In a flurry of fists that connected with his adversary's face, Robert managed to knock the big guy to the ground while his two friends ran away.

Straddling the guy, Robert never let up, every blow compounding the damage caused by the previous one.

The fight got the attention of the older guys hanging out at a nearby corner. They came over to watch Robert pound on a guy twice his size. With each punch, though, his knuckles felt the pain.

The crowd of older Italian boys who had gathered around him cheered him on.

"Give me that stick," Robert yelled. Moments earlier, his adversary had tried to use it on him.

Someone said, "No, Robert. Just use your hands."

So he did—until his hands hurt so much he couldn't throw another punch. The guy's mouth was bloody, and both eyes were swollen. Robert let him up, cussing him as the big guy ran over to the corner where his cowardly buddies were waiting.

"Some kind of friends they turned out to be." Robert rubbed his hands and tried to catch his breath, relishing his moment of glory.

So when Matthew Boccio realized it was Robert who was cutting in front of him, he didn't hesitate to allow him passage.

Robert turned to Angelo. "What's for lunch today?"

"You're buying?"

"Yeah, I left mine at home."

"You picked a bad day to forget it. We're having the manager's special, whatever that is."

Robert sniffed the air. "Macaroni and cheese. I betcha we get a side of turnip greens too."

"Again?" Angelo started ranting, swearing at the food and the lunch ladies. Apparently the expletive was loud enough to catch Sister Anne's attention—not to be confused with Miss Ann. Sister Anne, better known to the students as Sister Booger Picker, was a burly eighth-grade teacher who was as mean as she was big. Her rosy cheeks and distinct accent gave away her Irish roots. With the exception of Tommy Garfield, center for the YMCA basketball team, she towered over most of the seventh graders. Tommy was only thirteen years old and was already over six feet tall. Robert was struggling to break the five-foot barrier. When he stood next to Tommy, his line of sight was somewhere between his chest and navel.

It wasn't much different with Sister Anne, although she was a lot thicker than Tommy. She must have been waiting in line to buy her lunch, since she had her pocketbook with her. Her eyes on fire, she marched over and planted her feet right in front of Robert. "Which one of ya said that?" Her voice was about as deep as Principal Aquinas, as Irish as St. Patrick's Day.

Robert stared at the wooden cross dangling from the silver chain around her neck.

"Said what, Sister?" Angelo said with the voice of innocence.

Robert still didn't look up, but the air forced through her nostrils brushed across his face. He felt like he was in the presence of a raging bull.

"Ya know what—the *S* word."

"Which one is the *S* word?"Robert knew he should have kept his mouth shut, especially after his meeting with Miss Howell. But at that age, his mouth was its own entity.

Some of the kids around them snickered.

Robert smiled.

Sister Anne thrust her hands onto her hips—or at least in the general vicinity—and leaned over so she could be on Robert's level. "Young man, you know good and well what the *S* word is. It's what you're made of."

After just snickering at Robert's joke, the kids gasped.

He was stunned for a moment, caught off-guard by her remark. He was a punk kid, definitely not a saint. He was expected to be disrespectful and have an out-of-control mouth. On the other hand, she was a nun, one of God's workers. She was supposed to be more like an angel and only say good things. Unfortunately, the staff and faculty knew Robert's reputation as a smart aleck, and she seemed determined to go toe-to-toe with him and win.

Feeling the pressure to spout off a comeback line, Robert crossed his arms and leaned against the cafeteria's cinderblock wall, avoiding eye contact with the giant nun. "Is that what you ate for breakfast?" He waved his hand in front of his nose, grinning as he looked around for approval.

Instead of satisfying laughter from his peers, all he got was a bunch of saucer-eyed boys with gaping mouths staring back at him. With his focus on them, he never got a chance to dodge Sister Anne's pocketbook swinging toward his head. With a hard smack on the nose, his head slammed into the cinderblock wall. Once again, he was stunned, this time with a lot of pain. He tried to act like the tears resulted from his nose being hit, but everybody knew he was crying.

That woman packed a punch that would knock Sonny Liston for a loop, and here she was, smacking a kid one-fourth her size with a loaded pocketbook. When he finally looked and saw her smirking, satisfied that she had humbled him before his classmates, his crying immediately turned to rage. Unfortunately for her, she misjudged Robert's tenacity and the pride that fueled it. His most-valued possession was his newly found reputation, and he wasn't going to let anyone take that away, not even a nun. She was as loathsome as the Bushwick Boy who had come into F&R territory and picked a fight.

With all his fury he flailed at her with his fists. He never landed what he would consider good blows. Her face was too far out of reach. But that didn't matter.

Two of the brothers who taught at the school came to Sister Anne's aid. After restraining Robert, they dragged him down to the principal's office. The fact that he attacked a nun was enough to be suspended from school. In fact, it was the last straw for Aquinas, who tried to send Robert to another Catholic school in the area, but no one was willing to take him off his principal's hands.

When the suspension was over, Robert had to come back to Our Lady of Lourdes.

FOUR

June 1969
Age 14

Robert looked down both directions of Herkimer Street with a cautious eye, then pressed through the darkness to the Oldsmobile idling in front of the empty lot where neighborhood kids played football. At the driver's window, doublechecking to make sure no one was around to see the transaction go down, he pulled out some bills folded over.

"Hey, Blaise." Robert handed him the money.

Blaise examined the bills under the lamppost light. "Whatcha got here?"

"Eighty dollars."

"You take your cut yet?"

Robert shook his head.

Blaise unfolded the bills and handed Robert a twenty. "Twenty-five percent. You sold them all?"

"Every last black cat."

"No hassle from the cops?"

"None."

"Good." Blaise chuckled as he confirmed the count of the remaining bills. "Money's gonna be good even after the Fourth. Hey, Robert."

Robert was startled by the sudden pronouncement of his name.

Blaise didn't notice. "How about them Mets? You think they have a shot this year?"

Robert looked down the road again. "Oh yeah. For sure. Seaver's pitching like a champ, and they're finally swingin the bats."

Blaise laughed. "Well, don't get your hopes too high, kid. Put your money on football. I like the Jets. I think they have a chance to make the playoffs this year."

"As long as Namath stays healthy."

"You're right about that. That guy can rack up some yardage." Blaise studied Robert. "I got a shipment of Italian knits coming in a few days. Think you can help me get rid of em?"

Robert perked up. "You bet."

"Good. In the meantime, I'll bring youse some more fireworks. Be here in the morning. Ten o'clock."

"Sure thing, Blaise."

Blaise rolled up the window. The tires of the Olds screeched as he sped down the street and disappeared around the corner.

Robert headed in the direction from where he came, where several of the members of the F&R waited for him at the street's edge.

After Robert's induction a few years earlier, the faces of the gang had changed. Marty Iacocca, Vinny Gotti, and James Augustus had either moved out of the neighborhood or had turned their interests to girls and cars. Joey Iacocca, Jamesy Reed, Alley Boy, and Robert's brother Frankie remained. Added to the gang were Robert's best friend, Angelo Sali, a couple of other kids, and Peter Petralli. That night, all of them were there except Frankie.

There was no formal declaration regarding who the leader of the gang was, but over the last few years, Robert had forged a reputation as a crazy kid who loved to fight. That reputation earned him the respect of the other gang members, who willingly followed him into battle.

As he approached, he held up the twenty.

The others looked on in admiration.

"Tomorrow, sodas and candy bars. My treat."

"Why not now?" Jamesy said.

"Because it's your bedtime," Joey said. "That's why."

Jamesy swore at Joey, who ignored him.

Joey stepped away from the curb. "Besides, it's Robert's money. He can do with it what he wants, when he wants. Let's head on back."

As they passed Eastern Parkway and came up to the apartment building where Robert lived, Joey pointed to a dark figure several buildings up. "Hey look, Robert. It's your favorite Puerto Rican." He was referring to Juan Garcia, owner of a small store a few buildings away. He and Robert had butted heads when the neighborhood kids were playing and a punch ball hit the store window, which didn't break, but Mr. Garcia scolded the kids. With his newfound boldness, Robert jawed back at him, and the two almost fought.

Mr. Garcia was locking up for the night. As he turned and saw the gang, he paused and said something in Spanish, loud enough for all of them to hear.

Robert flipped him off as he turned away and ducked into the alley with the F&R crew. "I hate that old man." He sat on a crate against the wall.

"I know what you mean," Joey said. "I don't know why he has to come over to our neighborhood to have a store. It's like he's rubbing it in our faces."

Robert's hatred for Mr. Garcia simmered inside him. Not only was Garcia hateful toward the F&R, but he broke the unwritten rule of racial boundaries when he entered an Italian neighborhood for business. The gangs understood those boundaries. Why couldn't he? It was clear to them that he was being disrespectful. With that in mind, Robert stood. "I changed my mind. I'm gonna go to that old man's store and get something to drink. Anybody with me?"

Alley Boy looked at Robert as if he were an idiot. "He just locked up and went home."

Robert stared at Alley Boy, his expression making his intention clear.

Peter Petralli, one of the newest members of the gang, said, "You gonna bust in?"

"Shh!" Robert signaled with his hands. "Keep it down." He looked around at the rest of the crew. "Who's in?"

Joey raised his hand. "I hate that old man as much as you."

"Me too," Peter said.

Alley Boy looked at those who had yet to commit. "I guess we all are."

Robert nodded. Redemption was in the making.

~~~~~

The next day, the F&R gang was playing punch ball with Michael Cotillo, a long-time friend, and some neighborhood kids on Fulton Street, directly in front of Robert's apartment building. Robert was in the outfield with his eyes fixed on the hitter when Mr. Garcia approached him from behind.

"I know it was you," Mr. Garcia said. "You broke into my store last night."

Startled by the angry voice, Robert turned to face Mr. Garcia, only three feet away, his hands on his hips. "What?"

"You broke into my store. Stole beer and soda. I know it's you."

Robert smirked. "You don't know nothin, old man." He turned around to join the game.

"I'm gonna call the cops, tell them it was you."

Robert felt the heat rise from his neck, effectively cutting off any sensibility. He turned to face Mr. Garcia again. "You call the cops, and I'll burn your place down."

Mr. Garcia was shocked by the sudden outburst from such a small kid. He backpeddled to the sidewalk, turned, and walked to his store several doors down.

"Yeah, that's what I thought." Robert aimed a finger toward Mr. Garcia.

By then, Peter and Alley Boy had eased over to Robert.

Alley Boy glanced left and right. "What did he say to you? Does he know?"

"Says he's gonna call the cops, but he don't know nothin. Don't be so nervous."

"Maybe somebody saw us and told him."

"Alley Boy, just relax. Nobody saw us. He's just tryin to get me to confess. That's all. I'm tellin ya, he ain't got nothin on us."

With the game interrupted and the sun overhead, the boys went inside Joey and Peter's apartment building to cool off—just two doors down from Mr. Garcia's store. They sat along the hallway outside their apartment.

"Hey," Peter said. "Don't we fight the Bushwick Boys tonight?"

Gang fights were a common summertime ritual among Brooklyn kids, one of the many ways the boys would combat boredom. The fights usually started with an exchange of words from bordering streets, or in community areas, such as Spinners Supermarket. If tempers were high enough, challenges would be made.

"Yeah, at six o'clock."

"We need to do something big this time," Joey said.

"Like what?"

"I don't know. Just something that'll let em know we mean business."

All the boys agreed, nodding and nudging one another.

"So Joey … got any ideas?" Robert said.

"No."

"Oh, great. You get us all worked up about somethin and then you got no idea. That's good. That's really good."

"I got an idea," Peter said. "I saw these guys on TV throw gasoline bombs at the cops. When the bottles hit the ground, a big fire ball blew up in front of the cops."

"What?" Alley Boy said. "Are you crazy?"

"Yeah, he's crazy," Angelo said.

Robert waved them off. "No, that's perfect. I can see those guys running for their lives after we toss a few at em. It'll be an easy win. After all, it's about to be the Fourth, and we need to show a little patriotism."

"Do we have stuff to make em?" Alley Boy said.

Peter pointed behind him. "There's beer bottles in the alley."

"I wonder where they came from?" Robert said, inciting more laughter.

"I saw some rags out in the trash," Joey said. "What about gasoline?"

Robert hesitated. "I ain't got no money."

"You got a twenty." Alley Boy raised an eyebrow. "We all know that."

"Oh, yeah." Robert dug into his pocket and pulled out the single bill. Gasoline wasn't exactly what he wanted to buy with the money, but fifty cents was a small price to pay for the fun it would buy.

"You can take my bike," Alley Boy said.

Robert nodded as he crammed the bill back in his pocket. "Okay. Youse guys get all the bottles and rags while I'm gone."

~~~~~

At five o'clock, the F&R gang sat on the stoop outside Joey and Peter's apartment building. The fresh air was a relief, since the fumes from the gasoline bombs lining the hallway inside had given them headaches.

"I ain't got a lighter," Robert said.

"My old man's got one in his drawer," Peter said. "You can use it."

The boys never saw the patrol car until it stopped in front of Mr. Garcia's store. Two cops got out. Mr. Garcia came out and met the cops on the sidewalk. They talked for a moment, with Mr. Garcia pointing toward Robert and the rest of the gang. When they were done, Mr. Garcia went back to his store, and the cops approached the boys.

"Hello, officers," Robert said.

They both held identical poses—legs spread apart, both hands on the buckles of their utility belts.

"A couple of cowboys, that's for sure," Robert whispered to the group. They laughed quietly.

The cops were not in the mood for jokes.

Pointing to Mr. Garcia's store, the one on the left looked at Robert. "Did you threaten to burn down that store?"

Robert smirked and shrugged. "I ain't gonna burn nobody's store."

"He says you threatened him this morning."

Robert shook his head as if that was the most ridiculous thing he'd ever heard.

"Says you just rode by on a bicycle carrying a gas can. Is that true?"

Robert froze. He never intended to go through with his threat against Mr. Garcia. But now he realized he had just passed by the old man's store, holding a gallon of gas. What else was Mr. Garcia going to think?

"No, I ain't got no gasoline."

"Boy!" The cop sniffed the air. "I could blow up this whole block right now, just by lighting a match. You boys wreak of gasoline fumes."

The other cop nudged his buddy. "How about I take a look inside?"

"You do that while I babysit these boys."

He came out holding one of the gasoline bombs. "That wouldn't happen to be yours, would it? Where do you live?"

"What?" Robert said. "But I didn't—"

"Tell me where you live, or you'll have to come down to the station with me."

~~~~~

Two weeks after he was busted, Robert—along with his distressed mother and tight-lipped father—appeared in family court before Judge Hardaway. Instead of the tough-guy persona he had learned to portray, Robert was genuinely scared, as evidenced by his trembling. Even though the courtroom was crowded with other teens and their parents, Robert was surprised to see two particular persons. One was the fire marshal, adding to Robert's nervousness, since he figured the judge called him for expert testimony. The other was Alberto Devacio, who stood as Robert passed, first shaking his parents' hands and then holding Robert by his shoulders.

He leaned in close.

"Just stick to your guns, and you'll be okay. Got it?"

Robert nodded.

The judge saw a few other cases before Robert was called. Two of the teens—one of which Robert knew—walked away from the judge's bench in tears, headed for juvenile detention. Robert thought of what it would be like locked up in jail, never seeing his parents, his friends, or his brothers and sisters. His stomach knotted as he feared he would face the same judgment.

As Robert and his parents approached the bench, the judge was buried in the manila folder in front of him. After a minute of silence, Judge Hardaway spoke. "Robert Engel, you have been charged with assault and manufacture and possession of an illegal weapon." He took off his reading glasses, laid the folder down, and stared at Robert. "How do you plead?"

"Not guilty, sir."

Judge Hardaway never took his eyes off Robert. "From here on out, you will refer to me as 'Your Honor' or 'Judge.' Understood?"

Robert tried to swallow but his throat wouldn't cooperate. "Yes, sir. … I mean, yes, Your Honor." He felt as if he had just added another nail to his coffin.

"The judge tapped the folder. "Says here that you were on a stoop when the police officers approached you. That you smelled of gas. Why did you smell like gas?"

"I had just got gas to mow my aunt's lawn."

"In Brooklyn?"

"It's a very small yard, Your Honor."

Robert heard snickering from the gallery. Everyone knew Brooklynites don't have lawns.

"Says here you threatened the storeowner down the street. You said you were going to burn down his place. Is that true?"

"No, Your Honor."

"Then why did the storeowner say you said it?"

"We play punch ball on the street in front of his store, and he doesn't like it. So he's just tryin to get me into trouble."

With pursed lips, the judge nodded. "What about the Molotov cocktails the police officers found in the building? Did you make them?"

"Molotov cocktails? Your Honor, I'm too young to drink alcohol."

Robert heard more snickering.

Even the judge grinned a little. "A Molotov cocktail is the name for a gasoline bomb made like the ones found in the building."

"Oh, the gasoline bombs. No, Your Honor, I had nothin to do with that."

"You're telling me that even though the storeowner said you threatened to burn down his store, and even though you smelled like gasoline, and even though the police officers found you on the stoop of the building in which the hallway was lined with Molotov cocktails, you had nothing to do with it?"

"That's right, Your Honor."

The judge stared through Robert, looking for the truth. He then asked Robert and his parents to step back and signaled for the fire marshal to approach the bench. The two conferred in voices too low for Robert to hear. After a few minutes, the fire marshal returned to his seat.

The judge called Robert and his parents back. "I asked Fire Marshal Evans to come today so he could give me his expert opinion on this case." He cleared his throat. "Mr. Engel, how old are you?"

"Fourteen."

The judge nodded. "You do understand that the charges brought against you are very serious?"

"Yes, Your Honor."

"Threatening to burn down someone's business is a stupid thing to do, even if you don't intend to follow through with the threat."

"Yes, Your Honor, it is. That's why I would never do that."

The judge smirked. "I'm not so sure, Mr. Engel. Personally, I think you're as guilty as sin. But at best, the evidence is circumstantial. Between you and the storeowner, it's his word against yours. No one else heard you make that threat. And no one saw you make the Molotov cocktails, nor were you actually found in possession of them. Even though a Molotov cocktail is fairly easy to make, the fire marshal here seems to think you're too young to make one, much less a dozen. Without any hard evidence, I have no choice but to dismiss your case. I release you to the custody of your parents."

Robert's eyes grew wide in disbelief as his mother squeezed his shoulder.

"But …" The Judge pointed a finger at Robert. "If I ever see you in my court again, you can count on me tearing your case apart until I find something I can put you away with. And as for you two"—he pointed at Robert's parents—"keep a tighter leash on this kid."

Robert's father placed a hand on Robert's shoulder. "You can count on it."

The two of them turned and exited the courtroom, Robert's mother close behind.

Robert's father pushed his glasses up onto his nose. "Gonna be a lot of changes around our place. One is, you're not gonna get to hang out past dark. Second, you're gonna …"

Robert's attention was drawn to a scene across the hallway outside the courtroom. Alberto Devacio was walking over to shake hands with a smiling Fire Marshal Evans. After a few words and a couple of pats on the arm the two men parted, with the fire marshal stuffing green bills into his pocket.

Robert looked up to Devacio, who was about to enter the elevator.

Devacio smiled at him and winked.

FIVE

L eaves crunched under Robert's feet as the cold northern winds hurried him into the welcoming warmth of Thomas Edison High School.

Just inside the glass doors—amid the hustle and bustle of students rushing around, the noise of the warning bell drowning out an intercom message—he saw Louis Cafora leaning against the wall, hands in the pockets of his green-and-white New York Jets jacket.

"Louie" was a curly-haired funny guy with a goofy sort of nature. He was a year older than Robert and was somewhat on the heavy side. He was Robert's only friend from school.

The area around Fulton and Rockaway had been changing, and a gradual influx of Puerto Ricans had overtaken the once predominantly Italian neighborhood. By the end of the summer of 1969, almost all of Robert's classmates from Lady of Lourdes Catholic School had moved away. Angelo and his family were still around, but he had to repeat eighth grade due to failing grades. Robert, on the other hand, advanced to ninth grade, not because of good grades, but because Principal Aquinas wouldn't subject his faculty and staff to another year of Robert's unruly behavior.

Louie befriended Robert the first day of high school. They already knew each other casually from the neighborhood but nothing more than that. Robert's reputation as a wild, tough kid preceded him, and Louie was impressed with some of his antics, especially the episode with Sister Anne a year earlier.

Robert walked over to him, rubbing his hands. He looked down to the floor and saw a large brown paper bag. "Where you goin today?"

Louie looked around and then grinned like a kid who'd just received every gift on his Christmas wish list. "Match Game."

Up to that point—nine years before his alleged involvement in the Lufthansa Heist, the largest cash robbery in American history—Louie's reputation was built on a quirky passion: being part of studio audiences for TV shows. He often skipped school to make the train trip to Manhattan. Robert knew this was his plan, because Louie always carried the large paper bag—usually filled with several sandwiches, a bag of Lays potato chips, moon pies, and a soda—on the days he went.

"Are you comin?"

Robert shook his head. "I can't today."

"Why not?"

"I got a thing." Robert nudged the bag with his foot. "I told Mr. Gordon I would help him with the newspaper. We're running a piece on the Miracle Mets—with pictures and all."

Louie shook his head. "Man, that's lame."

"Louie, it's the Mets. They just won the World Series. It's kinda special, you know."

"You're telling me you'd rather go to class than a game show? You gotta be crazy."

Several times, Robert had gone with Louie to Manhattan and knew the trip was a lot better than trying to stay awake in his classes. He wasn't long into his first year of high school, but it proved to be even harder than the past eight grades, especially since he didn't retain much of what he was taught. Listening to his teachers' droning lectures over mathematical terms or grammar rules amounted to nothing by the time he tried to apply them. He was the type of kid who had to put his hands on them, feel them, experience them before he could understand. Out of all school had to offer, the printing press was the only thing that allowed Robert to learn in such a fashion. It was meticulous work: gathering all the letters, placing them on the platen in the correct sequence, and such. Besides, printing was apparently in his blood, since his father worked at a print shop, and it was something that Robert was actually good at that didn't get him into trouble.

As he contemplated the possibility, he noticed the poster next to Louie—a picture of a man in a puffy white suit and helmet, reminding him of the Michelin Man. He was standing in gray, desolate terrain. The caption at the bottom said, *That's one small step for a man, one giant leap for mankind.*

Robert nodded toward the poster. "Who's that?"

"Neil Armstrong. You know, the guy who walked on the moon."

Robert furrowed his brow. "Somebody walked on the moon?"

Louie gasped. "Are you kidding me? He did it just this past summer. Where were you?"

Robert shrugged. "Not on the moon." He turned toward his locker.

"So what's it gonna be? You gonna make me go by myself?"

Robert kept walking as he gave Louie a nonchalant wave. "Maybe another time."

~~~~~

The newspaper meant more to Robert than what might be expected from a street hoodlum. Throughout his entire life he had always taken pleasure in destruction. He might be breaking windows in an abandoned warehouse or beating a car with a bat, just because it was parked in the middle of their punch ball field. At home, his father never asked him to work on the car or help with repairs around the house. He was never expected to clean the bedroom he shared with Frankie and Richard. His only duty was to stay out of the way until suppertime.

Now, he was experiencing what it was like to do something constructive. He felt proud and liked the attention that came with it. It also made better sense than doing something that got him into trouble.

Print shop was during second period. His first class was geometry, which was on the second floor. Elbowing his way through the crowd, which prompted dirty looks, he made it to the stairwell. Taking two steps at a time, he bounded all the way to the landing. It wasn't that he was in a hurry to get to class. His nature was to move quickly, wherever he was. At the landing, he ran into a kid nicknamed Grubber, so called because he had a reputation for eating not only his food but also mooching off others.

Among the ninth-grade boys, making fun of how Grubber ate everyone else's food was an ongoing joke. There were, "Grubber ate the Brussels sprouts of everyone at our table," "Hey, let's get Grubber to eat it. He eats everything," and "I heard Grubber ate his little brother before he came to school this morning."

Robert was always looking for an opportunity to be the funny guy.

The day before, Grubber was handing his tray to the lunch lady, finishing the last couple of bites of his pizza.

"Hey," Robert said to the people at his table, "I just saw Grubber grab that pizza out of the trashcan."

Everyone looked at Grubber in astonishment, gasping and gagging.

Grubber saw them, but at the time, he had no idea what Robert had said.

Fire in his eyes, Grubber stood beside Robert on the stairway landing, hands on his hips. "You Robert?"

"Yeah, what of it ... Grubber?"

Others taking the stairs slowed down and were watching them.

"You told Tony I ate out of the trashcan?"

Robert smirked as he looked around. "Yeah, what of it? Get out of my way, you slob." He started to go around.

Grubber stepped in front of him. "You take it back."

"You take it back? What? Are we on the kindergarten playground or somethin?"

Several onlookers laughed.

Grubber, like most of the other teenage boys, was taller and heavier than Robert. "Take it back. Tell everybody I didn't eat the pizza out of the trashcan. Tell em you lied."

Robert smirked. "Get out of my way, you big sissy." He tried to walk on past him.

Grubber pushed him into the wall.

As Robert's anger flared and his street-honed instincts kicked in, all the excitement about printing the newspaper and the pleasure he got from positive attention was swept away. He crouched, keeping wild eyes on Grubber as he reached into his back pocket, pulled out a strap razor, and flipped it open. The crowd stepped back.

Grubber's eyes widened but showed no less desire to avenge his dignity.

Hoping the threat of the blade would make him back off, Robert swiped the razor through the air. The swipe was perfectly timed with Grubber's lunge, slicing across the bridge of his nose. A girl in the crowd screamed as Grubber stumbled backward, holding his face with both hands, blood trickling through his fingers.

Robert stood there, his adrenaline-flooded heart pounding in his throat, ready to cut again if he had to.

Grubber didn't retaliate. He sat on the first step of the landing and applied pressure to his nose as blood dripped onto his pants.

The girl who screamed knelt to help Grubber. "Somebody get Principal Andersen. I need a towel." She looked with fiery eyes, not saying a word to Robert.

Slowly, Robert folded the strap razor, a thin line of blood along its edge. He put it in his back pocket and then took off running back up the stairs. A hundred yards from the school, he surprised Louie.

"Decided to come along, eh?"

"Yeah." Robert tried to catch his breath. "Change of plans."

~~~~~

The next day, Robert was unsure where he stood in regard to the incident with Grubber. He wasn't about to show that he was a coward by *not* showing up at school. After all, Grubber had started the fight by pushing him. What was he supposed to do? Just stand there and let the kid disrespect him in front of the whole school? His reputation was all he had. If he had to slice somebody to protect it, then that's exactly what he was going to do.

As soon as he entered, he saw two cops patrolling the lobby, noting each student as they walked by. Robert put his hand up to his face and turned to leave. Halfway to the street, he felt a firm grip on his arm, pulling him back. He turned, ready to pop someone in the mouth.

"Hey! Easy, kid." The police officer grinned. He was the same cop who busted him for making Molotov cocktails. "I remember you. The gasoline bomber. For some reason, I knew we'd see each other again. Get in the car."

"What?"

"Get in the car. We're taking you to the precinct."

Reluctantly, Robert walked toward the patrol car.

~~~~~

Robert was sitting on the precinct bench, just inside the front entrance, when his mother showed up, bundled up in her full-length gray wool coat and red scarf. She barely glanced at Robert as she went to the front desk and quietly spoke to the sergeant on duty. After five minutes of conversation and several head gestures toward Robert by the sergeant, his mother turned toward him. "Robert," she said, sounding like she was commanding a dog. "Come!"

The sergeant at the desk nodded, acknowledging that it was okay to leave.

Although visibly upset during their walk to the train station and the subsequent ride, his mother was quiet. As she kept a brisk pace, her coat drawn tight, the clopping of her heels echoed against the brick walls along Fulton Street. Robert followed, a couple of steps behind. Inside the apartment building, she fumbled with the key before she steadied herself enough to unlock the door. Instead of hanging her coat and scarf like she usually did, she threw them across the back of the couch.

Robert stood and watched, agonized that she wouldn't say anything to him, contemplating whether or not he should break the silence.

After a few minutes of dangling her fingers over the radiator, she started to cry, covering her mouth and nose with a semi-warmed hand.

Robert couldn't stand it anymore. "Ma, I'm—"

"Don't … say anything." She pointed a trembling finger at him. "Don't say anything."

At supper, silence still dominated the atmosphere, but Robert could tell that his mother had not told his father about the incident at school, nor that she had to retrieve him from the police station. Otherwise, Robert would be out looking for a place to stay the night instead of being seated at the table, eating his pasta.

After his father went to bed, Robert's mother called him into the kitchen. "They decided not to file charges against you." She rinsed a bowl in the sink.

Robert nodded. "Okay."

His mother glanced at him. "They're transferring you instead."

"Transfer? To where?"

"East New York."

In disbelief, Robert shouted, "East New York?"

His mother put her finger to her mouth. "Keep it down. I don't want your father to know. It's already hard enough around here as it is."

"But Ma, that's an all-black school. The guys who go there—I fought a lot of em. I'll get killed."

She swatted him with the hand towel and whispered, "I said, keep it down."

Robert paced the kitchen floor like a caged lion, biting a fingernail and shaking his head. "I'm a dead man."

"Well, maybe you should have thought of that before you decided to use a knife on that kid."

Robert wasn't about to correct her regarding the weapon. "I'm just not gonna go."

"Yes, you are. You gotta. The police said, if you don't go, then you'll be arrested for assault. And this time you won't get away with it."

Robert threw his hands up. "Then you might as well start diggin a grave, cause that's where I'll end up."

"You don't got a choice."

Robert shook his head and slammed his hand into the sink countertop. He marched out of the kitchen, grabbed his coat from the hall tree, and went outside. Headed down Fulton Street, he lit up a cigarette and let it hang from his lips, his hands tucked inside his jacket pocket.

He was angry because almost all his friends were gone, leaving him there to fend for himself. He was angry because, for once in his life, he had found something legitimate to do that he liked, and he blew his chance. He was angry because it seemed like everywhere he turned, trouble found him.

He turned south and charged down Eastern Parkway for a couple of blocks, his warm breath hitting the cold night air, forming clouds over his head like a steam engine. He slowed his pace as he came to the intersection of Atlantic Avenue and Eastern Parkway. The building on the corner housed the Italian-American Social Club, a place where he worked in the summer when he was twelve years old. Alberto Devacio owned the club—the neighborhood businessman who had befriended Robert since he was a little boy. He also owned the candy store next door, which doubled as a front for his blackmarket business ventures of stolen cigarettes, Italian knits, and anything else that might make money.

Robert enjoyed working at Devacio's club, where he stayed busy serving food and drinks to Devacio's pals who came to play cards and chew the fat. He also ran errands for just about everything, from cigarettes or cigars to aspirin and Pepto-Bismal®. Anything the club didn't offer, he would get—except for alcohol, which was strictly forbidden in the club. There was lots of loud laughter, and the men always tipped Robert generously.

As he stood in front of the blacked-out storefront window, he heard explosions of muffled laughter over the noisy traffic passing by on Eastern Parkway. Robert spun around as he heard the blast of a horn fit more for a locomotive than a car.

Devacio was pulling his white 1969 Cadillac Eldorado into a parking space just behind him. "Little Robert," he said as he got out of the car, carrying a brown grocery bag.

Robert took the bag, which smelled the distinctive aromas of an Italian deli.

Devacio patted him on the head. "Always a hard worker, ain't that right?"

For the first time since his printshop teacher asked him to help with the newspaper, Robert felt the warmth of acceptance.

Devacio opened the door of the club, which was covered in green curls of peeling paint. "What you doin out this late at night? Don't you got school in the morning?"

Robert shook his head. To the left side of the room, several of Devacio's buddies were sitting at the table, concentrating on their fanned-out cards in front of them. He recognized Anthony Trentacosta, known in the neighborhood as Tony Pep.

"Look who I found camped outside the door," Devacio said.

"Hey, Little Robert," Tony Pep said. "How's it goin, kid?"

"It's all right." He looked at Devacio. "Where do you want me to put this?"

"Just set it on the table." Devacio opened the bag and served his buddies. "Meatball sub." He handed the sandwich to a man Robert didn't recognize. "Who ordered ham and Swiss?"

Tony Pep raised his hand. "That's me."

Devacio pointed to quiet the stranger across the table. He was stocky, with dark hair.

"Hey, Nicky, you know Robert?"

He looked up from his cards. "No."

Robert shook his hand.

"Are you the Robert who works for my kid brother Blaise?"

"Yeah, that's me."

Nicky's expression was blank. "Good."

Devacio rummaged through the sack. "So Nicky, what did you order?"

"I got roast beef."

After serving everybody, Devacio waved Robert to the back, where they entered a small kitchen. He folded the brown bag and put it in a cabinet with a dozen more. He leaned against the countertop. "Tell me, Robert. You get kicked out of school again?"

Robert stared at the floor. "Yeah."

"Hey." Devacio grabbed Robert by the chin and forced his head up. He had an expression of anger, but without the fire. "Don't be lookin down like some whipped dog. You got nothing to be ashamed of."

"But I got into another fight."

"And?"

"I cut a kid with a razor."

Devacio's stare turned to a smile stretched across his face. Within seconds, he was laughing so hard the countertop bounced under his weight. He shook his head and wiped away a tear. "I knew I was right about you."

"What do you mean?"

Devacio grabbed Robert by both shoulders. "Kid, you got what it takes." He patted Robert on the cheek.

Robert's face felt cold enough for his smile to crack. Devacio always made him feel good about himself. When everyone else was upset at his antics, Devacio celebrated them. When everyone else offered no hope, Devacio painted a bright future. Clearly, the family that most cared for him was not by flesh and blood but by a whole different set of rules, one in which members looked out for one another. They didn't judge a person for the bad things but embraced those things as a part of a person's character.

"Robert, how old are you now?"

"Almost fifteen."

"Good. In another year or so you'll be old enough to make your own decisions. Take my advice. Do whatever it takes to get by and get along. When you turn sixteen, you'll be a free man to do whatever you want. I'll be sure to help you out with that. You hear me?"

"Yeah, sure."

"Now, how would you like to earn a couple of dollars tonight?"

"Okay."

Devacio pointed to the other room as he handed Robert a twenty-dollar bill. "Serve these bums in there. Treat em like family." He took Robert's chin in his hand and forced him to look eye-to-eye. "Cause that's just what we are, Little Robert. We're your family."

SIX

S weat dripped off his brow onto the cumbersome cardboard box, which Robert loaded into the back of the tractor-trailer. The forklift operator had loaded the rest of the cargo but overlooked the box. Robert happened to catch the discrepancy on the shipping order, just as the driver was about to leave for Pennsylvania.

The driver shook Robert's hand. "Thanks, kid. You just saved me a lot of hassle."

After turning sixteen in December 1970, Robert followed Alberto Devacio's advice, dropped out of high school, and spent two months of freedom watching TV. His mother told him he couldn't lie around the house all day. He had to get a job. The next two years, he worked for a courier service, then as an attendant at the Cypress Hills Cemetery with his Uncle Barry. After he was laid off from there, Blaise Corrozo hooked him up with a job at Jet Air Freight as a dockworker. It was hard, physical labor, with little shelter from the harsh weather. Many evenings, he went home to his family's new place on Richmond Street, plopped down on his bed, and slept until morning. He liked his boss, who had no problem letting him leave early or take a day off.

His penchant for fighting lay dormant after he sliced Grubber with the strap razor, in part because he lost all contact with anyone who knew him as Robert the tough, crazy kid with the mile-wide anger streak and sharp weapons. Therefore, he had no reputation to uphold. Instead, he built his status at work as the respectable kid who made everyone laugh.

Robert paused as he watched the semi pull away, taking a well-deserved breather.

"Robert!"

Robert turned and ran toward the tall, lanky man standing outside the door to the white office, dwarfed by the massive warehouse in which it was built.

"Time to clock out, buddy."

Robert nodded and went inside.

~~~~~

Robert didn't have a car, so he depended on public transportation to get him to and from work. The six-mile bus journey of drop-offs and pick-ups usually took forty-five minutes to reach home.

Completely exhausted, he slouched down in a seat near the back of the bus, crossed his arms, and shut his eyes, hoping that if he dozed off, he wouldn't miss his stop at Richmond Street.

The noise of the air brakes disengaging startled Robert. He opened his eyes and saw two elderly women slowly negotiating their steps down the aisle. A young guy about Robert's age and height, but thinner, followed behind them. The bus was always crowded around this time, since most of the blue-collar workers were calling it quits and heading home. A man at the front got up and offered his and the empty seat to the ladies and took the next single seat in the bus's midsection. As far as Robert could see, the only other seat remaining was the one next to him.

The young guy saw it too, and picked up his pace to claim it as the bus lurched forward. As he fell into the seat, he cursed the bus driver. "Couldn't wait 'til I sat down, could ya?"

Robert grinned. "Freakin city workers, I tell ya."

The guy nodded. "Yeah. Maybe he'd think different if I punched his lights out." He held out his hand. "Joe Dadona. Everybody calls me Little Joe."

Robert shook it. "Robert. Everybody calls me … Robert."

Little Joe gave Robert a half grin. "Where you from?"

"I live off Richmond Street. Just headed home from work."

"Hey, that's my stop too. Where you work?"

"Jet Air Freight. Been there almost a year now."

"Oh yeah? How did you manage to get a job there?"

"A friend named Blaise hooked me up."

Little Joe sat up. "Blaise Corrozo?"

Robert held up his hands. "Is there any other? You know him?"

"Yeah, I know him."

For the next forty minutes, Robert and Little Joe talked without regard to the other passengers or their choice of words. Within a few short minutes they discovered a family tie—distant cousins related through Robert's mother and Little Joe's grandmother. Through that connection, Little Joe knew he was talking to the same Robert he had heard stories about—the small guy not afraid to fight anyone, how he took on a rival gang of black kids by himself and won, and how he was arrested for making Molotov cocktails with which he threatened to torch the Catholic school after getting kicked out for fighting a nun. Little Joe's versions of Robert's antics were slightly twisted, but Robert didn't say anything to correct him. The exaggerated version made him sound more legendary.

Little Joe had credentials of his own. He was the godson of "Fat Andy" Ruggiano, one of only a few made men within the Gambino crime family. Fat Andy and Little Joe's father had been close friends. Before Little Joe's father died of cancer, Fat Andy promised to look after Little Joe. Fat Andy's son Anthony and Little Joe grew up together and were like brothers.

As they were exiting the bus, Little Joe put his finger in the bus driver's face. "The next time you take off before I'm seated, I'll break your freakin neck."

The driver was in his fifties and apparently experienced at dealing with people like Little Joe. He held up a hand. "Hey, I'm sorry, I didn't mean to."

Little Joe smirked. "Yeah, right." As they got off the bus, he said to Robert, "Ralph Cramden back there needs a good butt kickin."

They walked over to the streetlight.

Robert pulled out his pack of cigarettes and offered one to Little Joe.

After a drag, Little Joe said, "Hey listen. If you ain't got nothin goin on tonight, come hang out with us at the pizza joint on the corner of 93rd Street and 101st Avenue. I'll introduce you to Anthony and the rest of the crew."

~~~~~

After showering, Robert slept for an hour before getting dressed. It was only a mile to the pizza parlor, but Robert opted for the bus, having no desire to be soaking wet with sweat when he arrived. As he walked from the bus stop to the pizza parlor across the street, he saw Little Joe and three other guys standing outside.

Little Joe noticed him and met him at the curb. "Robert, glad you made it." He led Robert over to the rest of the group and introduced Anthony, Herman Locke, and Tommy Mancini.

"Been hearin a lot about you," Anthony said.

"Yeah?"

Anthony nodded. "I heard about the F&R gang even before Little Joe started talking about you. You know Alberto Devacio?"

"Sure. I worked for him."

"He's an associate of my father's. Always talking about the tough kids in his area. Whose crew you been hanging out with lately?"

Robert shrugged. "Nobody, really. Just punching the time clock, that's all."

"Little Joe said you work at Jet Air Freight. How long?"

"About a year. Puts money in my pocket."

After talking for a while, they walked inside the pizza parlor and sat at the back of the dining area. Anthony ordered two large pizzas and a pitcher of beer. He told the owner to put it on his father's tab. The owner's expression said he knew he would never see a penny for the pizzas but could do nothing about it.

Robert didn't care. He was famished, and he felt like part of something important, an elite group perched high above the social order of commoners.

After both pizzas were gone, Herman Locke left for the restroom.

Robert watched him with a wary eye. He said to the rest of the group, "Have any of you noticed that Herman is a black kid?"

All three laughed.

Little Joe wiped his face with a napkin and tossed it on the table. "Yeah, but he's cool."

This was a new experience for Robert. Until then, the only contact he had made with an African-American was in a negative setting—gang fights with the Bushwick Boys, getting jumped on his way to Catholic school, being taunted the few days he actually attended East New York High School, and with the junkies and boozers. All led him to believe the racism taught among Italian-Americans was justified.

Herman seemed to be a laid-back guy, and he smiled a lot, which was disarming that Robert felt uncomfortable.

"So you trust this guy?" Robert said.

All three nodded as they glanced at one another. "Yeah. Of course."

Robert shrugged. "Well … okay. I guess any friend of yours is a friend of mine."

After Herman returned, they walked out, waving to the pizza parlor owner. No one left a tip.

"Greaseball," Anthony said under his breath as he pushed through the door.

At the corner, Robert asked, "So what do youse guys do for fun?"

Little Joe's grin suggested "fun" must be qualified by something not so nice. "Well, if Anthony here isn't at the movies smoochin with his girlfriend …"

Anthony shoved Little Joe, laughing. "Yeah, youse guys are just jealous, that's all."

Little Joe straightened his shirt. "To be quite honest with ya, Robert, that's part of the reason I asked you to meet up with us. You see, we run into *situations* at times." He threw a couple of uppercuts into the air. "If you know what I mean. You up for that?"

Robert's stomach flipped. It had been a long time since he let those juices flow. Now, just the thought gave him an adrenaline rush. He threw a couple of jabs of his own. "Just show me who to punch." He looked at Herman. "I'm guessin it ain't gonna be a gang of black guys."

Herman laughed. "Naw, man. We liked to stir it up with pretty boys from other crews. They think they are all that. We show em they ain't."

~~~~~

The next morning, Robert was an hour late for work. As he walked into the office, the shop manager looked up from his clipboard, his eyebrows raised.

"Sorry, boss." Robert slipped his timecard into the clock. The sound of stamping the card rattled Robert's throbbing head. "I missed the bus."

"Looks to me like you've been out all night." The shop manager tapped his clipboard with his pen several times.

Robert stared at his boss, not sure what to say.

"Forget about it." The shop manager kept writing on the shipping order attached to the clipboard. "We've all been there. Just don't make a habit of it."

Robert nodded.

The shop manager was right. Robert and his new friends were out until 4:00 a.m. Now, Robert was tired, and his head was about to roll off his shoulders. But he didn't regret taking Little Joe up on his invitation. It had been a while since he had felt excitement in an atmosphere of conflict—or the camaraderie among guys who thought and felt like he did. Ever since he and his family moved to Richmond Street—even before, when his friends moved out of the Fulton/Rockaway neighborhood—his life had been docile. But now, the old self who had grown dormant over the last two years was awakened by last night's minor skirmish with a crew from Ozone Park. Again he felt like he was part of something exclusive, something that had its own set of rules, something that could bowl over anything in its way— and he liked it. As he considered these things, he remembered the words of Devacio, a man who in Robert's eyes was very wealthy, and who happened to be an associate of Fat Andy Ruggiano, the father of his new running buddy Anthony: *We are your family.*

~~~~~

The day dragged on, and by the time early afternoon arrived, Robert was wishing he was anywhere but at work. His head was not as woozy, and the tiredness was not as heavy, but his heart was not in it—demonstrated by his slow work pace and loading cargo onto the wrong trailer.

Robert was on the dock, taking a smoke break, when a Cadillac pulled up—the same car as the bar-hopping night before. Anthony, Little Joe, Herman, and Tommy got out, shirtless and in swim trunks. An innocent-looking blonde in a bikini remained in the back seat. Robert's weary eyes were now fully alert.

"Hey, Robert!" Anthony yelled as he hung on the opened driver's door, waving for Robert to come over.

Robert jumped off the dock and ran over to the car.

"I want you to meet someone." He looked to the girl. "Robert, this is Sunny."

Robert's grin was big as he took her hand. "Hiya, Sunny."

Her smile was a little uneasy, as if she was unsure of what she was doing. "Hi, Robert."

"We were headed to the beach. Thought we'd stop by and see if you wanted to join us."

"Me? Oh, hey, I'd love to, but I still got a few more hours to go before I'm off."

"Can't you ask off?"

Robert ran off for a few minutes and came back shaking his head. "Boss man says he's got too many guys out, and he needs me. He's usually good about letting me off, but—"

"You don't need this stinkin job," Anthony said, cursing.

"Yeah, I do."

Anthony put his arm around Robert. "Listen, come with me, and I promise you won't need to worry about workin a sucker's job again."

"Really?"

"Yeah, really. So come on. Let's go."

Robert never went back to his boss to tell him he was leaving. He and the others went straight to the beach, where Robert took his knife and cut off the legs of his blue jeans. He stripped off his shirt and shoes and enjoyed the afternoon with his new friends and Sunny.

Death at Club

Brings Arre

Forest Hills,
Brooklyn man ac
ally shooting a
man in a brawl i
ightclub in Dece
rres yesterday
er c y New Y
olic
Po aid the su
ohn o, 23, unempl
as ed out by wi
t a me t the
Hills,
ouse ve
ng o
alled M
aste
ng E le
Ro
illing
who p

PART II

AN UP AND COMING STAR

EW YORK CITY
POLICE
QUEENS

24224

SEVEN

Summer of 1973
Age 18

ey, Ricardo!"

"Fat Andy," Ruggiano said to the restaurant owner, as Robert and Anthony were waiting to take numbers from another customer.

Fat Andy exuded toughness. His broad shoulders bore a set square jaw and an equally square chin that had taken the brunt force of many punches over the years. There wasn't a single hair out of place, each one combed back and held in place by an abundance of hair grease. He dressed sharply, usually in dark suits and wearing gold rings, looking like a well-dressed boxer.

Sitting next to Fat Andy was a man named Giuseppe, wearing an off-white apron with faint yellow and red stains. He was expressing his concern to Fat Andy over his declining street-vending business.

Ricardo came out of the kitchen, wiping his hands on a dishtowel. "What can I do you for, Fat Andy?"

"You been downtown to visit those two new skyscrapers? The World Trade Center?"

"Yeah. They just finished. Me and the wife went last week."

"They got many street vendors there?"

Ricardo put his hands on his hips and looked up. "I don't remember seeing very many."

"Much traffic?"

"Oh yeah. You know those two towers are the tallest in the world, right?"

"That's what I heard."

Ricardo nodded. "Yeah, and more to come."

Fat Andy looked back at Giuseppe. "There you go. Just move your business to Manhattan, and set up your cart in front of those buildings. You ought to make a killing."

Giuseppe didn't look pleased. "But Fat Andy, it's a long ways to Manhattan from where I am. I would have to put my cart on a truck and—"

"I can't work out all the details for you. That's *your* job. In the meantime, grab ya a plate. Dinner's on me." He pointed to Anthony and Robert. "Then see to it you place your numbers with my son and his friend over there."

Robert never returned to his job at Jet Air Freight. Instead, he hung out with Anthony every day. Anthony taught him how to "work the numbers," a game based on the last three numbers of the amount of money handled by a racetrack on any given day.

Currently, Robert and Anthony were taking bets for the Belmont number. They would make a percentage of what monies they collected, which was more than he had ever hoped to make working the docks.

With more time on his hands, Robert stayed out with Anthony and his crew, who barhopped routinely. They often got into fights. It was nothing for Little Joe to punch a member of another crew, just for bumping into him or accidentally stepping on his foot. Some smart-aleck guy said something about Anthony being the spoiled son of Fat Andy. After a couple of teeth were missing, the guy realized that Anthony was quite capable of standing on his own merits.

No matter who started the fight or why, Robert managed to use every opportunity to build his reputation as a crazed fighter who backed down from no one. He didn't care how big the other guy was or how great his reputation was. Robert loved the fight and the attention he got from it. He took on anyone willing to go toe-to-toe with him, and he would do anything to make sure he won—even if it meant using a weapon.

Ricardo escorted an unsatisfied Giuseppe to an empty chair at the other end of the table, then disappeared into the kitchen.

Fat Andy signaled for Anthony and Robert to come over. "How's it goin, boys?" He shoveled a forkful of spaghetti into his mouth.

"It's good." Anthony revealed the layers of bills and slips of paper that he and Robert had collected over the evening.

Fat Andy wiped his mouth with his napkin. "You boys hungry?" His words were distorted by the food still in his mouth.

"Starvin."

"Pull up a chair. The pasta's great tonight."

Robert and Anthony took seats at the opposite end of the table and filled their plates.

After letting Robert and Anthony eat a couple of bites, Fat Andy tipped his head toward Robert. "Good stuff, right?"

With his mouth full of pasta, Robert grinned and nodded.

"Anthony said you're doin a good job. You just need to keep that knife in your pocket and stay out of trouble—when you can."

The "knife" was the one Robert used on a bartender in the middle of a brawl about a year ago. The bartender jumped over the bar to break up a fight, and Robert thought he was coming after him. So Robert lunged toward the bartender and sunk his knife into the side of his chest. He and the rest of the crew escaped that night, thinking the bartender was dead. Fat Andy sent Robert and Anthony to Florida until things cooled down. After they got to Miami, they found out that the bartender had not died. Ten days later, Robert and Anthony returned to New York with tans and the surety that the bartender had not and would not give them up.

Once again, Robert's problems disappeared without repercussions.

"I don't even carry a switchblade anymore," Robert said. It was the truth. He had opted for a box cutter, which prevented him from being charged with a weapons felony if he were ever caught.

"Just don't leave yourself vulnerable. You got a lotta friends, but you're makin a lot of enemies too."

Fat Andy was right. Not long after Robert and Anthony returned to New York, a gang of bat-wielding hoodlums chased down Robert for slicing up the face of one of their friends—an incident he didn't even remember. As they were about to do the same thing to him, an undercover cop drove up and saved him from being mutilated.

"I'll be sure to protect myself," Robert said.

~~~~~

After Robert finished eating, he left Fat Andy and Anthony with the take for the night, minus his percentage. He met up with Little Joe, Tommy, and Frankie at a nearby club, where they bellied up to the bar for the evening. Eager to buy some clout with the cash he had earned taking numbers, he ordered drinks for his friends and a couple of girls at the club. It had been a pleasant and uneventful evening.

As they stepped into the night's muggy air, they were about to get into Frankie's car, intending to drive to a nearby diner for a bite to eat. Before Robert could open the car door, a man of massive proportions approached them. Robert thought he was high, and apparently he wanted to stay that way.

The man looked desperate. "Youse guys got any drugs?" His hands were in his pockets, and he bounced a little.

This was trouble he didn't want. "No, man. We don't do that kind of stuff." Actually, the others often smoked pot, and Robert had dabbled with some pills before. All his life, Robert had lived around junkies, and the telltale signs of drug abuse were emanating from this man.

The big guy grew more agitated and asked again.

Robert grabbed one of the girls and moved toward the car. "Man, you got the wrong guys."

"You think this is funny?" The big guy was staring at Tommy, his nostrils flared.

Before Tommy had a chance to say anything, the guy's left arm was wrapped around his head, and his right hand held a knife to his throat. He moved back a couple of steps while Robert and the others spread out, expletives flying.

"I want my drugs now!"

"We told you," Robert said. "We ain't got no drugs. You're askin the wrong guys." He reached into his back pocket and gripped the box cutter. His brother Frankie was wielding a bat, which he must have pulled out of the car.

Robert nodded toward him. By now, fighting was routine. Since joining Anthony's crew, he had brawled several times. But fighting a giant hopped up on drugs was a completely different and uncomfortable scenario. He cursed the guy. "Just let our friend go. He ain't done nothin to you."

The big guy slowed his breathing and relaxed his grip on Tommy.

"Yeah," Robert said, still maintaining his defensive position. "That's it. We don't want any trouble."

For the entire time, Tommy had been struggling to free himself. He tried to maneuver out of the man's loosened grip, but the big guy clamped down on Tommy's forehead with his bulging arm and drew the blade of his knife across his throat. Blood spewed from Tommy's neck as the big guy let go.

Tommy dropped to his knees.

The guy kicked him in the back toward the rest of the crew.

Tommy lay on the ground, not moving.

Robert felt his heart jump from his chest to his throat. He pulled out his box cutter.

Frankie charged the guy, screaming at the top of his lungs, and took a swing at him. The bat was blocked by the big guy's forearm and went flying in one direction while Frankie went flying in another.

Robert's fear turned to rage, just like it had many times before. On his right, Little Joe had his knife drawn. They stepped toward the big guy, whose sinister grin made Robert even angrier. As soon as Little Joe made his move and the big guy swiped at him with his knife, Robert went behind him and sliced through his hamstring. In a single motion, the big guy had been dropped to one knee.

With only primal instincts guiding their actions, Robert and Little Joe never let up until the big guy had let go of his knife and was flat on the ground.

"Okay, okay," the big guy said, blood oozing from his wounds. His bare hands stretched out, empty of any weapon. "That's it. You got me."

Robert was breathing hard, his saliva and sweat falling onto the giant.

Little Joe stood next to him, his knife hanging by his side, blood dripping from its tip.

Robert cursed the guy, made sure the man was incapacitated, and ran toward Tommy, who was still laid out on the street.

Frankie caught him from behind. "Somebody'll take care of him. Let's go!"

Little Joe nudged him. "Come on, Robert."

They got into Frankie's car, along with the two girls.

Frankie drove to his and Robert's parent's home on Richmond Street.

"You go on," Robert said to Frankie, looking at his bloody shirt. "I can't go in like this. Give me your keys."

Frankie handed him the keys. "Where you goin?"

"Not sure," Robert said. Actually, as he pulled away from the curb, he knew exactly where he was going.

After he realized that Robert was going back to the club, Little Joe said, "The cops'll be swarming all over the place. We'll get busted for sure."

As he turned up 93rd Street, Robert said, "I can't leave Tommy lying in the street like that."

Before they came to the intersection where the club was, they saw the reflections of red and blue lights pulsing against the buildings across the street. As they slowly drove by, they saw the big guy still sprawled out on the street. None of the ambulance attendants seemed to be in a hurry to help him. Tommy was nowhere in sight.

Little Joe said, "Somebody probably took Tommy to the hospital."

"Yeah." Robert took one last drag from his cigarette and flicked the butt out the window. He passed through the intersection and sped away to the diner nearby, where he and Little Joe used the restroom to wash up.

Ever since Alberto Devacio showed up at court when he was accused of making Molotov cocktails, Robert knew his back was covered. After all, he was part of a special family. His only concern was not getting caught. If by chance he did get caught, the odds were high that somehow he would still get away with it.

In regard to remorse, he had none. By slitting Tommy's neck, the big guy was the one who brought the fight. Were they supposed to stand there and let him get away with it? What kind of man would do that? A coward. In Robert's mind, the only choice was to take this guy out or end up like Tommy.

After he was attacked by the gang that wanted to mutilate his face, he swore that he would never let anyone have the ability to come back after him. So he did what he had to do.

~~~~~

The next morning, Robert called his house to check on Frankie.

His mother answered the phone. "Robert, what did you do?" Her voice was frantic.

"What is it, Ma?"

"The police just left with your brother in handcuffs."

"What?"

"They say he killed somebody. I know he was with you last night. What's going on?"

"I don't know, Ma. I'll call you back after I find out." He hung up before she had a chance to ask any more questions.

He sat there for a moment, his heart racing, angry that the big guy had brought this about.

Little Joe sat on the bed across from him. "What is it?"

"The police just hauled off my brother. That S.O.B. who attacked us last night is dead."

Little Joe got up, swearing by all things holy. While he paced the floor, Robert called his sister Anna, who gave the phone over to her husband, Paulie.

Robert said, "Somebody gave Frankie's license plate number to the cops."

"Listen," Paulie said. "You two need to keep a low profile. Where are you at?"

Robert told him the name of motel where they and the girls were staying.

"Look, ditch the girls. I'll call you back after I make some calls."

After hanging up with Paulie, Robert told Little Joe the gist of the conversation and sent the girls home.

In a few minutes, Paulie called back and said his brother offered for them to stay at his place.

They checked out of their room and left for Brooklyn. They stayed cooped up in Paulie's brother's apartment, adhering to the order given by Fat Andy not to go out in public, which caused them to get a little stir crazy. During that time, after the police were unable to find any evidence against him, Frankie was released.

After a couple of weeks of hiding out, Anthony showed up. After hugging both Robert and Little Joe, he stood in front of them for a while, shaking his head. "You know, you two are crazy. Taking on a psycho monster like that."

"He slit Tommy's throat," Robert said. "What were we supposed to do? The guy got what he deserved."

"I know he did. You can never trust a dope head. They're too unpredictable." He paused. "I don't know if you heard, but Tommy's gonna make a full recovery."

"We heard," Little Joe said. "That's great."

"Yeah." Anthony leaned against the door. "Get packed. You're going away for a while. Upstate. Dad has some friends up there. They'll take care of you two."

EIGHT

Summer of 1973
Age 18

L eeds, New York was a postage stamp compared to
Brooklyn. Outside its Main Street of antique shops and
quaint cafes, there was nothing around for miles. For guys
like Robert and Little Joe, this was a setting for insanity.

Fat Andy arranged for the two to hide out in the town of
about 300 while the fire from the killing settled down. They
stayed at a sprawling ranch once owned by the 1930s mobster
"Happy" Maione, one of the infamous members of Murder, Inc.
He was the grandfather of Anthony's girlfriend, and Robert
figured that connection made the ranch available. With the tiny
population came the certainty of everyone knowing everyone
else. Considering this and the fact so many people knew the
infamous ranch was still owned by the mob, two hoodlums like
Robert and Little Joe would be easy pickings for the county
sheriff. Again, they were given strict orders to stay inside.

Five months after Fat Andy sent them to Leeds, Robert and
Little Joe were sitting in the living room, watching the Mets slam
the Astros, doing their best to fight the boredom and anxiety.
They heard a knock at the door.

Robert got up quickly and turned down the TV.

Little Joe went to the door. "Who is it?"

"It's the cops, you freakin moron. Let us in, or we'll blow your
little house down."

Little Joe looked at Robert and smirked as they both recognized the voice. He opened the door to Anthony and Angelo. Anthony had been there several times, but this was Angelo's first visit. After everyone exchanged handshakes and hugs, Angelo took a case of beer into the kitchen and set it on the countertop while Anthony dropped a bag of groceries next to it.

"What brings you two here?" Robert examined the contents of the bag.

"Thought you could use a little company."

"Are you kidding me? You already kept us company several times. You need to get us out of this hell hole."

"Hell hole?" Anthony examined the room. "What? All day, all you have to do is sleep, eat, and watch TV in this gorgeous place. Can't you ride horses here?"

Little Joe smirked at the horse comment. "It's driving us crazy. You can take just so much. It's like being locked up with no bars."

Robert handed four beers from the fridge to Little Joe and their guests, and then popped his while he took his place at the dining table. "Give it to us straight. How long before we get to leave this place?"

Anthony sipped his beer. "Soon. Things are in the works."

"What does that mean?"

"That means that things are in the works, just like I said. Got a lawyer workin on the situation. Got elections coming up in November."

"Elections? What does that have to do with us?"

Anthony sighed. "Well, if certain individuals are elected, then we should be in a better situation ... if you know what I mean."

"No, I don't know what you mean."

"I mean, certain individuals are in our back pockets. If they are elected—like, certain judges and such—then we should see a lot of leniency, just in case you have to go to court."

"Oh. Okay." Robert scratched his head.

"But we're gonna try to avoid all of that. Just stay out of trouble. Do as you're told."

~~~~~

Soon after Anthony and Angelo's visit, Fat Andy ordered Robert and Little Joe separated. Robert supposed Fat Andy split them up so if one got busted, the other would still be free. Whatever the reason, Robert never knew. He stayed in Rochester for a short stint, right before he was summoned to New York. His brother-in-law Paulie picked him up, and they drove to an unfamiliar bar in Brooklyn. The sign on the door said *Closed*. Robert sat in silence, trying to figure out what was going on. He didn't think he was in any kind of trouble, even though he had griped about his situation over the last few months. It wasn't that he lacked gratitude for what was being done for him. On the contrary, the attention he was receiving made him feel important, like he was somebody. His problem was refraining from his usual activities of going to clubs and having a good time with his friends. Still, complaining wasn't going to get him into water hot enough to warrant a clandestine meeting with someone unknown. He considered the possibility that he could be meeting a lawyer who would represent him in court, since that was something he and Anthony had talked about.

As he and Paulie sat in the car, another vehicle pulled up behind them. Out stepped Little Joe and his uncle.

"Let's go," Paulie said. He and Robert got out of the car.

As the four men came together and entered the bar, no one said anything. The light was dim, with the wood paneled walls and the predominant cove lighting adding to the effect. The jukebox was playing "Bad, Bad Leroy Brown."

Robert took in his surroundings. At the back corner of the bar were the dark figures of three men sitting at a table, shrouded in a fog of smoke. As he got closer, he saw Fat Andy with a cigarette clamped between two fingers. He felt he should recognize one of the other men, but nothing was coming to him.

"There's the boys," Fat Andy said as Robert and Little Joe stopped at the table. "I want you to meet some friends of mine." He motioned to the man Robert thought he knew. "This is Nicky."

Nicky held out his hand. "We met before. At Alberto's club."

"Oh yeah." Robert shook his hand. "I was a kid at the time."

"Alberto had a lot of good to say about you."

"Is that right?"

"Yeah. Said you had a lot of spunk." He motioned across the table. "This is my friend Lenny."

Robert and Little Joe both shook his hand.

"Have a seat," Fat Andy said.

The four men pulled up chairs to the table and sat. After ordering drinks, Fat Andy got to the business at hand.

"I brought you two here because I'm about to call in a favor. You two need to keep moving so the cops don't find you. So I'm sending you to Jersey with these friends of mine." Fat Andy pointed to a table across the room, where three other men were sitting. The one in the middle nodded toward them. "These guys'll take care of youse. Nicky and Lenny here are gonna be the go-betweens. You need anything, these two will get it for you. Got it?"

"Yeah," Robert and Little Joe said.

After the meeting, Robert and Little Joe drove with the three men, who belonged to the Campesi crime family, to New Jersey, where they stayed at a hotel. After two weeks, they were moved to an apartment.

Robert and Little Joe were upset with the situation, because they were told they had to earn their keep by working at the Campesi-owned restaurant, washing dishes. Robert thought he was well above such menial work. Fortunately for him and Little Joe, the cops busted the guys hiding them out before any trouble arose. Out of options, Fat Andy was forced to bring Robert and Little Joe back to New York.

NINE

May 1974
Age 19

Ten months after going on the lam, Anthony drove Robert and Little Joe back to New York, where they stayed with a Jewish guy named Squinty, in his apartment on Pacific and Sachmann. For the first two months, it was more of the same—stay inside and don't cause any trouble. Robert was still going stir crazy, but he knew this was what he had to do, although he and Little Joe would take an occasional nighttime stroll. People would come around and bring food, or give money to Squinty to buy food.

Summertime rolled around again. Blaise took Robert and Little Joe to Corona, Queens, where they met a guy who gave them fake driver's licenses. For now, Robert would be known as John Rosato.

Afterward, Blaise dropped Robert and Little Joe off at the apartment.

~~~~~

Over the next few months Robert learned a lot about Nicky. He was a thick-blooded Brooklynite whose parents were immigrants from Italy. He was short like Robert, actually two inches shorter. But Robert soon found out that Nicky wasn't a guy you'd challenge. He was tough as nails, and his intelligence made him a daunting adversary.

Nicky didn't have the clout of Fat Andy, since Fat Andy and a few others were the only made men at the time. But he and his associate Lenny were genuine mobsters, dedicated to that lifestyle.

Robert started driving for Nicky, which meant he was no longer cooped up at Squinty's place. Nicky had a 1973 Cadillac El Dorado, and Robert loved to drive it around, especially when Nicky didn't need him. He'd pick up Angelo, and they'd cruise around, trying to impress girls. For the first time in a while, Robert was experiencing the freedom he was used to, not to mention the increased status.

Even with a fake driver's license, Robert knew he needed to play it safe, which meant avoiding the cops. After going to work for Nicky, his relationship with Anthony cooled.

Anthony's crew had already lost Tommy. After surviving the attack, Tommy quit hanging out with them, leaving Herman and Little Joe as Anthony's crew. But in October, Little Joe was arrested for the murder of the big guy.

In December, on his twentieth birthday, a large group of friends took Robert to a club—Broadcasters Inn, so named because it was housed in the building that used to be a radio station. The communication tower was still mounted on top. It was one of the most popular dance clubs in the area. Every night it was open, long streams of high-heeled girls in sequined dresses and guys in silk shirts lined its perimeter.

Robert and his party—which included Angelo and Herman—arrived at 10:00 p.m. and walked inside the large foyer, still decorated with colorful lights and garland left over from Christmas. Since they were known for ringing up healthy bar tabs, they were able to skip the long wait and the $5.00 cover charge.

"Hey, Robert," the doorman said as he unhooked the thick satiny rope on the stanchion dividing the foyer from the rest of the club.

"Hey, Jake, good to see you," Robert said. "I see the place is packed tonight."

"As usual," Jake said. The unusually buff doorkeeper kept an eye on the line of commoners trying to wiggle into the warmth of the foyer.

"Do you have a place for us?" Robert passed a twenty to Jake as he shook his hand.

Jake pocketed the twenty. "I got some tables reserved for youse guys in the back." He looked toward the dance floor and signaled a club employee, who hurried over. "Help my friends out here, will ya?"

Robert and his entourage followed the young man past the first group of booths and tables, past the dance floor to the tables near the back, close to the club's inoperative kitchen.

After ordering and finishing off their first round of beers and Scotch whiskey on rocks, Angelo brought out a white quarter-sheet birthday cake with "Happy Birthday Robert" written in red. He pulled out his lighter and lit the single large candle in the center as everyone sang "Happy Birthday." When half the cake had disappeared, most of the party moved to the dance floor. Robert and a few others went to the kitchen.

"I got a little somethin for ya. Angelo led Robert to the corner of the kitchen, where several rows of white powder were lined up like a plowed field of snow. "Go ahead." Angelo offered Robert a straw cut to one-third its original size.

Robert was accustomed to recreational drug use. Since the time he was a kid sniffing model airplane glue, he had tried several drugs—including cocaine—with no signs of addiction. Still, he was a little hesitant, because he considered himself a mobster, and the usage of drugs was strictly banned.

Then again, it was his twentieth birthday, ceremoniously moving from the teenage years into adulthood. Just one line of coke never hurt anyone, right?

Robert took the straw, brought it up to his right nostril, and lined it up with one of the white rows.

~~~~~

Robert was having a great time, especially after meeting a girl named Sharon and her friends, with whom he returned to the kitchen for more cake and coke.

Close to midnight, he noticed a group of Puerto Ricans walk in. They scoped the place out, seeming to evaluate the possibilities of either scoring or fighting.

It wasn't hard for Robert to recognize the potential for trouble. He nudged Herman and nodded toward the other guys, who were now at the bar.

"Yeah," Herman yelled over the blaring music. "I saw them when they first come in."

"Keep an eye on em." Robert turned his attention back to Sharon.

As the night turned into morning, Sharon had to leave, so Robert escorted her into the foyer. As he reached for the handle, the door flew open. On the other side was one of the guys from the other crew, breathing a frosty cloud into the chilly night. Robert locked eyes with him.

Hatred seethed from both men.

Sharon thought the guy was holding the door open for them and started to go through. As she put one foot in the doorway, the man shut it, and she screamed in pain.

Without a thought, Robert threw his shoulder into the door, knocking the guy on the other side to the ground. He reached down and picked him up, cursing him and his family. "You think it's okay to hurt a lady?"

Before the guy had a chance to reply, Robert had him up against the wall and was relentlessly pounding him with his fists, never giving the guy a chance to throw his own punches. When his hand got sore, he took his gun from his pants and beat him.

Robert's opponent slumped to the ground.

"Not such a tough guy anymore, huh?" Robert wiped his runny nose with the back of his hand. He kicked the guy in the ribs before opening the door and going back inside.

Another fight had broken out inside the foyer, with several of his friends and members of the other crew. In the middle of the ruckus, Robert saw someone lying on the floor. With his gun at his side, he walked over to the guy. Robert couldn't see his face, but he knew the guy wasn't one of his friends. As he was putting the gun into his pants, he tried to release the hammer, but it slipped. A bullet rifled into the floor next to Robert's feet, setting off shrieks by the female patrons standing close by.

"He shot him!" One of the women was pointing at Robert.

"What? No! He was ... my gun just ..."

Someone screamed, and Robert made a quick escape through the front door, with Angelo and Herman right behind him, disappearing into the frigid night.

TEN

T he weather had turned bitter cold, and the plows were pushing snow to the edges of Liberty Avenue. Robert marched up the sidewalk and slipped into an after-hours joint at the corner, where Angelo, Little Joe, and Herman were waiting for him at the bar, nurturing their drinks.

"Cold as a meat locker out there." Robert rubbed his hands together and blew on them.

The others acknowledged him with a nod.

He signaled the bartender, who came over, wiping his hands on a towel.

"Get me a beer."

The bartender got a mug, drew a draft from the tap, and placed it in front of Robert, who was scouting the rest of the place. Fat Andy was at a table in the back. Anthony was sitting next to him. Robert waved toward them.

Fat Andy tipped his head, but Anthony only stared coolly at him.

After Robert fell into the care of Nicky, he unofficially became a part of his crew. This hadn't set well with Anthony, who felt betrayed.

With Anthony's cold reception, Robert looked down at the end of the bar and saw another member of Fat Andy's crew, a guy called Nunzi. The beautiful, shorthaired blonde next to him happened to make eye contact, and he recognized the girl.

Robert asked Angelo, "Isn't that Janice's sister?"

"Yeah, I think so."

The words had barely left Angelo's mouth when a shot glass flew through the air and hit Robert on his right eye. In pain, he covered his eye with his hand.

"What are you gonna do about it, you freakin punk?" The remark came from Nunzi, who was now standing and facing Robert, bowing his chest, his arms in the air.

Electricity raced through Robert's body, tensing every muscle. The bar stool fell over as he stood and charged Nunzi. But Angelo, Herman, and Little Joe pulled him back.

"I'll kill you!" Robert yelled at Nunzi.

"Come on, you punk."

"Hey!" Fat Andy's strong voice was clear. The fight was over.

Rage still saturated his veins, and Robert considered ignoring the order. After a few breaths, he released the tension in his body, and his friends let him go. Angelo picked up his stool, and Robert sat on it, staring at Nunzi.

A few minutes later, Fat Andy called Robert over, saw the cut on his eye, and stared at him for a moment. "You look upset."

"I was disrespected," Robert said.

"What do you want to do about it?" Fat Andy's grin was small but said a lot.

"I wanna kill him."

Fat Andy shook his head. "Robert, your temper's gonna get the best of you someday. Don't you know if you take Nunzi out, you're gonna have to kill everybody else in this place?"

Robert called Fat Andy and Anthony a few choice swear words. "I don't care. I'll kill em all if I have to."

Fat Andy looked at Anthony, then back at Robert. "I'm not gonna give you permission to kill Nunzi. Besides, you need to learn a thing or two about respect."

Robert didn't move, staring straight ahead at nothing in particular. Fat Andy's response shouldn't have been a surprise, since their relationship had been strained for some time. Yet he still felt Fat Andy should maintain a sense of honor and stick with it, no matter what the circumstances or persons involved.

Feeling set up and betrayed, Robert got up abruptly, knocked over his chair, and left.

~~~~~

It was four in the morning. After leaving the club, Robert went directly over to Nicky's apartment and banged on the door.

A disoriented Nicky answered and let him in. "You need to relax, Robert."

"Ain't gonna happen." Robert paced the living room floor.

"You're too cocky." Nicky yawned and adjusted his robe. "You think you're indestructible, and that kind of thinking'll get you killed. You gotta be smart. Play it cool."

"But Nicky, I can't let him get away with this."

"It's a little cut. No big deal."

"Maybe to you, but not to me."

Nicky stuck his hands into his robe pockets. "You know, you're probably signing my death warrant as well as yours." He sighed. "Okay, kid. Do what you have to do."

The truth was, Robert didn't care about the repercussions or who was affected. He was only concerned with his reputation, and presently, his reputation as a fighter was tarnished. There was no option but for Nunzi to pay.

With the idea of putting a bullet between Nunzi's eyes, he drove Nicky's car back to the club and parked a block away. He pulled the car to the side of the street, turned off the engine, and waited for him to come out. He pulled a cigarette from his pocket, then remembered Nicky's strict no-smoking-in-the-car rule. After looking around, he got out of the car. A wintry blast made him turn up the collar on his brown leather jacket. As he moved to the sidewalk, he turned his back to the wind and lit the cigarette with his Zippo lighter.

Halfway through the cigarette, his ears were frozen, and a dusting of snow covered him. He threw the cigarette to the curb, got back into the car, and started the engine to get warm. After warming his hands, he turned on the radio, laid the seat back, and watched the club entrance through the veil of snow.

Three hours later, Robert woke up to the tapping on his frosted window. With cobwebs in his head, he rolled down the window to the face of a police officer.

"Hey buddy, I need you to step out of the car."

Robert rubbed his eyes. "I was just … waiting for my girlfriend."

The cop scanned the inside the car. "I need you to step out of the car, show your I.D. and registration."

Adrenaline rushed through Robert as he realized the gun he planned to use on Nunzi was under the seat. "Hey, it's okay. I'll just move the car." Robert started to put it in drive.

"Sir," the officer said with a much more stern voice, "turn off the engine and step out. Now!"

Reluctantly, Robert got out and handed him his fake driver's license and the car's registration.

In searching the car, the officer found the gun and took him to the local precinct on 106th Street in Ozone Park. He was booked under a false name, so no warrants were found. He stayed in the holding cell overnight and was released after his lawyer, which he didn't know he had, gave him $400 and told him to post bail. Robert found that to be strange, since he hadn't appeared before the judge yet. But the judge set the bail at exactly $400. Robert paid it and was out of there with the idea of never coming back.

He had a problem though. After he was arrested, Nicky's car was impounded. Nicky wasn't mad about that, but he told Robert he had to go back to court so he could get it out.

Robert returned to court a couple more times, each time trying to get the car released. The last time he went, he was arrested again. Robert and Nicky didn't know standard procedure. Cops try to match shooting crimes with those arrested for illegal possession of a weapon. They brought in witnesses to the killing at Broadcasters Inn and matched Robert's mug shot with who they thought was the shooter. When he went back for the weapons charge, they arrested him for the Broadcasters Inn murder that had happened on his birthday.

In handcuffs, with his jacket folded over his hands, Robert was brought to Central Booking. As he entered the lobby, someone said, "Hey buddy, look here."

A photographer from *Newsweek* was poised with a camera, but Robert used the jacket to hide his face.

"You moron," Robert said. "Get lost!"

That same day, the police tied Robert to the killing of the giant junkie a year and a half earlier. They tried to get him to implicate others in the murder cases, but Robert's dedication to his friends ran deep. He wasn't about to give anyone up, just for a little leniency in his case.

He stayed locked up for three months, waiting on a more merciful judge who would set a bail that he could make. The bail was finally set at $40,000. Nicky and Lenny called in a favor from a friend to put up a couple of properties and with the help of Robert's mother and sisters, they pooled enough money to get him out of jail with the order not to travel outside New York.

ELEVEN

Tension was brewing in Brooklyn, but no one seemed willing to acknowledge it. Nicky was a good earner for Fat Andy, so Fat Andy had promised to recommend Nicky once the books opened up. But both men knew that as soon as Nicky was a made man, he would be equal to Fat Andy, which meant Fat Andy would no longer get a cut of Nicky's earnings.

Nicky was aware of this and knew, when the time came, Fat Andy would drag his feet regarding the proposal. With that in mind, Nicky came up with a plan.

Near the end of 1975, Robert drove Nicky and Lenny to the Ravenite Social Club, an establishment belonging to Aneillo "Neil" Dellacroce, the Gambino crime family's underboss. He had held that position for over ten years—first under Carlo Gambino and then with the new boss, Gambino's cousin Paul Castellano. Even though he was second in command, most of the family felt like he was the actual backbone of the organization. He and a capo named Charles "Charlie West" deLutro were running a couple of clubs in the area, making money off illegal gambling schemes.

Nicky, Lenny, and Robert walked to the back of the club, where Neil was playing cards with a few friends. Robert ran his fingers through his hair and tucked the back of his shirt. Meeting Neil was like meeting the president of the United States. As they approached the table, Charlie West stood, and Nicky and Lenny kissed him.

After shaking hands, Nicky made the introduction. "This is Robert, our up-and-coming star."

Robert's heart fluttered. Nicky had used those very words before, but hearing him say it in front of the second most powerful man in the Gambino family made Robert swell with pride.

Neil was expressionless as he extended his hand.

Robert shook his hand. "It's a pleasure to meet you."

Neil turned to Nicky. "Sit down. We were just getting started with a friendly game of pinochle. You're my partner."

As they played cards, Robert stood guard from a dark corner a few feet away from the table, where cards were zipping across like Frisbees amid a cloud of lazy smoke and a steady stream of crude humor.

Later on, Robert realized that Nicky wasn't just playing pinochle. He was also stacking the deck. His direct connection with Neil and Charlie West was all part of a strategy to ensure his place at the table of made men, once the books opened.

~~~~~

After dropping Lenny off, Robert parked the car outside Nicky's apartment in Canarsie.

"Come on inside," Nicky said.

In the short time he and Nicky had associated with each other, he had come to admire Nicky as a son marveling a heroic father. Nicky showed true interest in Robert and was willing to share with him the ins and outs of the business. He also gave Robert money for no reason, and when Robert's services weren't needed, he let Robert drive his car.

Nicky wanted to take Robert under his wing, show him the ropes, and teach him to become somebody. And when Robert did get into fights or stirred up trouble, Nicky was understanding and never came down on him, since it was a part of Robert's nature.

Sure, what Robert was learning was mostly illegal moneymaking tactics, and it could land him in jail. But that didn't matter. He'd learned from people like Principal Aquinas and Sister Anne—authority figures who should have been more of a guide than a hindrance in teaching him the due diligence of justice. But if he was going to get somewhere in life, he had to play by his own set of rules.

Nicky shut the door to the apartment. "I think Neil liked you."

"Oh yeah? How could you tell?"

Nicky laughed. "He wrote the book on how to wear a poker face. That's something you need to learn. Never let nobody know what you're thinking."

Robert nodded, a student absorbing the wisdom of his mentor.

"And"—Nicky waved a finger toward Robert—"never let nobody know what you're feeling. In this business, you never know who you can trust, and you never know who you might be asked to whack." He turned his finger straight up. "Hold on a second. I got something for you."

When Nicky returned from his bedroom, he handed Robert a business card and blue-star sapphire ring. "I want you to have these. Fat Andy gave them to me when I was young. I want to pass them on to you."

Robert read the card aloud. "You are now a member of the Mafia." He laughed. "I guess this is supposed to be my official membership card, huh?"

Nicky smiled. "Put it on."

Robert slipped the ring onto his left pinky.

"Robert, you're going places. You're a likable kid. You're tough. After I show you what I know, you'll have everything you need to go far in the family."

~~~~~

Soon after Nicky's meeting with Neil and Charlie West, Nicky and Lenny opened crap games in Manhattan—a source of income they had yet to tap into—a way for Nicky to prove his savvy. He was aggressive in his approach toward the endeavor and opened three locations at three different times. One was in a factory building on Mott Street. It opened at noon and closed at 4:00 p.m. on weekdays. The second one was at night on Flatbush Avenue, opening at 8:00 p.m. and closing at midnight. The third was on Elizabeth and Houston Streets, open on weekends.

Robert worked at all three of the crap games, mostly as a ladder man. His job was to stand on a ladder overlooking the tables and make sure everybody was being honest. If he caught someone cheating, he tossed him out. Occasionally he dealt cards at the poker tables.

"Robert!" Lenny was at the base of the ladder, waving him down. Standing next to him was Antonio, another one of the crew.

Robert climbed down and straightened his shirt.

"I need you to go with Antonio here," Lenny said. "Me and Nicky got to step out for a couple of hours. When you finish, meet us back here."

Rumor had it that—as predicted—the books had opened for official membership into the family a few months earlier, and several people they knew were proposed, including Robert's childhood hero, Gene Gotti. Now, he sensed the time had come for Nicky and Lenny to be inducted. But no matter whether that was what happened or not, it was taboo to talk about and something any member was required to deny.

Robert grabbed his brown leather jacket, followed Antonio out to his car, and got in on the passenger side.

Antonio was someone Robert knew as a kid, but the two weren't acquainted until he started working for Nicky. Unlike Robert, Antonio was married and had kids. Beyond work, Robert had no other relationship with him.

On top of picking up what they called "policies" or "slips"—which amounted to the person's name, three numbers scribbled on a piece of paper, and the cash—Antonio had a regular route selling black-market cigarettes for Nicky. Several times, Robert had gone with Antonio and helped him unload cartons at homes and factories in the East New York, Canarsie, and Mill Basin areas.

Running numbers was a chancy scheme, and the police arrested Robert more than once for the crime. One morning, he heard the pounding on his front door and cops yelling. Instead of surrendering, he ran out the back, wearing nothing more than his briefs. After finding some clothes, he met up with Nicky and the rest of the guys. They agreed to turn themselves in. Robert had no desire to go on the lam again, especially for an illegal sports gambling charge.

Nicky didn't either, saying, "You can't make any money when you're on the run."

Of course, Robert's reputation among the police was well known. After his arrest for the murder at Broadcasters Inn and subsequent release after making bail, it was not uncommon for him to be pulled over a couple of times a week—if only for the purpose of letting him know they were watching him.

Still, he continued the life of illegal gambling and selling contraband. The business was lucrative, and Robert made money quickly and with little effort.

Nicky encouraged Robert to ease up on the barroom brawls, since all it caused was trouble for him and others. On occasion when Nicky needed an outstanding debt to be collected, he allowed him to express his hostilities. At first, Robert found it a little strange to beat up someone who hadn't ticked him off. In time, though, he learned to transfer his anger from some other source—being mad at his girlfriend, some chump at a bar, or his broken radiator in his bedroom that caused him to freeze at night—onto the one he was beating up.

~~~~~

By the time Robert and Antonio returned to Flatbush Avenue, the celebration party had already started. Many of Nicky's and Lenny's friends and associates were there. Neither Fat Andy nor Anthony were there. Food was abundant, spread across three banquet tables. Among the usual beer and liquor were bottles of champagne.

"Robert, glad you made it back." As he patted Robert on the shoulder, Nicky's smile looked permanently fixed on his face. His eyes were equally jubilant. "Grab a glass. We're about to make a toast."

Robert took one of the fluted glasses from the tray held by one of the kids working the club. He was about fourteen years old, with dark hair, and he had light patches of freckles on each cheek. He smiled at Robert and was quick with the right words, but his eyes told a completely different story. They revealed a hunger that Robert recognized from his youth, and it made him realize that even after all these years, he was still trying to relieve that same hunger. Perhaps now that Nicky and Lenny were made men, his day of reckoning was not too far away. Perhaps he would soon ease the pangs that had been haunting him for so many years. After all, satisfaction wasn't that difficult to attain, was it?

From his pocket, Robert handed a twenty-dollar bill to the boy. "Keep the change."

"Thanks." The kid tucked the twenty securely in his pants pocket, at first hesitant to leave, thinking he needed to do something more to earn the generous tip. Finally he moved to the next group of men.

Nicky raised his glass. "I'd like to make a toast to all you slime balls here."

Everybody within earshot laughed, some a little too hard.

"May you have great health and lots of prosperity. Because when you're healthy and wealthy, I'm healthy and wealthy. Cheers!"

The sound of glasses clanking together echoed throughout the place as the men celebrating the unmentionable induction sipped their drinks. Nicky downed his entire glass of champagne.

Nicky threw his arm around Robert. "This is just the beginning. You think you're making nice money now? Wait until you hear about where we go from here."

Robert laughed. "You know, Nicky, you're crazy."

Nicky drew Robert in tight and smiled. "Yeah. Crazy like a fox."

TWELVE

T
hough things were going well for Robert, and he was making a lot of money, he still had the murder charge lingering over him. He stayed in and out of court for a couple of years, dealing with not only the murder at Broadcasters Inn but also the murder of the big guy several years back and the charge for illegal possession of a weapon. During that time, he was arrested on unrelated charges but never spent more than one night in jail.

For a cool $12,000, Nicky and Lenny attained the services of a lawyer named Maurice Brill, who handled all three of Robert's cases. He assured Robert that he would see little, if any, prison time.

Yet, as Maurice began working on the case, he realized the situation was more difficult than it seemed at first. The DA had labeled Robert as a bad apple and wanted to put him away for a long time. With this in mind, Maurice believed it was in Robert's best interest to work out a plea bargain for all three charges. He finally got the DA to agree to ten years, which at that time meant Robert would probably serve eight years in a state penitentiary. Maurice encouraged him to take the plea, and Robert really considered it, knowing that a lost trial could send him away for at least twenty-five years, if not for the rest of his life. Still, he wanted to talk to his family and see if they agreed with him. A slightly annoyed assistant DA told him that he either made the deal now or it was off. This angered Robert. It was his life at stake here, not anyone else's. He cursed the prosecutor and told him he would see him in court.

Maurice wasn't too happy with Robert's outburst, but he never said anything. Since Robert was caught red-handed with the gun, he started working on the weapons charge. Not long before the trial, an agreement was made on the weapons charge: one to three years, but it was understood that nothing could be done about it until the two murder cases were done.

According to Maurice, the murder case at Broadcasters Inn would be the most difficult to beat. Five witnesses swore that Robert walked up to the guy and shot him while he was on the floor. Since he was innocent, Robert thought he shouldn't have anything to worry about. Maurice's confidence was not equal to Robert's.

As Robert sat next to Maurice at the defendant's table, dressed in a suit with a tie, his hands sweated as they waited for the judge to enter the courtroom. He pulled at his shirt collar.

The door to the judge's chamber opened. A tall, clean-shaven black man with small wire-rimmed glasses moved quickly through the doorway, floating in a sea of rippling black silk.

"All rise," the bailiff said. "The Honorable Kenneth Brown presiding."

"You may be seated," the bailiff said after the judge took his seat. "Court is now in session."

Robert's tie had worked its way out from inside his buttoned-up jacket. He tucked it in as he sat in the uncomfortable wooden chair. For the first time, he looked toward the twelve men and women who would be deciding his fate. All were focused on the judge, who was running through procedural jargon with them.

One of the large doors leading into the courtroom opened with some low-level rustling. His mother in one of her two church outfits was leading a tardy entourage that included his father, sister Anna, and his girlfriend, Phyllis. Behind them was Michael Cotillo, a longtime friend who recently went to work for Lenny after his business went belly up.

Opening statements began the trial. The assistant DA claimed that Robert started the brawl. While the victim was down on the floor of the club's foyer, he walked over to him, pulled out his gun, and shot him in the head. The man was full of indignation, as if it were his own brother who had been killed. He pointed his finger at Robert several times. It was all Robert could do to keep himself from jumping over the table and breaking the DA's finger. Apparently Maurice sensed the tension and discreetly placed his hand on Robert's arm.

After enduring the false accusations for a good ten minutes, Maurice stood before the jurors and began his discourse. He told the jurors how the fight started, when one of the decedent's friends injured a young lady. Robert was defending her honor outside when someone else shot the decedent in the foyer.

Over the next two days, the prosecutor called each of the five witnesses against Robert, who were all friends of the victims. Each witness's testimony appeared to corroborate the stories of the other four.

Robert wished he had taken the plea bargain.

When Maurice began the cross-examination, he meticulously went through the witness's account, having him restate his location prior to and at the time of the incident, what type of gun Robert was holding, and where he was in relation to the body. His story was the same as before.

Robert began to wonder whose side Maurice was working for.

But then Maurice did something that threw a wrench into the prosecution's case. He asked the witness what Robert did after supposedly shooting the victim. The witness stammered over his answer.

Over the first two days of the trial, as Maurice cross-examined each of the five witnesses, each one of them had a different answer regarding Robert's actions after his gun went off. A chink in the prosecution's armor-clad case had been found.

On the morning of the third day, Maurice called the club's doorman Jake, who testified that Robert was outside, fighting someone else when the gunshot occurred. He then called several expert witnesses who testified that, according to the coroner's report and forensic evidence, the victim was shot standing up and from the front, not the back as the witnesses said. Also, the weapon used to kill the victim was a 9 mm, which flew in the face of the witnesses' testimonies that Robert was carrying a revolver.

On the fifth day, the jury went in for deliberation while Robert and Maurice waited in the bullpen.

The bailiff came in. "The jury's asked for a portion of the testimony," he told Maurice. "Thought you'd like to know."

"Thanks, George," Maurice said. As the bailiff left, Maurice buried his mouth into his right hand and covered his stomach with the left. He looked as if he were about to vomit.

Robert turned to face Maurice. "What's wrong?"

Maurice shook his head without saying a word.

"Need some water? Tums? A doctor? Tell me what's going on."

Maurice sat up. "Usually, if they ask to review testimony ... It's been my experience that they're about to return a guilty verdict."

"But I'm innocent."

"Robert, sit back down." Maurice tugged on his sleeve. "And keep your voice down."

Maurice's disposition lightened when the bailiff returned so soon to inform them that the jury was back after only two and a half hours of deliberation.

Robert's stomach flipped when the judge asked him to stand for the reading of the verdict.

Maurice stood with him.

As the jury foreman's voice became obscured among Robert's thoughts, he couldn't help but think about how a good portion of his life—if not all of it—was going to be spent in a penitentiary. For Robert, that meant no more Scotch on the rocks at his favorite clubs, no more girls, and no more partying until he felt like going home. It meant no more Aunt Rosie's pumpkin pie on Thanksgiving, laughing at an inebriated Uncle Barry dressed as Santa Claus, or trying to get the right present to the right child. It meant no more of his mother's home-cooked meals, especially her Italian meatballs and pasta. The remainder of his birthdays would amount to a card or two in the mail. His status as an up-and-coming star among his Mafia associates would be yanked out from under him, since jailbirds are nothing but consumers, wards of the state.

From what he understood, doing time in prison was nothing like doing time in jail. The prison was for hardened criminals, the type who had no problem sticking someone with a shank just because he wouldn't give up his mashed potatoes at chow time. The truth be known, that wasn't much different from Robert's way of thinking, so he knew he could handle it. Yet it was not the way of life he wanted, nor the place.

He was young, and there were still things he wanted to do and places he wanted to see. Las Vegas sounded like a perfect fit for him—lots of money to be made, plenty of women to be had, partying all day and all night, living by his own rules. Sin City was where he belonged.

The jury foreman read the verdict. "Not guilty."

Robert heard the words, saw Maurice's smile, and felt the pats on his back, but its meaning didn't immediately sink in.

The judge called his name. "You are free to go. After you sign some papers and process out."

An hour later, with Phyllis hanging off of his arm and his family close behind, Robert floated across the street to a restaurant. They found a large booth in a corner where they could celebrate with a little privacy.

Michael Cotillo, who was sitting next to Robert's father, was the first to say something about the trial. "What were you thinking when they came back so soon with the verdict?"

"I tell ya," Robert said. "I thought I was a goner."

After the waiter took their order, his mother said, "You know you got some good friends who helped you out. Thank God." She crossed herself. "Your father and I are relieved. I pray to God every day to send his angels to watch over you."

"Yeah." Robert looked at his father, toying with his fork. His smile was slight, but Robert knew what it meant.

Even though trouble was so prevalent and caused his mother a lot of heartache, his father enjoyed the credibility given to him by his bar pals because of his son. For him, it was sort of a badge of honor to have raised such a tough kid, one who was important enough that some of the most powerful men in New York went to a lot of effort to make sure his son walked out of that courtroom a free man.

His father looked up, and Robert mirrored his grin.

"You've sown your wild oats," his mother said. "You need to think about settling down, starting your own family." She smiled at Phyllis, who turned her eyes toward the menu.

Robert grinned. "Come on, Ma."

When they left the restaurant, all Robert could think about was getting back to Nicky and Lenny and soaking up the notoriety he earned for beating the case.

~~~~~

Eventually, the DA dropped the murder charges against Robert and Little Joe for the killing of the big guy. The incident had occurred many years ago, and the DA wasn't able to produce witnesses.

Robert was sentenced to one to three years for possession of an illegal weapon but was released on an appeal bond. Eighteen months later, his lawyer Maurice notified him that the case was dropped because an illegal search was performed on the car.

His relationship with Phyllis didn't work out so well. She broke up with him soon after the trial. He was devastated.

Unfortunately, there would be no settling down for Robert for a long time.

THIRTEEN

November 1977
Age 22

O f all Robert's friends and acquaintances, none of them were quite like Michael Cotillo. He was a handsome young man who had a reputation of being one of the nicest guys around. He was popular among the ladies. His and Robert's mothers were good friends. When Robert and Michael were toddlers, the mothers took turns babysitting the other son. As the boys grew older, Michael was drawn to athletics while Robert opted for the F&R Gang and fighting. But the two remained close, even after Michael's parents separated. Michael never spoke harshly to anyone. He always had a good attitude, even when his situation was less than stellar. To Robert, Michael was a stand-up kind of guy he greatly admired, who didn't deserve the tragedy that would soon befall him.

~~~~~

A few months before the Broadcaster Inn murder trial, Michael called. "I've got a fruit stand on Jamaica Avenue."

"Yeah," Robert said, "I know that. What? Is somebody giving you a hard time? I can take care of that."

"No, it's nothing like that. It's ... the business flopped. I'm broke."

Robert had become well-known as Nicky's righthand man, and as a result, many of his old friends came looking for a handout or a job. He loved to help others. He was no Mother

Teresa, but he enjoyed the notoriety that came with such acts of good will. It also gave him the opportunity to build his own crew.

"So you need a couple of dollars? I can loan you—"

"No, man. I just need a job and thought maybe you could help me out."

Robert scratched the side of his nose. "Sure, I can get you a job. You know where the club is on Pacific Street? Come by later on. I'll see what I can do."

Michael showed up that night, his eyes shifting from one end of the building to the other. When he saw Robert signaling from one of the card tables, he smiled and walked over.

Robert hugged him. "My man, it's been a long time." He looked at his dark, curly hair. "Did you always have an Afro, or is this something new?"

Michael laughed. "Always had the curly hair, but the Afro's been around for a couple of years."

"Looks good on ya. Hey, let me find Nicky and Lenny so I can introduce you."

Robert looked around.

"Could I talk to you first?"

Robert took Michael back to the storage room near the back of the building and shut the door.

Michael said, "Hey, man. I just wanted to tell you how much I appreciate you doing this for me."

"Sure thing. You stood up for me many times when I was a kid. Remember when no one would pick me to play punch ball? But when you were captain, you always picked me, just like my sister did. That meant a lot to me."

Michael smiled. "Well, like I said, I appreciate it." He paused. "I know the … line of work you're in. To be honest, I don't think I could do some of the things you guys do. Like the rough stuff."

"No worries, man. I got you covered. Just trust me." Robert patted him on the back as he opened the door. "You good at math?"

~~~~~

Robert introduced Michael to Nicky and Lenny, and before long, Lenny had Michael running routes, picking up policies for him—the same thing Robert did when he started working for Fat Andy. Although illegal, it required no "rough stuff," as Robert had promised.

For several months, the only time Robert saw Michael was in passing. Occasionally, Robert invited Michael to go out on the town, but Michael always declined.

Within the Gambino family, several factions were friendly toward one another, but some were intolerable. Most fights involving Robert were with members of other crews. This was unlike his days as a kid in the F&R gang in Brooklyn, fighting other street gangs, when ethnicity dictated the hatred. That same hatred existed, but now it was based on greed, lust, and jealousy, brewed within the ranks of the Italian culture.

Just as Charlie West headed up several crews that included Nicky's, an established mobster named Charlie Wagner was in charge of a another part of New York, which included the crew from Ozone Park. Gene Gotti, Robert's childhood hero, and his brother John were a part of this crew. Nicky and John had been rivals from childhood, both growing up in two different street gangs fighting each other—Nicky from Eastern Parkway and John from Robert's old neighborhood.

Unknown to Robert, Michael was dating a girl who was the former girlfriend of an associate in Charlie Wagner's crew. Among mobsters, this was a major taboo, even if the girl was no longer dating him.

Soon after the trial, Robert finally convinced Michael to go out on the town with him. They stayed out late, jumping from one bar to the next. At 4:00 in the morning, Robert, Michael, and a couple of other guys went to the Blue Fountain Diner, a popular place to eat after a long night.

A girlfriend of Phyllis's named Cathy met him at the steps. She looked irritated. "Hey Robert, there's some jerk in there named Vito giving Phyllis a hard time."

Robert and Phyllis were no longer dating, but he still had strong feelings for her. Since she was the daughter of reputed mobster Freddy DiCongilio, Robert enjoyed a higher status among his peers. On several of their dates, they dined with the famous and not-so-famous at the Copa Cabana. Even though Robert wasn't going out with her anymore, he wasn't going to let some guy hassle her.

Robert snuffed out his cigarette against the brick wall. "Where are they at?"

"She's in a booth. On the right. Lois and Martha are sitting with her."

As Robert walked in, he immediately saw Phyllis, leaning away from a long-haired guy in blue-jeans and silk shirt. He had one hand on the back of their booth and the other on the table.

When Phyllis saw Robert, her eyes conveyed desperation.

Robert strolled with conviction down the aisle to the booth. "Phyllis. You all right?" He looked at Vito, who now stood facing Robert.

"She's fine," Vito said, his arms crossed in front of him.

"I wasn't talking to you," Robert said, referring to Vito as an unflattering part of the human anatomy.

"Who are you?"

Out of respect for the owners and the girls, Robert didn't want to stir up trouble inside the diner. So he got within a few inches of Vito and whispered, "Why don't you come outside and find out?" Robert turned toward the exit.

Apparently, Vito was up for the fight, since he followed him outside. To avoid disrupting the flow of business into the Blue Fountain Diner, they went to the other side of the street. Before they came to blows, Robert heard another commotion on the other side of Cross Bay Boulevard. The guys in his crew were fighting another group of guys. Under the streetlights of early predawn, Robert saw Michael in the middle of brawl, a fish out of water. Forgetting his fight with Vito, Robert ran to Michael, who stumbled toward Robert with his shirt open, holding his chest. Only a small cut. Very little blood.

"He stabbed me," Michael said, just before he fell to the ground.

Robert knelt next to him. "Who stabbed you?"

"I don't know who he is. Some guy." He pointed back to where the incident occurred.

The men were gone, just as a police officer arrived. Together, he and Robert got Michael into the back of his squad car.

Robert got in next to him as he tossed his keys to one of the other guys. "Meet us at the hospital."

After a few hours in the waiting room with his crew, Robert approached the doctor when he came out. "How's he doing?"

"We're waiting on a heart specialist. The knife apparently punctured his heart." The doctor explained that they likely would be able to stitch him up and send him home. But they wanted to consult a specialist first.

Robert thanked the doctor and turned back to the other guys. "Well, I guess he's gonna be okay."

Nods of relief and *Thank God* rolled through the waiting room.

After running home and taking a quick shower, Robert returned to the hospital. Several of his friends were still there.

The doctor looked up and saw Robert. He closed his chart and went through the door that separated the waiting room from the triage area.

"How's my brother doing? Michael Cotillo?" Earlier he had told the nurse that he and Michael were brothers so he could get information about him. He expected the doctor to have some sort of definitive word from the cardiologist.

The doctor took a deep breath. "I'm sorry. Your brother passed away just a few minutes ago."

Robert's head got light. "What? But you said you were gonna stitch him up—"

"Apparently, the damage to his heart was more than we suspected."

"More than you suspected?" No longer lightheaded, his face flushed with anger. "But you said he was gonna be all right." It took what little self-control he had to keep from strangling the doctor. Instead, he buried his head in his hands. After a few slow breaths, he asked, "Can I see him?" The words were barely audible.

"Sure. Let me tell the charge nurse so she can make those arrangements. Just wait out here. She'll call you back when Michael is ready."

~~~~~

The only time he ever saw Michael get into a confrontation was when he accidentally hit one of their punch-ball buddies in the eye with the ball. The kid got mad at him and hit Michael in the eye. Michael did nothing to retaliate, even though it was an accident. That was just the kind of guy he was. There was no way anyone could have a beef with him, especially one who would cause his death.

But here Michael was—in a small, dimly lit room, lying motionless on a cold steel table, his face white as chalk. Only a white linen sheet covered his body up to his chest. On his left side, close to his armpit, was a red dot on the sheet, about the size of a pencil eraser.

Robert pulled the sheet down enough to reveal a inch-long wound. He replaced the sheet and wept.

Many times, Robert asked Michael to party with him and was turned down. Now, the one time he said yes …

"I don't know who did this to you, Michael, but I promise … I'll get him."

~~~~~

The next day, Robert went to Phyllis's house. His remorse over Michael's death was genuine, but his self-centeredness caused him to use the situation to gain sympathy from her. She answered the door sniffling and with a tissue in her hand. She wrapped her arms around him and cried. After a few minutes of sniffling on each other's shoulders, she invited him into the living room, where the three friends from the diner were seated on the couch. After they had all hugged him, they sat back down to ask questions.

"Do they know who did it?"

"Not yet," Robert said. "But when I find out, I guarantee you he's a dead man."

"Oh, Robert." Phyllis looked concern and squeezed his arm. He patted her hand, encouraging a rekindling of their relationship, then looked at the others. "The funeral's in a couple of days."

"They're not going to make it," another voice said. It was Phyllis's father, Freddy DiCongilio. "Hello, Robert," Freddy said, shaking his hand. "Sorry to hear about your friend."

"Thanks," Robert said, thinking it strange that Freddy referred to Michael as *his friend*, since he had known him as long as Robert.

"Why can't we go to the funeral?" Phyllis said.

"Not now, Phyllis."

Robert said, "But I don't understand—"

"Sure you do." Freddy put his arm around his daughter.

~~~~~

Except for his father, who was too ill to make it, Michael's funeral was attended by family members and friends. Robert was dramatic, crying and weeping on others' shoulders, which drew scorn from Nicky, who had taught Robert to never show his feelings. Actually, Robert felt remorse, but the drama was more about getting attention.

A month later, Michael's father passed away.

Soon after the funeral, Jo Jo Corozzo, one of Nicky's other brothers, came by the crap game on Mott Street and picked Robert up in his car. Nicky and Lenny were down in Florida at the time, and Jo Jo went to a meeting regarding Michael's death. While they drove around, he explained to Robert what had happened.

"It seems your friend Michael was messing around with some guy's girlfriend or wife or ex—I'm not sure who she was. It doesn't matter. Anyway, this guy's part of a crew that hangs out with a guy named Charlie Carneglia."

"Never heard of him," Robert said.

"He runs with the likes of Genie and Johnnie." Jo Jo was referring to two of the Gotti brothers. "From what I hear, this Charlie is one bad dude. So his buddy tells Charlie about your friend Michael messing with his old lady. I don't know how it happened, but somehow they knew Michael was there at the diner."

After a moment of silence, Robert said, "So they set us up."

"What do you mean?"

"There was this guy Vito, hitting on Phyllis. While I was dealing with him, they killed Michael. They got me away from Michael so they could kill him. This Charlie guy, is he the one who killed Michael?"

"Yeah."

"Who gave the order?"

"Nobody. He took the matter into his own hands."

"Great. Then point me in the right direction. and I'll take care of it."

"That's the thing, Robert. This guy Charlie's untouchable."

"Nobody's untouchable."

"It's an order straight from Neill. Charlie's done a lot of favors for Neill, if you know what I mean."

Robert was frustrated. He swore as he hit the dashboard of Jo Jo's car.

"Hey, easy on the interior." Jo Jo wiped his hand over the dashboard. "Listen, there's nothing you can do about Charlie. But Neill said you have his permission to take out one of the other guys who was there."

"Did he kill Michael?"

"Well, no."

"Then why would I wanna kill someone who had nothing to do with Michael dying? That's just stupid."

Jo Jo held up his hand. "Well, that's the only option you got. Otherwise, you're just gonna have to drop it."

FOURTEEN

June 1978
Age 23

A new year came, and with it, a new lease on life for Robert. His reputation as Nicky's crazy righthand man became more widespread. Nicky told him that was a good thing. It kept people on their toes when he was around.

Robert would never admit it to anyone, but his toughness was a byproduct of fear. As a kid, he was afraid when he was forced to travel through the turf of other gangs, just so he and his brother could get to school. He was scared when the mob of angry guys chased him down, looking to cut up his face. He was afraid when he had to fight the big guy hopped up on drugs, after he slashed open Tommy's throat.

For sure, fear was a major component in the development of Robert's persona. It was either beat or be beaten, kick or be kicked, shoot or be shot.

But none of those fears compares to the fear he experienced when the Mafia wanted its money and was hunting him down to get it.

~~~~~

Illegal gambling was big business. Nicky and Lenny were soon bringing in major cash for their captains, running numbers schemes and crap games. To assure the security of the money collected at each of the three crap game locations, accountability was assigned to one of the trusted members of the crew.

Robert was working the crap game at the Mott Street location, where Antonio was in charge of the bank.

Antonio approached him. "You seen the price of gasoline?"

Robert took a drag from his cigarette. "Yeah. I just filled up Nicky's car. Eighty-six cents a gallon."

"Were there lines? Where I went, a line of cars wrapped around the block."

"I pretty much got in and got out."

Antonio swore. "I guess we're the ones getting shakin down. Can I talk to you for a second?"

"I thought we were."

Antonio gave him a nasty look. "Okay, okay. I got a thing at two o'clock today, so I'm gonna have to leave early. I was wondering if you could cover for me."

"Sure. What do you need me to do?"

Antonio handed him a set of keys. "Lock up the place around four. And be sure to take the bank with you."

"The bank?"

"Yeah. Marty'll count it for you. Make sure you watch him, and count it yourself."

Robert pocketed the keys. "Don't worry. I got you covered."

The game wound down that afternoon. After shooing everyone out and locking the doors, Marty sat at the small desk next to the craps table. He unlocked the metal box on the desk, took the money out, and sorted the various denominations. As he counted each stack, he wrote the total on a yellow pad.

In contrast, Marty was more of the accountant type than a tough guy. He was rail thin, wore glasses, and spoke softly, no matter who he was talking to or what he was talking about. Since Marty would have been an easy target for anyone familiar with the routine, Antonio counted on Robert to assure the money's safe keeping.

When Marty finished adding the numbers, he pushed his glasses back up the bridge of his nose: "$12,800."

Robert looked over his shoulder and added the numbers in his head. "Looks good to me."

Marty secured the individual stacks with rubber bands and handed them to Robert in a brown paper sack. He then locked the metal box, and they walked out the front door.

Robert locked the door. "Take it easy, Marty."

Marty nodded and smiled, avoiding eye contact.

Robert searched up and down the street, then headed straight home in his new brown Cadillac, forgoing his usual night on the town.

He got up early the next morning, with the idea of going to the horse races at Belmont, a practice that had become a habit. He took the money to the track with him so he could drive straight to the factory on Mott Street after the races. As he parked the car at Belmont, he hid the bank under the car seat. It was too warm to wear a jacket that could conceal his gun, so he stowed it with the bank. He figured that would be the best place to have it, just in case someone tried to rob him. He didn't know he was the one the bank needed protection from.

The line at the window was short. Robert dug into his pocket and found two crisp hundred-dollar bills. Sensing the wind of good fortune was blowing, he pushed them through the window's opening.

"Two hundred on Jersey Sal ... to win," he said, counting on a tip he received at the Mott Street crap game that the race was fixed. Jersey Sal was sure to come in first, despite the 24 to 1 odds. He smiled.

The cashier wasn't smiling. "Have a great day."

After finding a seat, Robert looked over the program to see which horse he would bet on in the next race, using the winnings from Jersey Sal. Another horse promised a healthy payoff, which he marked as the horses for the first race entered the starting gate.

Jersey Sal crossed the finish line in the back of the pack.

Robert stared at his ticket as if some error had been made. With no money in his wallet, he left the grandstand for the parking lot, dropping his ticket into the trashcan along the way. He sat in the driver's seat, wondering what he was going to do for the next two hours before he had to be at work. Mindlessly, he took $100 from the bank under the seat, went back to the same cashier, and placed a new bet.

"Jersey Sal didn't work out that well for ya, huh?"

This time, Robert didn't have a smile for her.

~~~~~

On the seventh race, after losing most of the bank on the previous races, Robert bet $2,000 to win on Painted Wagon, ridden by the most famous jockey of all time, Willie Shoemaker. Until that point, Robert had bet on long shots. But the odds on Painted Wagon was 7 to 1. He was sure to win back the money he had lost.

A horse ridden by a young jockey named Steve Cauthen, a 28-to-1 longshot, won the race. Instead of being up nine grand, he had lost over $10,000 of money that didn't belong to him.

Worse yet, it belonged to the Mafia.

Robert was a dead man. No matter how likable he was, no one in the mob was going to be okay with him gambling away their money without repercussions.

His first thought was to rob a bank to replace the money he had lost. He still had time before he was due to arrive at the Mott Street game, but it wasn't worth taking the risk of going to jail— or being gunned down by a bank security officer. So he did the second best thing: he took what money was left and did everything possible to stay away from anyone associated with Nicky's crew. It was either that or he really would end up dead.

For the rest of the afternoon, he hung out at one of the clubs with old friends, living large as a man with a death sentence. After throwing a few beers down, he called his mom. She told him Antonio had called.

He took a deep breath and returned Antonio's call.

"Robert, where are you?" Antonio said. "You were supposed to be here hours ago with the bank."

Robert considered making up some story about being robbed, but no one would believe that. Feeling brazen enough to admit the truth, he said, "I got some bad news, man."

"What did you do now?"

"I lost some of the bank." He hesitated. "I went to the races." Antonio was quiet for a moment. "Okay, okay. Don't worry about it. We can make it up."

Antonio's answer was surprising, and Robert felt relieved. Then he considered that maybe this is the way guys who borrow the Mafia's money without permission are set up before they're fitted with cement boots.

"How much did you lose?"

The bartender slid a shot of whiskey over to Robert, who downed it in one gulp. "Ten grand," Robert said.

"What? Are you freakin crazy?" Antonio yelled and cursed, saying Robert was going to get them both killed. Then he hung up.

~~~~~

During the following week, Robert was cautious enough to make sure he didn't go to the places Nicky and the crew knew he would be, hanging out mostly with friends on Long Island, who knew nothing about what was happening.

Several days later, buddies from his old neighborhood told Robert that they got roughed up by Nicky and Lenny because they wouldn't tell them where Robert was.

Robert told them that if anybody other than Nicky or Lenny hassled them again, he would kill him.

At 4:00 a.m., a week after losing the money, Robert had been hanging out at clubs all night and was tired. Since the whole ordeal began, he hadn't been home. He hadn't had a decent night's sleep. So he decided to go to his parents' house on Richmond Street in the old neighborhood, which was where he was living at the time.

Most everyone recognized his Cadillac, but since it was so early in the morning, he thought he would be safe. Still, he had two guns beside him, just in case a shootout occurred. He eased up to the traffic light at Fulton Street, just a couple of blocks from the house. An Olds 98 pulled up to the light on the opposite side.

Robert perked up, adrenaline now coursing through his body. The car belonged to Lenny DiMaria, Nicky's partner. Robert looked down at the pistols next to him. When he looked up, someone was getting out of the car. Nicky, running toward Robert, with his hand in his pocket.

Robert had never been in such a dilemma. Even though he had the two guns with him and had no problem shooting anyone who shot at him, he never thought he might have to use one of them on Nicky. He was Robert's mentor, his father figure, the one who gave him a chance to be somebody. There was no possible way he could shoot Nicky.

He considered staying there and hearing Nicky out. But as Nicky got closer, and Nicky's hand was still in his pocket, Robert felt the risk was too great. No one was above the law of the Mafia. His light was still red, but he took off anyway, running stop signs and traffic lights. He glanced back in his mirror. They were right behind him, headlights off. As they approached Logan Street, Robert was desperate to get them off his tail. He turned onto Logan, the wrong way on a one-way street. Even though they were traveling in the wrong direction, Lenny and Nicky continued to follow him. Robert made a quick right onto Ridgewood Avenue. As he came up to the intersection at Norwood, he didn't notice the other car. Coming from his left, the car broadsided him, knocking him to the other side of the street. Stunned, Robert continued driving down Norwood for another hundred feet. By that time, the car was just limping along, so he parked it just before Force Tube Avenue and took off on foot, leaving the two pistols behind. He sprinted for a couple of blocks before running out of breath and stopped, resigning to his fate.

Lenny pulled the car in front of Robert.

Nicky was the first to get out, punching him in the face, followed by blows from Lenny. Even though they were giving him a good beating, Robert didn't go down, nor did he fight back.

"What?" Nicky said. "Are you coked up or something?" Obviously, he knew about Robert's secret. After their fists grew tired, Nicky pushed Robert against the car. "You freakin idiot." He rubbed his sore knuckles. "What do you think you're doing?"

Robert didn't answer.

After cursing him a few times, Nicky motioned toward the car. "Get in."

Robert had sworn that if the mob ever decided to get rid of him, he wanted his mother to know he was dead. He couldn't stand the thought of her wondering, hoping he might be alive, when in fact, he was fish bait at the bottom of the bay. Therefore, getting into the car was not an option. He wiped blood from his face with the sleeve of his shirt. "Just kill me now."

"What are talking about? I'm not gonna kill you, you moron. You need to go get your car."

Robert was still skeptical. "I can't. I left my guns in it."

He had been arrested several times for illegal possession of a weapon. If he went back to the car, the police responding to the accident would surely arrest him again.

Nicky rubbed his brow and said something indiscernible. "Listen, I've been trying to find you so I could tell you that I replaced the bank with my own money."

Robert squinted, feeling the pain from his swollen left eye. "Really?"

"Yeah, really. We said you got arrested, was locked up."

Relief washed over him. At that moment, Robert knew that Nicky had saved him from certain death.

Nicky looked around. "We need to get out of here. Hop in the car."

"I'll catch a cab."

Nicky scoffed. "Okay, have it your way." He went around to the passenger side of the car. "Go home. Get some rest. Then call me tomorrow."

After Nicky and Lenny left, Robert hailed a taxi and went to his sister Anna's house, since he didn't want his mom to see him bloody and beaten. He stayed there overnight.

The next day, Robert called Nicky, who said it was okay for him to come back to work. He also told him that he would have to pay off his debt. Robert thought twelve grand was a lot of money to pay back, but the alternative was much worse. At first, he paid Nicky $100 a week. At that rate, it would have taken years to pay off the balance.

Before long, a big payoff fell into his hands. Robert had a crew of his own, a few guys younger than him who were looking to make a name for themselves. They burglarized a home in Long Island that had some valuable coins. One of them alone was worth $90,000. The value of the coins would bring them lots of money, but more important to Robert was the chance to redeem himself in Nicky's eyes. When Robert brought the coins to Nicky, he was pleased and ended up squashing his entire debt to him.

Regarding the car wreck and the two guns: Robert reported his car stolen. The insurance company sent him a check for the loss.

PART III

SHE
DON'T
LIE

FIFTEEN

Warmer air from the south had invaded the East Coast, and with it came the incentive for New Yorkers to get out of their homes and into the city parks, or take walks along neighborhood streets. Robert and Angelo opted for the walk, strolling down a busy Liberty Avenue in the middle of the bright afternoon. Between Forbell and 74th Streets, he gestured toward a place that sold knishes—a favorite Jewish delicacy of Robert's since experiencing them with Squinty while on the lam a few years ago.

"Let's go in here," he said to Angelo.

As they approached the counter, a petite brunette with a smirk met them with a pad and pen, ready to take their order. "What can we get for you?"

Robert got a good look at the girl's face. "Hey, I know you."

Her smirk widened. "And I know you too, Robert."

"Yeah, you're Rose's friend. Cookie, right?"

Rose was a girl Robert dated some years back, when he and Anthony Ruggiano were still running together.

"Wow, you have an amazing memory." Cookie's eyes were fixed on the pad.

"Yeah," Robert said. "That was quite a while back."

Cookie finally looked up from the pad, turning to Angelo. "As I remember, we met him and his friends at the Fudge Factory."

Angelo took a half-step back and raised an eyebrow. "The Fudge Factory? You went to a gay bar?"

Robert shrugged. "Hey, all the straight pretty girls were there. It was like shooting fish in a barrel."

"Yeah, we went there to hide from guys like you," Cookie said to Robert, pleased with her sarcasm.

"Well," Robert said, "I have to tell you, word got out fast. How is Rose?"

"I don't know. Haven't seen her in a while." The bell dangling over the door sounded as another customer came in. Cookie returned her attention to the pad. "So are you gonna order or waste more of my time?"

Robert glanced at Angelo. "Boy, she's one tough cookie, isn't she?"

Cookie glared at him.

"Okay, okay. Just tryin to break the ice here. We'll have six knishes."

~~~~~

After leaving the knish place, Robert and Antonio headed back the way they came.

Angelo rinsed his mouth with a gulp of his Coke. "So … that's the same Cookie—"

"DeSimone," Robert said. "Tommy's wife."

Tommy DeSimone was the hottest topic among the members of the Gambino family, but only in quiet, small circles. His reputation was a hot-tempered gunslinger who took much pleasure in killing and not getting caught. Even those who were close to him called him a psychopath. He was tight with Jimmy Burke—the father of Robert's friend Frankie Burke and the mastermind behind the infamous Lufthansa Heist in which over $6 million in cash and jewelry was stolen from the JFK International Airport.

Robert was familiar with Tommy's ways. He once drove Nicky and Lenny to a meeting that included Tommy. Nicky gave Robert the order that Tommy coming out of the meeting before they did would mean that Tommy had killed them. If that were the case, then Robert would have to kill Tommy. Fortunately, Nicky and Lenny appeared in good health, and no one had to die.

At the beginning of the year, Tommy disappeared. Lots of rumors were floating around, but the most reliable word was he was whacked because he killed two of John Gotti's close associates without permission, several years earlier. Another rumor was he went into hiding to avoid being killed.

Robert wasn't sure which story was true. He was interested in Cookie, so he had to make sure Tommy was indeed out of the picture before he even considered asking her out. The opportunity came the next day, when he was driving Nicky to Manhattan for a friendly game of pinochle as Neil Dellacroce's partner.

"He's gone," Nicky said in response to Robert's question.

"Like, he's gone gone?"

"Yeah. You don't have to worry about him. Are you sure you want to go out with Cookie? You know she's not exactly take-home-to-mother material, right?"

"She seems like a fun kind of girl. It's not like I'm gonna marry her or anything."

The next day he marched into the knish place and asked Cookie out.

She accepted.

~~~~~

Robert and Cookie partied every night, drinking excessively and snorting coke. Their relationship was extremely volatile due to two flammable contents—Robert's jealousy and Cookie's desire for attention from more than one man. Robert dealt with Cookie's flirtatious ways by either beating somebody up or relying heavily on the numbing effect of drugs and alcohol.

As the drugs grew in prominence in Robert's life, a wedge was driven between him and Nicky, who was adamant about upholding the Mafia code prohibiting their use or sale. He told Robert it made a man unstable and therefore, unreliable. But Robert saw Nicky as one of the old-schoolers who wasn't up with the times. Many of the guys in Manhattan were selling and using, and he didn't see them as unreliable.

A year after Robert started dating Cookie, he met a guy named Cuchio, considered an expert on freebasing, popular as a recreational drug after Richard Pryor set himself on fire while trying to get high.

Until then, Robert had snorted coke with Cookie while out at the nightclubs with their friends. Freebasing was a "step up" into the realm of getting high. Anyone who was "someone" chose to freebase instead of snorting coke. When Robert snorted coke, he would be on a sleepless binge for several days. When he freebased, he got high at a more intensified level and then went home to crash. This led him to errantly believe freebasing was not as addictive as coke.

With a network of fellow freebasers, Robert was always able to maintain an ample supply of friends with whom to enjoy drugs. That was his intention with his friend Vincent Miniciello. Vinny was ex-military who received 100 percent disability for a mental disorder, which funded his drug habit.

On a Saturday night, Vinny invited Robert to freebase with him. Vinny told him a girl he had partied with before—a prostitute who worked at a brothel several houses down the road—would be partying with them and to meet him at her apartment. Robert accepted the invitation, but instead of going directly, he went to a nightclub on Long Island with Cookie. While there for several hours, he got into a fight and was arrested, landing him in the Nassau County Jail, where he spent the rest of the weekend.

The following evening, he strolled into the jail's common area. The news was blaring from the TV hanging overhead. At first, he started to move away from the TV and its loudness … until he noticed the two photographs plastered on its screen. The photos were of Vinny and the girl. The anchorman said the two had been found shot to death at the girl's apartment—the place he intended to be before he was arrested. His heart skipped a beat as once again, he had quite possibly skirted death.

Even though he was shaken up by the incident, the murder of his friend did little to deter Robert from his drug habit. He and Cuchio were freebasing regularly. Robert would bring his coke, and Cuchio would do his "magic," turning the illegal substance into a purer form that supposedly had fewer side effects. But one thing that surely remained was paranoia. As they continued their arrangement, Robert believed Cuchio was setting aside some of the coke for himself. Or perhaps he was selling it and not sharing the profits.

Feeling betrayed one evening, Robert went to Cuchio's apartment with two of his friends and found Cuchio asleep on his bed. Without waking him, Robert pulled a revolver from his pants and fired point-blank at Cuchio's head. Instead of sending a bullet through his skull, the gun exploded in Robert's hand, its parts falling onto the bed.

Cuchio woke with a scream and ran out of the room, passing all three men, who stood there in shock.

Several months later, Robert was parked along the street when Cuchio walked up to the passenger window and tapped on the glass. Robert unlocked the door, and Cuchio climbed in, as if nothing had happened. They shared a few minutes of small talk and a couple of hits on his pipe. After a strange moment of silence, Cuchio opened the car door and exited.

Robert never heard from or saw him again.

SIXTEEN

Fall 1980
Age 25

Robert looked at each of the men standing in front of him. "Everybody do your job. We get the score. We're out of there. Nobody gets hurt."

On an early fall morning, the sun was still hiding below the eastern horizon. Six men stood inside a friend's living room, inspecting weapons and ensuring they had the necessary supplies.

Like Robert, several guys were recreational drug users, but he wouldn't allow anyone to get high or drunk just before a heist. This was especially the case with this particular job, since it had the potential of being a large score.

A month earlier, a friend of Robert's, who worked at the Lemon Tree Club, gave him inside information concerning a jewelry store in downtown Brooklyn. From that birthed the plan for an early-morning robbery, just as all the employees arrived. The store was one of the larger jewelry stores and was sure to yield a good return.

Once they were sure their equipment was in good working order and the supplies were loaded in a single bag, they loaded into three vehicles outside his friend's house. They owned two, and the other was stolen. They drove to a predesignated area within a couple of blocks from the target, and then the men piled into the stolen vehicle and drove to the destination, parking just out of sight of the jewelry store.

"Okay, let's go." Robert was the first out of the car, exiting the front passenger seat.

After scanning the streets and neighboring businesses for potential problems, they entered the jewelry store, one at a time. Three men went inside, posing as potential customers. A fourth stayed posted at the door.

When all three were in position, they pulled out their weapons.

"Hands where I can see them," Robert yelled to the one man and two women employees. "Now!" All three were behind the same jewelry counter, eyes and mouths wide, hands in the air.

Two of the robbers walked over to them, and one nudged the man with his shotgun. "Get to the safe, old man. Ladies, you too. Move it!"

The three shuffled hurriedly to comply with the order while the other men smashed glass cases that contained the more expensive jewelry on display.

Robert followed the others to the safe. "Handcuff and tape the two broads. Pops, I need you to show me the big stuff."

The elderly man was shaking, but he didn't hesitate. Robert grabbed the more valuable pieces of jewelry and put them in his bag.

"Mail call." One of the other robbers had his gun stuck in the ribs of a mailman, a mailbag slung over his shoulder. "He walked in on us."

"Tie him up with the rest."

In just a few minutes from the time they entered, they were speeding off in the stolen car. After ditching the stolen car, they climbed into the two other cars, traveling in separate directions to get back to Robert's friend's house. The men were jubilant as they emptied their bags onto the dining table, tried on rings, and admired diamond encrusted brooches and pendants.

Robert slipped a princess-cut engagement ring on his pinky and held it under the light of a nearby lamp. "Look at that thing." He rotated his hand so the ring glimmered.

"Looks good on ya," one of the guys said. "But maybe you ought to give it to Cookie."

Robert studied the ring as he considered the suggestion. Even though his and Cookie's relationship was shrouded in deception and lies, he cared for her. But marrying her? He thought about Nicky's words the first time he told him he was interested in Cookie: *She's not the type you take home to Mama.* The memory broke the trance the ring had placed on him, and he slipped it into his pocket.

"So Jamesy, your guy can handle this sort of thing?"

"Oh yeah. Not a problem. He'll have it moved in no time."

~~~~~

Three days later, Robert met with the other guys, bringing the cash he had collected from the fence. They divided it evenly—around $40,000 each.

The following day he went to Cookie's house for supper. He had told Cookie to make sure the whole family was there, including Danielle, Cookie's young daughter from Tommy.

In the middle of the meal, Robert started a conversation. "Wow, it seems like winter's kind of early this year." He rubbed his hands together.

Cookie's father Sal looked up. "You cold?"

Mrs. DeVito started to get up. "I can turn up the heat if you want."

"No, no. It's fine in here. It's just kind of cold outside, don't you think?"

Sal shrugged as he forked a bite from his steak. "Pretty normal New York weather, if you ask me."

"I betcha it's not like this in Florida."

Cookie turned toward him with a suspicious look.

"Oh no," Mrs. DeVito said. "It's always nice in Florida."

Robert said, "It would be nice to be there right now, wouldn't it?" Everybody looked at Robert, whose smile stretched to the point of discomfort. "I bought me and Cookie and Danielle plane tickets to Orlando!"

"What?" Cookie said. "We're going on vacation?"

"To Disney World. What do you think of that?"

Danielle smiled and clapped her hands.

"That's right. We're gonna stay at the hotel there, right by Disney World."

Danielle shook her fists in the air. "Yea, I'm going to Disney World."

~~~~~

The temperatures were hovering in the lower 80s when Robert and Cookie strolled down to the pool, where fellow sunbathers slathered tanning lotion onto their pale bodies. They claimed two lounge chairs with a table not far from the water's edge.

Robert located a poolside waiter dressed in black slacks and a white jacket, lighting from table to table, and called him over. "Two piña coladas."

"Yes sir."

"Robert," Cookie said as the waiter walked away. "I didn't want a drink right now."

"Yes, you do." Robert adjusted his lounge chair.

"No, I don't."

"Trust me, you do."

"I don't trust you, and I don't want a drink."

Laughing, Robert lowered his sunglasses and looked at Cookie. "Don't make things more difficult than they have to be, okay?"

Cookie shook her head as she applied tanning oil to her arms.

Within a few minutes the waiter returned with the drinks. Robert tipped him a twenty.

Cookie said, "I told you I don't want that."

"I promise, you do." He handed the drink to her. "Here, take it."

Reluctantly, Cookie reached for the drink, but he wouldn't let go.

"What? You order me a drink, and then you won't give it to me?"

"Look."

"Look at what?" She looked around.

Robert gave her drink a slight shake.

"Just look. Right in front of your face."

As she looked at the glass, she saw the sparkle from the princess-cut ring on Robert's pinky finger, glistening in the bright Florida sun. Robert eased his grip from the drink as she took the ring from his finger.

"What's this?" she said as she inspected it.

"What do you think it is? Try it on."

Cookie placed it on the ring finger of her right hand. "That's nice." She held her hand out in front of her.

Robert sat on the edge of his chair, waiting for more of a response from Cookie. It never came. She reclined in her lounge chair, her eyes hidden by sunglasses.

More than just the sun was heating Robert up. He tried to keep his feelings inside, but words of retaliation refused to stay harbored inside. The words exploded from deep within. "That's nice? That's all you can say?"

As Robert rolled out a string of expletives for the next minute, Cookie leaned away. The commotion created a spectacle that drew the attention of nearby beachcombers. When he paused in the middle of his rant, he noticed the dirty looks of the parents. Some had their hands over their child's ears. He wanted to curse the parents as well, but he had no malice for the innocent kids. So he took a deep breath and sat back in his lounge chair.

In a quieter voice he said, "I risk my life just so I can take trips with you, just so I can buy you things, just so we can have a better life. And all you can say is, 'That's nice'?" He took a large gulp from his drink. "I tell you what, Cookie. You're a real piece of work."

SEVENTEEN

March 1981
Age 26

When Robert was a kid, Ronnie Trucchio was known as one of the toughest teenagers around. Unlike Robert, he was lanky, standing about six-foot-three by the time he was sixteen, with wavy, sandy brown hair and a crooked smile.

Ronnie got the nickname One Arm after being hit by a car. When twelve years old, he and neighborhood kids were trying to beat the summer heat by playing in the torrents gushing from a renegade fire hydrant. The high water pressure out of the hydrant knocked the kids off their feet, which was a big part of the fun. As bad timing would have it, Ronnie ran through the gushing water and was knocked into the street, just as a car was passing by. The driver couldn't avoid him. The car crushed his right shoulder, permanently disabling him.

Robert was at Mom's Bar, a neighborhood bar where he regularly hung out.

Ronnie came in and sat next to him at the bar without saying a word.

"Ronnie, you look like you seen a ghost." Robert finished a double of Scotch.

"Yeah, I might have messed up."

"What's goin on?"

"I got in Vinny Asaro's face."

Vincent Asaro was a made man from the Bonanno crime family.

"Why did you go and do something like that?"

"He was upset with me because I smacked around a girl."

Robert smirked. "Why would he care about that?"

"Because me and Michael ... his son? We hooked up with these twins. The one I was going out with got smart with me, so I smacked her. She went crying to her sister, and she went to Michael. He told his old man, and he came to me. And ... well, I didn't like the way he was talking to me."

"Vinny can talk to you however he wants. He's straightened out." Robert rubbed his forehead. "So what? You think he's comin after you?"

"I don't know, man. Maybe."

It wasn't the first time Ronnie felt the need to look over his shoulder. Another incident occurred when he and a buddy helped Jimmy Burke in a crime. Jimmy was known as a psychopathic killer responsible for the deaths of almost all those involved in the Lufthansa heist, including Robert's high school buddy Louis Cafora and his wife. Soon after helping Jimmy, paranoia got the best of Ronnie. He had heard how Jimmy methodically knocked off people who could tie him to a crime. Ronnie and his buddy were afraid Jimmy would do the same to them. Robert told Ronnie to go to Nicky, who assured Ronnie that he would take care of it.

Now, a similar predicament was presenting itself, and once again, Ronnie was turning to his old friend.

"Look," Robert said. "Don't worry about Vinny. We'll get some of the guys. Have em come here. Anyone tries to get to you, they gotta get through us first."

After a few calls from the phone behind the bar, Robert and Ronnie went to Jo Jo Corrozo's social club next door. Within twenty minutes five men, all carrying loaded weapons, formed an impenetrable human barrier around Ronnie inside the club.

Many of the kids in the neighborhood were "recruits" of Robert's crew, much the same as he was a recruit of Blaise Corozzo when he was young. And like the younger version of

Robert, they roamed the neighborhood until late into the night, trying to outdo one another in acts of bravery or stupidity.

When Robert first came to the bar, just as the sun was fading in the west, before going inside, he talked with some of the kids for a minute or two. Later, one of the kids burst into the club, sweaty and panting, and stopped in front of Robert.

"What's goin on?" Robert said.

"These three guys outside are stirring up trouble," the kid said, doing his best to make his message clear. "Bobby … he got stabbed." He was referring to was one of the kids in the neighborhood.

All the men jumped up and headed out to the street. A group of kids were gathered on the sidewalk, surrounding Bobby, who was holding his left leg.

Bobby pointed to three silhouettes across the street. "They stabbed me."

Even in the darkness, Robert saw the glistening blood on his pants. He took a couple of steps in the direction of the boys. "Hey, you three. Come here."

They didn't move.

Robert waved for them to come. "I said, come here."

This time, they moved, but running away from Robert. "Hey! Stop!"

~~~~~

Bobby was rushed to the hospital. The knife used against him severed a major artery, causing massive hemorrhaging. He died in the ER.

As for the three assailants: when they failed to stop on Robert's command, a barrage of gunfire rang out. When the noise settled, two of the young men lay in the street, their bodies riddled with bullet holes. The third one escaped.

EIGHTEEN

May 1984
Age 29

At the bustling LaGuardia Airport, Robert snatched his bag from the carousel, exited through the glass doors, and hailed a taxi.

It had been twenty-nine months since he walked in freedom among the rest of the New Yorkers. During that time, he served concurrent sentences at the Clinton Correctional Facility in Dannemora, New York, for illegal possession of Treasury checks and possession of a weapon. He also did time for a failed robbery.

He and Angelo Sali, his lifelong friend, had planned to rob the owner of a factory on 102nd Street, just off Atlantic Avenue. They knew he processed his payroll every week and paid his employees with cash. Robert was to take the man down as he returned from the bank, grab the payroll, and jump into the getaway car driven by Angelo. As they waited for the man, Robert grew impatient and got out of the car to take a walk, leaving his gun behind. Angelo continued his slow drive around the block. Before he made it back, the man showed up with the payroll. Instead of waiting for Angelo to come back around the block so he could get the gun, Robert assaulted the business owner in front of the factory. The man struggled with Robert, clinging onto the bank bag that held about $5,000 in cash. Some of the employees saw the commotion outside, the business owner in harm's way, and their hard-earned money about to be stolen. They went to the aid of their boss and pinned Robert to the ground.

From across the street, Angelo saw what happened and took off in the car, putting distance between him and the crime scene. But it wasn't long before he had a change of heart, rounded the block, and returned to try to convince the men to let Robert go. When the cops arrived, both Robert and Angelo were arrested after the gun was found inside the car Angelo was driving.

Prison time was less than desirable, but what was much worse to Robert was the mark of humiliation indelibly printed on his reputation.

~~~~~

After a reunion with his family, his brother-in-law Paulie told Robert that Nicky wanted to see him. Robert went to the Knights of Columbus meeting hall on Pacific Street, where he met Nicky.

As Nicky walked out the front door and hugged Robert, he said, "It's about time you came to see me."

"Yeah, sorry. I just—"

"I know what you've been up to."

The words were strong, but Robert didn't sense any malice behind them. Still, Nicky's mantra of "never show your feelings" settled in the back of Robert's mind. The uncertainty of the situation came with much angst.

"Let's take a walk." Nicky headed up the street with Robert. "Some things went on while you were away."

"Really?"

"I don't know if you heard, but a lot has changed."

Robert nodded, not sure where Nicky was going with the conversation.

"What's been going on with you? I haven't seen you in quite a while, even before you went to the pen."

"Just hangin out, Nicky. That's all. You know, make a couple of dollars here, a couple of dollars there."

"Yeah, I heard about all that too."

Robert bit his fingernail. "Look, Nicky. It's ... it's not like—"

"Forget about it. It's all water under the bridge. But I got to be honest with you, kid. For the stuff you pulled, anybody else woulda gotten a bullet in the back of his head."

Robert had done several things that made him worthy of being offed, so he wasn't exactly sure what Nicky was referring to. He could have meant the jewelry heist. Nicky never got his cut. He could be referring to his drug usage or the suicide attempts while in prison. Even though Robert was trying to manipulate the warden into giving him a furlough, Robert still looked weak in the eyes of his Mafia brothers.

Nicky shook his head. "This life? It's over for you." He took out a wad of twenty-dollar bills and handed them to Robert. He hugged Robert again, and then held him at arm's length. "Believe me, Robert, this is the better way for you."

~~~~~

Robert and Cookie had just finished dinner at Russo's and were walking toward the dim parking lot, lit only by two lampposts that had escaped the fate of the other six vandalized lights.

"I don't know if I want to go out tonight," Robert said to Cookie. His meeting with Nicky had left him in a foul mood.

"Why not?"

"I just don't feel like it." He handed her the keys. "Take me home. Then you can drive yourself home."

They got into the 1984 Buick Century and within a few minutes pulled in front of Robert's parent's place on Richmond Street.

"You can pick me up tomorrow," he said.

"What are you gonna do tonight?"

"I don't know. Watch the game. Sleep. I'm just not feelin up to hangin out tonight."

Robert shut the door and went inside. No one was home. After shedding his shoes, he got a beer from the fridge, turned on the TV, and found the New York Jets battling the Pittsburgh Steelers on ABC's Monday Night Football, an intensely close game near halftime.

Throughout the next two quarters, Robert yelled, screamed, and cursed at the TV, applauding his Jets when they made a great play, then calling them morons when the Steelers scored against them. He held on to the hope of a come-from-behind victory, but the Steelers ended up handing the Jets a gut-wrenching 23 to 17 loss.

Instead of winding down, the game energized Robert. After turning the TV off, he phoned Cookie to see if she still wanted to go out. After four rings, the answering machine took over, her voice informing all callers that they "know what to do."

Thinking she might be asleep, Robert called two more times, several minutes apart, and got the same result. He slipped his shoes back on and began the one-and-a-half-mile trek to her place. Even if she didn't want to go out, he could get the car and cruise around until he found his friends at one of their clubs.

Two hundred feet from Cookie's apartment building, even from that distance and despite the darkness, he could easily see that his car wasn't there. Instead of stopping, he walked on to Bruce's house, a friend who lived nearby.

With each step, his concern grew. He and Cookie had been together for about four years, and he knew how insatiable her desire for male attention was—whether his or someone else's. Only a few months ago, he had learned about an affair she had while he was in prison. The thought quickened his pace and fed his anxiety.

Bruce lived just down the street and a block over, so it wasn't long before Robert was at the basement knocking on the door. When Bruce answered, Robert looked past him and saw Cookie on the couch. Next to her was Bruno. Her arm was on his leg.

"Robert!" Bruce said, more to alert Cookie than as a greeting.

Robert stared at Cookie, then said to Bruce, "Tell her to come out."

"Robert, she—"

"Tell her to come out, Bruce. Now!"

By then, Cookie was at the door. She nodded at Bruce to let him know it was okay and closed the door behind her. "Robert, I thought you—"

Robert's roundhouse punch caught Cookie in the jaw, sending her to the ground, unconscious, his jaw clinched in rhythm with his fists. He was so angry, he felt like he could destroy the whole house and everyone in it, yet the small part of sanity that remained prevented him from doing it. He threw Cookie over his shoulder and tramped straight to the car. With his one free hand he opened the passenger side door and roughly put Cookie into the seat.

Cookie was coming around and starting to cry. "Just kill me. I'd be better off if you'd just kill me."

"I'm seriously considering it." Robert squealed the tires leaving Bruce's house.

By the time they arrived at Cookie's place, she was fully conscious, and Robert had lost his interest in killing her. He slowed the car enough to let her out and then sped away.

~~~~~

Sometime after the incident at Bruce's house, Robert, Frankie Burke, and Ronnie Trucchio were getting high when their supply ran dry. Frankie suggested they go to Howard Beach to replenish their coke stash, so they got into Robert's car and drove around for a while. During their search for more drugs, the conversation came up about the incident at Bruce's house.

"This is the worst kind of disrespect," Robert told them.

Frankie nodded.

"The worst," Ronnie said.

"I know where Bruno lives," Frankie said.

This surprised Robert, since Frankie liked Cookie, and Bruno was a friend of his as well.

"Do you wanna make a visit?"

At this point, revenge was not on Robert's mind, but since Frankie brought it up, he felt obligated to do something. "Yeah, let's head over there."

Bruno's place was across town, so Robert had time to build up his anger. They discussed the plan. Frankie would knock on the door. When Bruno answered, Robert would burst in while

Ronnie and Frankie prevented escape. They decided not to be concerned with disposing of the body.

They stopped in front of the red clapboard house where Bruno lived.

Frankie pointed to the right side of the house. "He'll answer that door."

Robert pursed his lips and nodded. He looked into the back seat where Ronnie was. "You ready to do this?"

"Looking forward to it."

He looked back at Frankie. "You lead."

The men looked in all directions for any reason to call off the hit. Feeling confident no one was around, they approached the unlit house, concealed by darkness. When they got to the porch, Ronnie unscrewed the light bulb in the fixture next to the door, just in case Bruno tried to turn it on. Robert gave the go-ahead nod as he removed his knife from his pocket.

Frankie knocked. No response. He knocked harder. "Bruno!" A light in the front room came on. When they heard the light switch flip, Ronnie grinned.

"Who's there?"

"It's me, Bruno. Open up." Frankie made sure he didn't identify himself, just in case an unseen witness was in earshot.

They heard the bolts being thrown, and the doorknob turned.

"What? You too stoned to remember where you live—"

Swearing, Robert threw his shoulder into the door, causing Bruno to stumble backward. "You think it's okay to mess around with another man's woman?"

He lunged at Bruno. The blade of his knife sunk into his neck. Robert pulled it out, ready to do stab him again.

Despite his injury, Bruno stayed on his feet and maneuvered around Robert, who failed to land another strike.

Ronnie and Frankie were waiting for Bruno at the open doorway. Initially they caught him, but during the struggle, Bruno managed to get free and run out of the house and into the darkness, which now played in his favor. They chased after him.

A voice yelled from the house next door. "What's going on out there? I'm gonna call the cops."

Instead of pursuing Bruno, the three men got back into the car and drove away.

~~~~~

Robert never saw Bruno again. After the stabbing, Robert avoided his usual hangouts and stayed at a friend's apartment. In the meantime, Ronnie was out and about, getting a feel for what the situation was like. He learned that Bruno had survived the attack and went to one of the wiseguys from another crew, seeking retribution. The wiseguy apparently told him he had no beef, since he shouldn't have been messing around with Cookie and added that he had better leave the neighborhood if he wanted to stay alive.

NINETEEN

June 1984
Age 29

I n the early evening, Robert was hanging out at the corner of Crescent Street and Liberty Avenue with some of his friends, when he heard someone call his name. He looked to the curb, where a dark sedan had just pulled up. His brother-in-law Paulie was getting out the back passenger door.

Robert met him midway.

"Hey, long time no see." Paulie took Robert by the shoulders and kissed him on the lips.

Robert was startled. "What's goin on?"

"It's Nicky. He wants to see you."

"He wants to see me? Why?"

"I don't know. I was just told to find you and bring you to him."

Robert hadn't seen Nicky since he was told that his life in the Mafia was over. Immediately, he remembered their last conversation and the mention of a bullet to his head. That thought brought concern.

But then there was the possibility that Nicky wanted him back. He had been his strong arm, an up-and-coming star. Did Nicky hold on to a glimmer of hope for him? Surely, he would know that Robert was still doing drugs. If there was anything Robert knew about Nicky, it was that he had eyes everywhere. Still, Robert gravitated to the idea that Nicky wanted his prodigal son to return.

"Okay. Well, let's go."

Paulie ushered Robert to the car and let him get in first. There were two other strange men in the front seat. The one driving locked all the doors.

It was then Robert realized the symbolism of Paulie's kiss, a familiar urban legend among those in the Family, supposed to have been administered to ill-fated members before their final demise.

The kiss of death.

The idea that Nicky wanted him back vanished.

I'm about to die. Nicky's finally given up on me altogether.

"Where you been lately?" Paulie asked.

"Just … hanging around."

Robert remembered the .38 revolver tucked in the side of his pants. If his brother-in-law was giving him up—

"Your sister's been asking about you. What should I tell her?"

"Tell her not to worry." The driver got onto Belt Parkway and headed west. "Where are we going?"

"Mill Basin," Paulie said.

"What's there?"

"Nicky has a friend who owns a catering hall there, just off the marina. He said to bring you there."

Right by the water, Robert thought. With much discretion, he moved in his seat to feel the gun against his back. It was still there.

His brother-in-law noticed. "What? You got ants in your pants?"

Robert didn't comment.

Except for Bruce Springsteen belting out "Born in the U.S.A." on the radio, the car was silent during the rest of the way to the marina. The driver got off Belt Parkway at Cropsey Avenue, went a few blocks, and turned left at 26th Avenue. From there Robert saw the choppy water that made up Lower New York Bay. A carnival was at the corner of Bay 41st Street and Shore Parkway. Soon, it would be littered with children and their parents chasing after them, but for now, it was minimally occupied.

They drove to the double doors of the red brick building where Nicky's friend ran his business. The simple white sign with black lettering above the double doors read *Mill Basin Catering*, with the phone number below. With the car in park, Paulie looked out his window, searching the area. Robert wasn't sure whether he was looking for Nicky's car or to see if anybody was around to witness his last breath.

Robert reached around with his right hand, brought his gun to his side, and under the cover of a cough, pulled back the hammer.

Paulie turned toward him and stared for an uncomfortable amount of time.

Robert felt his heart quicken as he reviewed in his mind the plan he devised during the drive to Mill Basin. He would kill the two men in the front seat before they could take him down.

At the end of the extended stare—which seemed like minutes but in reality was only a few seconds—Paulie glanced at his watch. He looked out his window again. "He's not here," he said to the driver. "Let's go."

"What are we doing?" Robert said.

"I'll take you back. Nicky's not here."

With that, Robert looked out his own window, not wanting Paulie to see any sign of relief in his face. He still sensed danger, but he released the hammer and tucked the gun back in his pants—again with much discretion.

The ride from the Mill Basin Marina to the corner of Crescent Street and Atlantic Avenue seemed much shorter than the ride there.

"Come over for supper sometime," Paulie said as Robert got out of the car. "I'll get Anna to call you."

Robert nodded.

TWENTY

Fall 1985
Age 30

Despite Nicky's pronouncement that his dream of Mafia stardom was over, Robert knew he would never work a legitimate job. Mafia life was in his blood. From the time he was a kid, those he looked up to helped mold him into the man he'd become. They encouraged the tough-guy image, including Nicky—especially Nicky. The fighting, shylocking, illegal gambling, and the occasional brutal collection of outstanding debts — all were engrained in his mind as ways of earning good money.

They were also instrumental in hardening his heart.

He was not only made for Mafia life, but it was all he knew. Outside of the few legitimate jobs he had as a teenager, the only way Robert earned money was by doing something illegal.

Robert and Angelo Sali walked the streets of their old neighborhood, the full moon lighting their way.

"Hey, look there." Angelo pointed to an old white house with a chain-link fence around the yard. They approached silently, amid the muffled barks of distant neighborhood dogs echoing in the crisp autumn air.

"That's Marcos's house," Robert said. "What about it?"

"See that over there?" Angelo motioned toward a dilapidated refrigerator on the side of the house.

"Yeah, so what?"

"I remember Marcos telling me about his stash, that he hid it in a fridge on the side of the house."

Robert studied the refrigerator for a moment. "That's stupid. There's no lock on it or nothin."

"Tell me about it."

"Anybody could just walk up and take it."

They looked at each other. Robert glanced at the picture window at the front of the house. It was dark. "Looks like nobody's home."

"Yeah. When they're home, they let the dog out."

A length of chain was attached to one of the porch columns. There was no dog on the other end.

Robert shrugged. "Hey, if Marcos is stupid enough to leave his stash out in the open and then brag about it ..."

Angelo nodded.

"Then let's do it." Robert checked both ends of the street and then opened the gate. He motioned for Angelo to go first.

Through the gate, the two men stayed to the concrete walkway as if they intended to go to the front door. Angelo's steps were sporadic, with a small step or two, and then a long stride, all with no rhythm. He was avoiding the numerous cracks in the concrete.

Robert shoved him, causing Angelo to step on the next crack.

"Hey!"

"What? You think you're gonna break your mother's back or somethin? Come on!"

Angelo cursed and moved onto the lawn on his right, headed for the refrigerator.

Robert checked the front window again before following.

The refrigerator was old—dingy white, speckled with rust spots, and only two thirds of its lever handle remained. Robert's mother would have referred to it as an "icebox." Angelo stopped in front of it and looked around.

"What are you doin? Open it up."

Angelo did. The door emitted a slight creak as a musty odor wafted out. With what little light the nearby lamppost provided, Robert viewed the abundant brown paper bags filling the refrigerator, neatly folded and stored on all the shelves.

"Great," Robert said. "You got us stealing a bunch of grocery sacks."

"Hang on." Angelo bent over, parted the bags, and stood holding a plastic bag. He dangled it above his head, the contents glistening in the sparse light. "See. Just like I told you," he said, unable to contain a smile.

Robert slammed the refrigerator door shut. "Let's go."

~~~~~

Several days later, Robert was driving across town to Steven's apartment. Steven was a younger guy, about twenty, and was part of Robert's crew. Like others, Steven enjoyed the status that came with being connected to Robert, who still had his reputation as a tough guy intact, despite his falling out with Nicky.

After stealing the angel dust from Marcos, Robert entrusted Steven with selling the larger portion of his take. In the past when Robert needed to unload a stash, Steven came through, proving that he had the capability of not only finding buyers quickly, but he also received premium dollars for the goods. It was only natural that Robert would first consider Steven. Still, Robert didn't give all of it to him, just in case he got busted.

When Robert arrived at Steven's apartment to collect the money, he parked his car on the street behind Steven's and passed between the two cars. As he stepped up on the curb, he heard a thud. He turned around and looked at Steven's car. Nothing. So he kept walking and approached the front entrance to the apartment.

Steven appeared at the door. His eyes were wide, and he was trembling. As he came out, another young man followed.

Robert didn't recognize him. Instinctively, he put his right hand to his side, where he kept his .357 magnum revolver. "Who's your friend, Steven?" He was careful to watch for the man's hands.

Steven looked back at the man, who had now cleared the doorway. Steven shook his head, unconcerned about the man.

"Robert, we got a problem." His eyes lacked focus and his speech was slurred.

"Steven." Robert stood within two feet of him. "You didn't smoke the goods, did ya?"

"No, no, it's … I got your money. It's …" He rubbed his nose as he glanced toward his car. "You know that guy Damien who runs around with Fat Andy's son Albert?"

Robert thought for a moment. "Yeah. What about him?"

Steven looked back at the young man behind him, moved a little closer to Robert, and whispered, "We killed him."

Robert stepped back. "What?"

"He was stealing from us. We couldn't let him get away with that, could we?"

The other guy was looking anywhere except at him.

Pacing the stoop, Robert ran his fingers through his hair. "Man, oh man. You really got yourself into a mess." He looked around to see if anyone was outside. Except for an old lady down the street, walking her little dog, there was no one. "Where's the body?"

Steven pointed toward his car.

"Show me."

At the back of the car, Steven pulled out his car keys and unlocked the trunk. An overpowering smell of urine permeated the air.

"Whoa!" Robert waved his hand in front of his nose and took a step back.

As the lid rose further, the trunk lights backlit a crumpled body. Keeping his hand under his nose, Robert leaned in to get a better look. Without warning, the pale head of Damien popped up, his eyes wide as silver dollars and blood shot, a white extension cord still wrapped around his neck. Expletives filled the air as Robert and the other two men scrambled to get away from the rising corpse.

Robert drew his gun and drew back the hammer, ready to shoot the zombie that once was Damien.

Damien held up his hands and yelled with a whispery voice, "Don't shoot."

Robert lowered his gun, simultaneously releasing the hammer and his breath. He nudged Steven, who was obviously struggling with the reality of the situation. "You didn't kill him." Robert returned the gun to his side. "He's still alive." He walked over to the trunk to help Damien.

"Is he really alive?" Steven said.

"Yeah, he's alive."

"How did that happen?"

"You didn't kill him, idiot." Robert held Damien's arm. "Now help me get him out of there."

Steven took Damien's other arm. "What do we do with him?"

"Take him inside. Clean him up."

"They tried to kill me," Damien said to Robert, his voice raspy and whispered.

Robert removed the cord from around his neck and patted him on the shoulder. "It's all right. Ain't nothin gonna happen to you now. Go get cleaned up."

Damien went inside with the friend while Steven got Robert's money. They were smoking outside on the stoop when Damien came out in a blue warmup suit. He glared at Steven, who crushed out his cigarette and went back inside.

"You okay?" Robert asked.

Damien just shook his head, more of an act of disbelief than to answer Robert's question. "You saved my life."

Robert shrugged off the comment. "Go home. Get you some rest. And do me a favor: don't tell anybody about this, especially Albert."

Damien nodded and headed down the street.

TWENTY-ONE

1986 thru 1987
Ages 31 thru 32

n December of 1985, a shock wave rolled through the
Gambino family after its boss, Paul Castellano, and his driver
were gunned down outside Sparks Steak House in
downtown Manhattan. Nicky Corozzo's longtime rival, John
Gotti, took his place.

Robert managed to stay out of prison all of 1986. He and
Cookie remained a couple, but her attitude toward him changed.
Ever since the incident at Bruce's house, where he knocked
Cookie unconscious, she displayed a genuine fear of Robert,
especially when they argued. She was no longer the smart-
mouthed girl who held her ground. Now, she made great strides
toward avoiding conflict.

During this time, drugs dominated Robert's life and consumed
a large portion of his funds. Whether snorting lines of coke at a
club or freebasing in the privacy of a friend's home, Robert's
"high time" was more often than not. Certainly, he had passed
the line of occasional recreational usage and teetered on the edge
of the abyss known as addiction.

Tito's became Robert's favorite after-hours hangout. He had
become acquainted with Tito's after he and Frankie Burke shot
up the place, destroying its exotic aquariums and liquor bottles.
The attack was in response to an act of disrespect by one of
Tito's patrons to one of Robert's friends. It was the lesser of two

evils. Robert had gone there to kill the man whose lack of respect had gone undisputed.

Afterward, Robert hung out at Tito's, parading around as if he were part owner, although that was far from the truth. Paranoia—induced by his drug usage—drove him to keep a Remington 12-gauge, double-barrel shotgun by his side as he strolled around the bar. He walked from person to person, greeting friends and strangers alike, never noticing their uneasiness as he precariously waved the shotgun around.

One evening, Robert was at the club, drinking alone at the bar. Due to a winter blast that had slowed down an otherwise bustling Brooklyn, business was slow. Around midnight, Robert's friend Angelo strolled in from the blistery cold, rubbing his hands together.

Angelo sat next to Robert at the bar, flapping the sides of his jacket to loosen the snow. "This kind of weather really makes me hate this town."

"Hey!" Robert shielded himself from the barrage of frigid wetness. "Keep that mess to yourself." He slid a bottle of Scotch to Angelo and signaled the bartender for a glass. "Here. This'll take the edge off the cold."

Angelo filled the glass and within a minute, consumed its entire contents. He refilled it.

"Where you been?" Robert asked.

Angelo shrugged. "You know, runnin here and there, tryin to make a couple of dollars."

The mention of money always piqued Robert's interest. "Oh, yeah? What? Are you talking about a score or somethin?"

Angelo nodded. "Yeah, maybe."

"You got my attention." Robert sipped his drink.

For the next half hour, Angelo provided Robert with the details of the scam.

"Sounds like a lot of money could be made," Robert said.

"Yeah. And it'll be hard to trace back to us."

Robert nodded. "Count me in." He set his glass down and pointed the shotgun toward the back. "Let's go."

They walked past the restroom to a room the owner used as an office. The dimly lit, dingy room was large enough to accommodate a desk, couch, and its own bar, where Robert refilled his glass from a different bottle while Angelo laid out several lines of coke. Within an hour, the coke was gone and the bottle empty.

Robert sat on the couch, the shotgun between his legs, pointed toward the ceiling.

Angelo was across from him, propped up on a barstool.

"This is all messed up." Robert pressed the release lever on the shotgun, allowing its double barrels to pivot down.

Angelo briskly rubbed his face with both hands. "Messed up? What's messed up?"

Robert removed one of the shells from the receiver and threw it behind him. "Everything."

The seconds that followed were darkened in Robert's mind, but when he recovered, the shotgun was locked and aimed at Angelo, whose hands were slightly elevated.

"Robert! What are you doing?"

Robert laughed. "It's not loaded, you idiot."

"Yes, it is!"

"No, it's not. I took the shells out."

"No, you didn't. There's still one in there. Now quit pointing it at me!"

Robert didn't listen. Instead, he continued to tease Angelo.

Angelo swore at him. "Put the gun down before you kill me."

Robert smirked. "You don't trust me?" He lowered the gun, placing the butt on the floor. "I'll prove it's not loaded." He leaned the shotgun toward him and positioned his mouth over the end of both barrels.

"No! Robert!"

As Angelo lunged forward to stop him, Robert pulled one of the triggers—but not before he moved the barrels to the side of his head. The force of the explosion generated by the single shell still residing in the shotgun's chamber sent Robert and the couch rocking backward. The couch crashed to the floor with Robert still in it.

Due to the tremendously painful ringing in his left ear, Robert couldn't hear Angelo, but his expression conveyed his angry message without the need for words.

Angelo helped Robert to his feet.

"I guess it *was* loaded," Robert said, his voice echoing deeply inside of him.

The bartender burst through the door and spoke to Angelo with lots of animation. At first Robert couldn't understand what he was saying. But then he pointed at Robert, followed by a thumb gesture, and the message to get out became clear.

~~~~~

In the first part of 1987, Robert had four pending cases against him, including bail jumping. With the heat rising in New York, he figured his best option was to get out of town before he ended up in prison again. He had always wanted to go to Las Vegas. Even though the tension between him and Cookie was heavy, she decided to go with him to Vegas, but only with the promise that he would stay away from drugs.

When they arrived, they stayed with friends who lived twenty-five minutes from the Strip. Cookie found a job at the Continental Hotel and Casino, while Robert did his best to combat his drug addiction.

Two months later, Robert received tragic news. On May 18, his good friend Frankie Burke was gunned down, fulfilling an omen Robert spoke over Frankie not long before he and Cookie moved to Vegas. Robert, Frankie, and an older guy named Tito (not to be confused with the Tito who owned the after-hours joint) were getting high together. Frankie spoke disrespectfully to Tito, an old school mobster, who threatened to kill him.

Robert told Frankie he needed to watch his mouth, or Tito would follow through with his threat.

Frankie blew it off, having the youthful mentality of invincibility and the false confidence that his father Jimmy's reputation would prevent any harm from coming to him. Frankie disrespected Tito again, who left and returned with a gun and shot him in front of a bar on Crescent Street.

Robert was floored by the news but decided it was best that he didn't return to New York for the funeral.

As hard as he tried, Robert failed to stay away from drugs. He and Cookie moved, this time to California, where another friend put him to work at his restaurant. Again, the drugs took over. After only a few months there, Robert and Cookie returned to New York.

The fragile foundation upon which their relationship was built finally collapsed. Robert had been drinking heavily at a bar one evening and surmised that something was up with Cookie. Not wanting the hassle of being hit with another weapons charge, he left his gun with the bartender and went to see Cookie where she was living. He looked through the window and saw her walking past, as if she were heading to her apartment upstairs ... with another "friend" of Robert's following her.

Robert ran around to the front door, which opened up to the stairs, and looked through the window. Cookie and the friend had stopped at the landing and were kissing. Empowered by his rage, Robert broke down the door.

Immediately, his friend ran toward the back door. Unable to get to him, Robert released his anger once again by hitting Cookie. This time she rolled with the punch and escaped to her apartment upstairs, where she locked herself in.

Robert staggered back to the bar and got his gun. When he returned, he went upstairs and continued arguing with Cookie while banging on the door.

A few minutes later, Cookie's sister arrived in her car. Apparently, Cookie had called and asked her to come get her. While Cookie stayed locked in her apartment, Robert went downstairs to the car. Her sister argued with Robert, calling him names and telling him to leave. Unconcerned about the attention he was drawing and infuriated by the tongue lashing, he cocked his .357 magnum, pointed it at her back passenger window, and shot. The glass spider-webbed in a million directions before collapsing into the backseat. After the screaming subsided and Cookie's sister slung several expletives Robert's way, she sped away.

Later, Robert was ordered to come to a "sit down" with two guys. One of them was a wiseguy from another family. Supposedly, they wanted to resolve the issue concerning the situation between Robert and the "friend." Cookie was there, as well as the family living there. Just before the sit-down got underway, the family left. Robert became suspicious when Cookie tried to leave, as well. Whether his paranoia was drug induced or not, he made Cookie stay, thinking nothing would happen to him if she were there.

Feeling that his life was on the line, Robert decided to play off the incident as a product of his imagination, due to excessive drinking. This apparently satisfied the two men. They stood, hugged Robert, and left.

TWENTY-TWO

March 1990
Age 35

A fter a while, the warrants dangling over Robert's head
caught up with him. In October 1988, he was arrested.
With the help of a lawyer, he received a sentence of one-
and-a-half to three years. He served eighteen months at
Marcy Correction Facility.

Prison was a place where Robert had time to purge his body of
the drugs that had dominated his life. When he got out in 1990
with a clear mind intact, he finally heeded the advice of his family
and didn't return to Cookie.

Since Robert was getting out of jail early, he had to serve the
remainder of his sentence under the watchful eyes of a parole
officer. Before he could be released, the parole board required
that he have a place to live and job prospects. Since his mother
and father had moved to Florida, Robert moved in with his sister
Anna while he got his feet back under him. With the help of
Nicky's father, who had connections within the labor union, he
got a job escorting large trucks around Kennedy airport. Other
times, he stood around all day at a job site, waiting for a licensed
contractor to finish his work. When he was done, Robert was
responsible for cleanup. He made good, honest money, working
thirty-five hours and grossing about $750 a week.

To help ensure that drugs and alcohol no longer played a role
in his life, the parole board required his involvement with
Narcotics Anonymous. Normally, new attendees attended ninety

meetings in the first ninety days, as recommended by NA. Robert's parole officer required only three times a week.

On his first day of freedom, Robert settled in at Anna's before walking to his first NA meeting at St. Helen's School in Howard Beach. When he reached the school campus, he was thirty minutes early, sweating due to the unusually warm April weather. Just to the left of the sanctuary, a white placard on the double doors had large blue AA letters. He wandered down the poorly lit hallway until he came to a classroom on his left, where the lights were on.

He leaned in through the doorway. In front of a table, a man was arranging cookies and drink cups, his back facing Robert.

"Am I at the right place?" Robert said.

The man turned around. "Robert!"

Robert was taken back. It was Anthony Ruggiano, his old running buddy and son of Fat Andy.

Anthony set the remaining cups on the table and walked over.

Robert was unsure how to react, considering their relationship had turned cold several years back. But as Anthony approached with a smile and open arms, it became apparent that whatever hard feelings he had harbored against Robert were no longer there.

The men hugged.

Anthony said, "I heard you got out, but I didn't expect to see you—at least, not here."

"Yeah. Well, it's part of my parole. And I need to get my life back on track, so …"

Anthony nodded.

Robert said, "What are *you* doing here?"

Anthony raised his eyebrows ever so slightly. "My dad. He told me I had to get clean, so he got me into rehab. When I got out, they recommended AA. I help out by hosting meetings." Anthony glanced at people coming in. "Listen, I gotta finish up. But we'll talk more after the meeting."

Robert nodded and found a seat near the back. During the meeting, he was a little nervous, waiting for his turn to introduce himself. As he spoke, the expressions of some attendees indicated that they knew who he was. After the meeting, several of them told how they knew Robert through so and so and asked if the events for which he was legendary really happened. Of course, Robert loved the attention, and he especially liked having new, admiring friends who were just as serious as he was about going straight. It made it easier for him to cut ties with old friends who were still involved in drugs and heavy drinking.

His social life revolved around the AA meetings, which he attended almost every night.

At one of the meetings, he met Linda, a sassy, dark-eyed Italian girl with long black hair. Their conversation was the natural result of two people who liked sitting near the back of the room. One of those conversations included information about her mother's basement apartment, which was vacant. Robert intended to live with his sister Anna until he could find a place of his own. From Linda's description, the apartment sounded like a nice place at a price he could afford. The only drawback, according to Linda, was that her mother was a tough lady. She even referred to her as a *gangster*. Robert knew he would like her before he met her.

On April 20, he went to the address on 106th Street. The clean, two-story house with white-shingle siding had a concrete stoop connected to the street by a sidewalk slightly fractured in several places by the hard freezes of many New York winters. On the side of the house was a dog run made of chain-link fence. Two Rottweilers were angrily barking at Robert, jumping up on the fence and furiously pacing. Without thinking, Robert reached behind his back, searching for a gun tucked away in his pants. For many years, he had depended upon a weapon for protection. As his hand groped at nothing but air, he knew his new life would have to depend upon his own abilities to get him out—better yet, keep him out—of any unpleasant situations.

Robert extinguished his cigarette on the curb and walked up to the stoop, careful to avoid the cracks in the sidewalk. He opened the French doors and saw the staircase that went to the upstairs apartment. Linda told him that she, her mother, and sister lived on the second-floor apartment and to knock on the door when he came. At the top of the stairs, an attractive young woman in her twenties came out with a basket of laundry. Looking much like Linda, the woman had to be her sister.

"Hey," Robert said, "let me give you a hand with that."

The woman was startled at first, looking like she was thinking about going back inside.

"It's all right. I'm here to check out the basement apartment, maybe rent it out. You must be Lauren."

Again, the woman didn't say anything.

"I'm Robert. I met your sister Linda. She told me about you and your mom."

"Oh, yeah." She shook her head. "Sorry. I just—"

"Hey, it's all right. Where you goin with this?" Robert reached for the basket.

Another woman appeared in the doorway. "She can handle it herself."

Robert assumed she was the gangster mother. In her fifties, she was a very pretty woman, with dark hair and the same hazel brown eyes as her daughter.

"Can I help you?"

"Yeah, Linda told me you're renting out your basement. I wanted to check it out."

The mother hesitated. "All right. Stay right there. I got to get the key. You," she said to Lauren, "get that laundry going."

Lauren scurried down the staircase and disappeared.

Robert wanted to follow Lauren, thinking her mother would catch up with them. But then, he didn't want the mother to think he was chasing after her daughter and ruin his chance of getting the apartment. So he stayed until the mother returned.

After an unusually long time, the mother finally returned. She had her cordless handset pressed against her ear as she signaled for Robert to follow her. "Yeah … yeah… that's what I heard. Listen, I got someone looking at the apartment right now. I'll call you later." She turned her attention to Robert as she made her way down the stairs. "I think this thing is going to grow to my ear one of these days. Okay, let's go check it out."

The entrance to the steps down to the basement was under the second-floor stairs. She chatted all the way down both flights, pointing out that her sister and family lived in the first-floor apartment. When they entered the basement, Lauren was putting clothes into the washing machine next to the dryer in the common area. She smiled at him and gave a nervous glance as her mother unlocked the basement apartment door.

"Anyway, let's go in," the mother said. "Name?"

"Excuse me?" Robert followed her inside.

"Name. Didn't you get a name when you were born?"

Robert snickered. "I get called lots of things, most of which I can't repeat. But you can call me Robert."

This time it was her turn to laugh. "We must hang around the same people. I'm Barbara. Where you from?"

"Brooklyn."

"What part?"

"Grew up around Fulton and Rockaway. Moved over to Richmond Street when I was older."

The door led directly into the bedroom. Like everything else he'd seen so far, it was clean and neat, with a full-size bed and nightstand.

"It's a two-room apartment, fully furnished," Barbara said as they walked from the bedroom into the next room. "You got the living room/kitchen area, and then the bathroom's through this door over here." She stood to the side as Robert glanced in. "The only downside is you might have to put up with a little noise from the washer and dryer. But that usually doesn't happen except a couple times a week."

Robert shrugged. "I don't think that'll be a problem." He motioned toward another set of stairs. "That leads to the outside?"

"The back yard. We have a pool. You're welcome to use it."

"How much is the rent?"

"I think $500 is a fair price. Do you?"

"Sure, sounds good."

She moved directly in front of Robert. "What do you do, Robert? I mean, for a living?"

Robert hesitated, his mind not totally wrapped around his new lifestyle. "I just started a job with a construction company."

Barbara stared at him. "You're an ex-con, aren't you? Don't try denying it. Linda already told me. Besides, I've been around enough of them to smell an ex-con a mile away—especially the mobster type."

Robert felt defiance arise but caught it in time to keep from saying something regretful. "Look, Barbara, I'm not looking to start any trouble. I just need a chance to get my life back in order. You can understand that, right?"

Barbara considered Robert's words. "You have someone to vouch for you?"

The only people Robert knew were involved with crime, so he said the name of the first person he thought of who wasn't. "My mom?"

Slowly, Barbara's smile grew to uncontrollable laughter.

Robert wasn't sure if the laughter should have been an insult, but he did know that it often produced good results.

"You're a funny guy, Robert." After wiping away the tears, she held out her hand. "Let me see the money."

Robert slipped his wallet from his back pocket and took out five hundred-dollar bills.

"Okay," she said with a pleased tone. "Keep your nose clean—and I mean absolutely no drugs—and we'll call it a deal."

~~~~~

To Robert, Barbara was very likable. She regularly invited Robert upstairs to eat with her and her girls. She chatted with him when he brought her the rent money. She had dated several men that Robert knew from his old life, including one who was close with Jimmy Burke.

What she told him about the laundry being done only a couple of times a week ended up being not so accurate. After he moved in, Lauren, who actually hated doing laundry, was in the basement almost every day washing, drying, folding, and hanging clothes.

Since Robert was no longer going out and getting high or drunk in the evenings, he spent a lot of his downtime in his apartment, often leaving the entry door open. This gave him the opportunity to have many extended conversations with Lauren in the common area, and eventually in his apartment, where they soon became intimate.

TWENTY-THREE

August 1991
Age 36

I n Robert's mind, the job in construction as a union laborer was a step down in social status. While a mobster, he had others waiting on him. Now, he was waiting on others, picking up scrap wood and metal, sweeping up the sawdust and dirt. Licensed contractors looked down their noses at him, as if he were no better than a slave to be used at their discretion, which made it difficult for him to avoid conflict.

The employment was sporadic. From the time he got out of prison to 1993, he worked from one contract to another, laid off in-between, which allowed the door to his old lifestyle to reopen.

As fate would have it, an opportunity arose for him to return to the days of his former glory. In 1991, he was involved in a credit card scheme, incorporating the skills of a guy named Pete, a thief who used to work with Anthony Ruggiano. After a dispute with Anthony, Pete went to work with Robert and his crew. His job was to go into Long Island and scope out the cars at jogging parks. Knowing that joggers usually didn't take their wallets with them, he broke into their cars, took one credit card, put the wallet back, and left the car with the break-in undetected. For several days, sometimes for weeks, Robert and his buddies purchased goods on the stolen credit cards and sold them to a fence. They usually got 50 percent of the market value of the merchandise, putting three to four hundred dollars a day into Robert's pocket.

Another source of illegal income was through a large amount of stolen traveler's cheques they acquired—over $1,000,000 worth. At first, they were selling the cheques at pennies on the dollar, but then wised up to a better plan and decided Las Vegas was the best place to put their plan into play.

After four years away, Robert returned to Las Vegas. Friends Dee Dee and Carmine and Robert's cousin Tony lived in Vegas. A couple of other friends came with him. All were included in the crew that would run the scam. Tony booked rooms at the Dunes Hotel and Casino, where they would set up their headquarters. After the nearly six-hour flight, Robert and his crew walked up to the front desk at the hotel.

"May I help you?" the bleached-blonde desk clerk asked.

Robert chuckled. "Honey, you already have." He looked to the other guys for approval of his little joke, either smiling or laughing.

The woman looked embarrassed. "May I have the name under which the room is booked?"

Robert gave her the false name under which his cousin had booked the rooms.

After searching her computer screen, she said, "I have two rooms on the seventh floor, rooms 707 and 709. Will that work for you?"

"Yeah, that'll be fine."

After Robert signed the necessary paperwork, the desk clerk asked, "Will there be any valuable items in need of safekeeping?"

"I think we're good for right now." Robert reached down and picked up the briefcase filled with traveler's cheques. "But I might want to put this away later."

"That's fine. Whenever you're ready."

At his room, Robert tipped the bellboy a healthy fifty and then called his cousin to let him know they had arrived. They ordered room service, billing the room for the food. He then turned off the TV and got all the men to sit down.

"Okay, the plan is simple. I'm gonna give each of you $1,000. We'll drive around to the souvenir stores, a 7–11, or any convenience store you see. One guy at each store. You buy something for a few dollars, maybe ten or fifteen. You don't want to buy a 50-cent piece of candy and hand them a $100 traveler's cheque and make them suspicious. Buy your stuff, pocket the change in cash. Nobody goes to the same store twice. Tony says there are enough stores around here to keep us busy for a while. And whatever you do, don't use any of the traveler's cheques in the hotel, especially the casino. Got it?"

~~~~~

The first day proved the plan was very lucrative, with nearly fifty unsuspecting stores falling prey to the scheme. They celebrated in the adjoining hotel rooms with champagne, cigars, and the purchases from the stores, which amounted to lots of bags of chips, cases of beer, boxes of Twinkies, and snow globes. Robert counted the cash—$4,400. He held the bills up in the air.

"It takes money to make money. Gentlemen, to the casino."

He divvied up the cash between the five of them and headed downstairs for the crap table. Within an hour he doubled his share of the take. Another hour later, he was even. Three hours into the gambling spree, he only had half the money with which he had started. Wanting to try his luck elsewhere, he collected his chips and went to wager on the ponies in another part of the casino. After several attempts, he scored on a trifecta worth $3,000. His yelling and whooping drew a couple of his buddies his way to celebrate with him.

The gambling and celebrating went on through the night and into the day. When Robert felt the weariness of a sleepless day hit him, he took the elevator to the basement, where he met up with one of the hotel's bellboys, who happened to be a friend of his cousin.

After staying away from alcohol for nearly a year, Robert fell off the wagon. Not long before leaving New York, he met up with some friends at a café after an AA meeting. He wasn't much of a coffee drinker, so he ordered a sandwich, but his friends ordered espressos sweetened with Sambuca, an Italian liqueur. As the evening went on, Robert decided he wanted to try the espresso. He took a sip of one of his friend's espressos, not thinking it would have any effect on him. He bought his own and drank it, then drank another, and before long, he felt a buzz. After calling it a night, he found a drug dealer in his old stomping grounds. Once again, his addiction took charge, sending him spiraling back into the vortex of drug abuse.

Now, Robert was meeting with the guy from the hotel to score some coke. After making the deal, he went up to his room and shared the illegal substance with a couple of the guys with him, negating the need for sleep.

This went on for several days. Robert got a daily share of traveler's cheques from the briefcase, now kept in the hotel's safe. He and his buddies converted them to cash. As fast as the money was made, it disappeared even faster. But it didn't bother Robert that he was burning through the money. After all, he had a briefcase full of traveler's cheques waiting to be converted into however much cash he needed.

About a week into their stay, Robert was watching TV, but before long, he got bored and went down to the casino. He had two hundred dollars, which he played on one roll of the dice … and lost. Bored and cashless was a bad combination for Robert. He ventured into his pocket and found his daily share of traveler's cheques. Just as mindless as he was the day he bet the mob's money at Belmont, Robert walked up to the cashier, completely ignoring his own decree of not cashing stolen cheques in the casino.

"How ya doin?" he said to the cashier, whose hairstyle was an exact replica of the one belonging to the desk clerk.

"I'm doing fine, thank you." She took the traveler's cheques. "If I could see some I.D."

Robert was caught off guard. He had planned to sign the traveler's cheques with a fake signature, not thinking he'd have to show identification. He opened his wallet and handed her his New York driver's license.

"Thank you," she said with a singsong tone. She wrote the information from the driver's license on the back of the cheques and then had Robert sign them. After she put them in her drawer, she counted out five one-hundred-dollar bills. Without another word, Robert went back to the craps table, determined to get his money back. He got five hundred-dollar chips from the dealer. But as it usually was with him, his luck had turned. Within minutes, his chips were mixed with those of the house.

He still had five more cheques. Since it worked once, he figured he might as well try cashing them again. As he neared the cashier's booth, the woman who had served him before was in a conversation with someone on the phone. She looked anxiously in every direction but his.

After she hung up the phone, Robert said, "I'm back again." He handed the other five checks to her.

"Hello, sir." This time, her smile was forced. "I'll have this processed for you in just a moment." Instead of asking for his identification, she opened a cabinet and squatted, as if she were looking for something in particular. When she stood and faced Robert, she looked to his right, then to his left.

Robert picked up on the body language and scanned around him. Two men in blue blazers and walkie-talkies were headed his way. Leaving the cheques with the cashier, he walked in the opposite direction. He looked over his shoulder. The two men were still following him and closing the gap. Without hesitation, he broke into a full sprint, crashing through casino patrons. One woman screamed at him as her cup of quarters spilled to the floor. He found the gray double doors that served as a fire exit, shoved the panic bar, and ran down the alley. The two security officers were still on his tail. He ran as fast as his legs would move, his lungs burning.

The border of the casino property was fenced, with barbed wire on top. Ignoring the damage the wire would cause him, he jumped the fence and escaped on the other side. For a while, he never looked back but kept running. He went inside a smaller hotel, slowing down from a sprint to a fast-paced walk. In the hallway was an ice machine. While no one was around, he moved the ice machine away from the wall and climbed in behind it.

Robert stayed there for several hours. He finally peered over the top, saw that he was alone, and climbed out. He couldn't return to his hotel, so he walked to his cousin's, who lived three blocks away. At his cousin's apartment, he immediately took a shower without explaining anything, washing off the crusted blood from the wounds the barbed wire inflicted. He borrowed some clothes and threw his away.

He called the hotel room, where he got in touch with Carmine. "Hey listen. Get everything packed and come to my cousin Tony's place. We're leavin town."

"Okay. What's going on?"

"I'll explain when youse guys get here. And don't try to get the briefcase out of the safe. We've been busted."

As Robert hung up, Carmine was swearing.

Robert and the crew from New York laid low for a day. They decided not to fly out of Vegas, fearing any one of them could be identified by airport security. Instead, they drove to California and stayed with one of Dee Dee's friends. While there, they used the remaining traveler's cheques they had on them to run the same scam. After four days, they had enough cash to purchase plane tickets back to New York.

~~~~~

Robert dropped three of his four pieces of luggage at the top of the stairs that led to his basement apartment, went downstairs, and opened the door. After throwing his bag on the couch, he went back to get the rest.

Lauren was at the door. "Robert," she said, surprised to see him.

"Hey," he said with a big smile. "Aren't you glad I'm back?"

Lauren didn't say anything.

"What's wrong?"

She didn't share his enthusiasm. "I ... didn't think you were coming back."

"What made you think that?" He headed back up the stairs to get the rest of his luggage.

"Well, Linda said—"

"Linda said what?" He picked up the largest piece of luggage and the garment bag and stood at the top of the stairs.

Lauren picked up the last piece. "She said you weren't coming back."

Robert laughed and headed down the stairs. "Why would she say something like that?"

"Just look, Robert. You took about everything you own with you."

"Yeah, I guess I did." He took the small bag from Lauren and threw it on the couch. "But she was wrong. I'm back. I never intended to be gone for very long from my best girl." He opened his arms and expected Lauren to fall into them, but she didn't. "Now what?"

"Well, I thought you weren't coming back."

"I get that. Is that all?"

"I … I started seeing someone else."

"What? How could you do that? I haven't been gone but a couple of weeks."

"I know, but …"

Two years ago with Cookie, he would have blown a fuse. But now, for reasons he couldn't explain, he didn't feel the need to lash out. "Okay. It's this simple. I'm back, and you can either hang with this other guy, or you can hang with me. You can't do both." He exhaled. "Listen, I'm kinda tired. Come see me tomorrow, okay?"

~~~~~

The next day, Robert woke to the smell of bacon. He got up, lit a cigarette, and walked into the kitchen.

"Good morning, sleepy head." Lauren was scrambling eggs in a frying pan. Unlike the evening before, she was wearing a smile.

"What time is it?" Robert scratched his head.

"About eleven. Hungry?"

"Starving."

Robert sat down at the small table in the kitchen area. Lauren loaded up a plate of eggs and bacon and placed them in front of him. He looked up at her through slits in his eyelids.

"Does this mean I made the cut?"

Lauren nodded.

"Good." He forked a bite of eggs and tore off a piece of bacon. Cause I really didn't feel like going out and killing somebody today."

TWENTY-FOUR

November 1992
Age 37

A s Robert and Lauren continued seeing each other, their relationship deepened. In 1991, they moved out of her mother's place and into their own apartment several blocks away. Through various illegal schemes, Robert was making a lot of money, including a lucrative robbery that netted him a cool $20,000. With the confidence that such an amount can bring, he decided to take the next step in their relationship.

A few days later, he took Lauren to a friend's store, which had a soda bar. After seating Lauren at a table, he ordered two ice cream sodas from the bar. Before bringing the sodas to the table, he topped Lauren's with an engagement ring bought with money from the robbery. He was a bit apprehensive, considering Cookie's response some years ago. But there were no similarities between Lauren and Cookie's personalities, including their reactions to Robert's gestures. As Robert had hoped, Lauren was ecstatic, and so were her mother and sister. Right away, they made plans for the engagement party, setting a date and securing the use of a banquet hall with a $5,000 deposit.

The outlook for Robert and Lauren's life together looked good except for one thing—his clandestine love affair with cocaine. At first, he was able to conceal his addiction from Lauren, who was not a user, nor did she condone its use. Using the cover of "work" as an excuse to stay away from home for days at a time, he regularly freebased with his friends. His money soon ran out, and it became quite clear to Lauren that Robert had reverted to his old ways. She pardoned him several times after promises that he wouldn't do it anymore, but each of those promises was broken.

Robert's lack of responsibility proved too much for Lauren. Within a couple of weeks of the engagement party, they decided to break up. Lauren moved back in with her mother, and Robert moved in with Angelo. Even though the engagement was called off, Lauren's affection for Robert remained, and they continued to see each other.

~~~~~

No matter the situation in her life, Robert's mother always managed to make Thanksgiving a festive occasion for her family. She loved the holidays—especially Thanksgiving—and how they brought her family together.

Because Thanksgiving made his mother happy, Robert liked it too.

The Thanksgiving of 1992 was going to be different. Robert was nearly thirty-eight years old, laid off from his job as a union laborer and fighting an addiction that had the upper hand.

He was broke. He had his occasional robbery or theft that brought in a little money, but that was usually blown getting high with friends. Without money, he couldn't buy a plane ticket to Florida, where his mother and father lived. Therefore, he would not be spending Thanksgiving with his mother.

Barbara's dinner invitations had ceased, and he wasn't expecting her to make an exception for Thanksgiving. His sister Anna and her husband, Paulie, would be happy to have him over, but he had led her to believe he had already made arrangements with Lauren.

So instead of spending the holiday with family, Robert did what he considered was the next best thing. He played basketball with friends.

Just after the tie-breaking third game had started, Robert's pager went off. He went to the bench where he'd left his belongings and picked up the pager with a towel. Two words shouted from the orange digital display: I'M PREGNANT.

It was a message from Lauren.

Robert felt the butterflies of impending fatherhood as he stared at the pager. He rubbed his face vigorously before viewing the pager again. When the reality of the situation set in, he shot his hand into the air and yelled, "I'm gonna be a daddy."

After the game, Angelo dropped him off at Lauren's place, where they celebrated together.

"This is so great," Robert said as he sat across from Lauren at the dining table, gorging on a plate of Thanksgiving leftovers she had brought home. "When's the baby gonna be here?"

Lauren laughed. "I don't know, I just found out I was pregnant."

Robert savored the thought that, in several months, he would be cradling a child of his own.

"You'll make a good father," Lauren said.

"You think so?" Robert imagined a tiny person calling him Daddy.

"I have no doubt. You've got a good heart. You just …"

Robert put down his fork and took Lauren's hand. "I know. I gotta stay clean. Hey, look." He held out his arms. "I'm playing basketball. Stayin out of trouble."

Lauren smiled.

"I'm gonna do whatever I gotta do. Cause this is it. This is what it's gonna take to kick the habit. I'm gonna be a daddy."

Lauren wiped her eye with her finger, taking a little eyeliner with it. "I believe you. And I believe in you. I think this is the chance you need to turn your life around. Cause this baby's gonna need you."

~~~~~

"Just sign your name and date it right here."

The in-processing administrator of Daytop Rehabilitation Center pointed to a line on the last page of the thick contract.

Robert used the pen she had given him to write his name. "What is the date, anyway?"

"April 1."

Robert chuckled. "That's appropriate. It's still 1993, right?"

As Robert promised the day he found out he was going to be a father, he stayed off the drugs ... for about a month. After a couple of on-again-off-again episodes, Lauren threatened to leave unless he got help. Since Robert had friends who had connections with the rehab facility, he got in without delay and without a penny out of his pocket.

While there, Robert experienced intense therapy, both group and individual. The focus was on forgiving someone who had caused him emotional pain. For Robert, that person was his grandfather. His sudden death was a traumatic episode for a little boy who viewed his grandfather as a hero. As multiple emotional layers were pulled back, revealing the anger and pain attached to his grandfather's death, Robert shed many tears. But he learned that the drug problem was only a manifestation of even deeper issues.

Robert felt confident that when he finished his six-month commitment to the rehab facility, he would be ready to become the father he so desperately wanted to be.

TWENTY-FIVE

July 1993
Age 38

T here was little relief from the unforgiving summer sun. Portable fans blew from two corners, supplementing the air conditioning, straining to cool the third-story room at Jamaica Hospital. On the glossy, tiled floor of the long, sterile room, six columns of blue rubber mats were five rows deep. Topping the mats were thirty women, their discomfort from lying on a hard surface somewhat relieved by the cushioning of multiple pillows. Their bellies were swollen from months of pregnancy. Behind each of the women were their coaches, propping them up. Some blotted their partner's brow with wet cloths while performing their duty of back supporter.

"Coaches," the instructor said loud enough so those at the other end of the room could hear. "Don't forget to help your partner with her breathing,"

"Did you hear that?" Lauren asked Robert as she held her bent legs at the back of her knees.

"What? Can't you breathe without thinking about it?"

"This isn't the time to be funny," she said in staccato syllables.

"Okay, okay. Ease up."

"Don't tell me to ease up unless you're willing to carry this baby for the next two weeks. Now, do the breathing technique."

Robert mimicked her from behind, smirked, and then started in with the patented Lamaze breathing technique.

Even though Robert was only three months into his six-month commitment with Daytop, the administrator agreed to release him so he could deal with a tragedy in his family. His brother-in-law Paulie had died suddenly from a heart attack, and he left Daytop for a week to grieve with his family. After returning, he finished the program, just in time to assist Lauren in the Lamaze class.

The instructor came up from behind, her arms crossed over a clipboard she held to her chest. "How's it going here?"

Lauren said, "Outside of the fact that I got a monkey for a partner? Just fine."

Robert looked up at the instructor, shrugged, and smiled.

"You might as well get used to the comments," the instructor said to Robert. "You just need to understand that at this moment, Lauren is very uncomfortable."

"I would be too if I had to lay on my back with my legs up in the air."

"Enough with the jokes," Lauren said.

The instructor laughed. "This is good practice for you. More than likely, she'll be calling you all sorts of names in the delivery room. But don't take offense. She won't mean them."

"Oh yes I will," Lauren said.

Again, the instructor chuckled. "It'll be worth it after you see your new baby."

"You hear that, Lauren? It'll all be worth it."

Lauren swore at him.

~~~~~

On the way home, both Lauren and Robert were quiet as they listened to Whitney Houston belt out the remake of Dolly Parton's hit, "I Will Always Love You." When the final chorus came, Robert joined in with Whitney to serenade Lauren.

"Iiiieeeye will always love you whoo oo ooao," he sang off-tune.

Lauren smiled, then burst into a full-fledged laugh. "Oh, please stop. You're gonna make me go to the bathroom all over myself."

Robert didn't stop. He sang with more intensity and animation, parting the air in front of him with his hand, lifting his head like a howling coyote. This only made Lauren laugh harder. As Whitney faded, Robert broke into a chorus of "A Lauren Song," a song he sang often to her. Soon, her laughter turned to a single sentimental tear down her cheek. She grabbed his free hand and kissed him on the cheek, thankful for his ability to turn her misery into happiness.

"Hey! You're getting me all wet here." Robert wiped the tear and kiss from his face.

"You look so much better," Lauren said. "You remind me of the Robert I met three years ago. I think this rehab thing was exactly what you needed."

"Yeah, me too. I'm just glad I got to be a part of all this. You realize, I'm about to be a daddy."

Lauren nodded.

"That's crazy," Robert said, wiping his face as if awakened from a dream.

~~~~~

Two weeks later, as the temperatures continued to scorch New York, Robert and Lauren were coming back home with Briana, their new baby girl. After Robert parked the car in front of the house, he ran around to the passenger side and opened the door for Lauren.

"Well, that's a first." She stepped out of the car, smiling as she shielded her eyes from the sun.

Robert returned the smile as he opened the back door to get the baby. He hesitated as he studied the straps and buckles that held Briana securely in place. "Uh, how do you … uh …"

"You get the stuff out of the back," Lauren said. "I'll get the baby."

Robert retrieved the baggage, plants, and gifts, trying to handle everything at once. He dropped one of the plants, breaking the pot.

"Robert! Just get one load and come back for the rest." She lifted the carrier out of the back seat.

"Okay." Robert balanced the load he was carrying, kicking the plant and its broken pot to the curb.

As they went inside, Lauren and the baby led the way to her mother's apartment on the second floor. Since Robert had shown progress toward overcoming his drug addiction, Barbara allowed him to return to the apartment. She even made her much larger bedroom available for the three of them.

"Surprise!" Barbara, Linda, and a slew of other relatives attending the welcome home party jumped out from behind chairs and around corners, startling the baby.

Lauren set the carrier on a nearby table and removed Briana, who was now wailing. "Aw, poor baby."

Robert continued on to the bedroom while enduring a gauntlet of congratulations and backslaps. After dropping his load, he went back to the car to get the rest of Lauren's baggage and plants.

Across the street, a neighbor pulled up in his truck, apparently getting home from work. He stared blankly at Robert and then looked at all the cars in front of Barbara's place as he walked up to his house and disappeared inside.

~~~~~

The celebration outlasted the searing heat as the moon overtook a sleepy sun. While some of the women put away dishes and pans in the kitchen, Lauren and the baby snuggled up on the couch among admirers. Robert, Linda, and several others went out into the street with fireworks leftover from Independence Day. While explosive lights overtook the night sky, screams of delight shook the atmosphere, and soon, disturbed neighbors occupied the windows and doorways of their homes. As Robert was about to light another aerial shell, he saw the neighbor across the street, dressed only in a pair of shorts, slipping around his work truck and walking his way. Several other neighbors were headed his direction as well.

The man stopped in front of him, hands on his hips.

"What can I do you for?" Robert said.

"I tell you what you can do. You can quit shooting off those fireworks. That's what you can do." By then, the other neighbors had gathered behind the man, as had Linda and the others.

"Hey man, I just brought my baby girl home from the hospital. We just wanted to celebrate a little."

"I don't care why you're celebrating." The neighbor pointed a finger in Robert's face. "Either you shut it down, or I'll make you shut it down."

Robert swore at him. "I'll do whatever the—"

Robert didn't see the roundhouse punch that caught him in the left cheekbone, knocking him to the ground. Lots of pushing and yelling resulted, with Linda in the middle of it all. Before Robert regained his senses, the neighbors and his family were in a full-blown street fight.

Robert ran inside the house to the nearest phone.

"Look on the table," Lauren said as she rocked the baby. "What's goin on?"

"Freakin neighbors jumped us." He dialed a number on the handset.

"Who you calling? The cops?" She knew good and well that Robert would never ask the police for assistance.

"What, are you stupid?"

"Then who you calling?"

A voice on the other end answered. Music was playing in the background of the club where he knew his friends were.

"Hello?"

"It's Robert." He turned away from Lauren. "Listen. Is Carl or anybody around?"

There was a pause. "I see Carl and Mario too."

Robert looked in a mirror hanging next to the doorway. His eye was slightly swollen and purplish. "I need you to do me a favor. Tell them I got some trouble at my house, and I need them to come over. Right now."

"Sure thing."

Robert hung up.

"Robert, don't get yourself in trouble," Lauren said as the women came out of the kitchen.

Robert didn't say anything as he ran out the door, down the stairs, and back into the street. By then, the crowd had already begun to disperse, and the neighbor who sucker punched him was nowhere to be found. Linda approached him, wiping sweat mixed with blood from her upper lip.

"Where'd you go?"

Robert didn't say anything but pointed to the car fast approaching.

Linda realized what Robert had done. "What do you think you're doing?"

"I'm gonna kill the guy."

Linda turned to him. "Robert! You're not gonna do that baby in there any good from behind bars."

"He made me look like a punk—"

"Who cares?" She held him by the shoulders. "Listen, my sister needs you. Baby Briana needs you. You've got a family to take care of now. You can't be goin off and doin things that's gonna land you in jail."

Robert smirked as he wiped a smudge of blood from her nose with his finger. "You're one to talk."

She wiped her nose with the back of her hand. "A fist fight's one thing. Killing someone is totally something else. Now, let's go back inside, get cleaned up, and call it a night."

Three men got out of the car after it skidded to a halt next to Robert and Linda. Two of them had their guns drawn.

Linda looked at Robert. "Tell them to leave, okay?"

Robert took a deep breath.

The three men came up to him. "What's goin on?"

Robert glanced at Linda. "Nothin. It's all over now."

TWENTY-SIX

September 1993
Age 38

Robert and Lauren's new life together with Briana was anything but routine. Sleep for Lauren was sporadic, her waking hours filled with dirty diapers and multiple feedings. At first, Robert made himself helpful by holding the baby while Lauren used the bathroom or tried to catch a few minutes of sleep, but as soon as the baby squirmed, cried, or smelled, he was calling for Lauren to relieve him. Before long, he was staying away from the house for long periods of time.

Lauren was standing in the living room with a crying Briana cradled in her left arm as Robert walked through the front door. Her eyes locked onto him. "Where've you been?"

"Down the street. Why?" With the shirt he'd just removed, Robert wiped the sweat collected on the end of his nose.

"Doing what?"

"What do you mean, doing what? Are you my mother now?" He walked to the back bedroom.

She followed him, lightly bouncing the baby. "You were at Rockies, weren't you? I know you were there, because I got people telling me you're there all the time, losing money on that Joker Poker machine."

Robert threw his shirt on the floor. "You got spies out watching me now?"

"No, I don't have spies. People just tell me. And they say you're losing a lot of money. Is that true?"

"Maybe." He opened the dresser drawer and pulled out another shirt.

"You can't be gambling our money away, Robert. We got bills to pay." She hesitated. "Are you doing drugs again?"

"What?" Robert threw his hands in the air. "I can't believe this. You're accusing me of doing drugs?"

"Well, are you?"

Robert said nothing as he shook his head, went into the bathroom, and shut the door.

"How much did you lose, Robert?" Lauren was standing at the door, the baby still crying.

"I don't have to tell you nothing. It's my money."

"It's *our* money. We have a baby to take care of. And if you can't be responsible enough for that, then—"

Robert opened the door. "Then what?"

Lauren shifted her weight to her other foot. "Then maybe you just need to leave."

Robert's jaw dropped. "You want me to leave?"

Lauren hesitated. "If you don't quit throwing the money away on that stupid Joker Poker machine, or whatever else you're blowin it on, then you can't stay here."

Robert felt his anger rise. "Fine." He walked to the dresser, opened the top drawer, and found the rolled-up hundred-dollar bills in the back. After removing the rubber band, he counted out $7,000 and laid it out on the dresser. He held up the remaining bills. "See this?" He tucked it into his pants pocket. "My money." After he grabbed a few of his clothes from the closet, he stormed out of the house.

~~~~~

Within minutes of arguing with Lauren, Robert was knocking on the door of his new friend, a young man named Bean.

Bean was a quiet guy who lived in the basement of his mother's house, just a few blocks from where Robert and Lauren lived. He not only enjoyed the notoriety that came with being a friend of Robert's, he genuinely enjoyed his company. But with that companionship came Robert's ability to persuade others to indulge in his bad habits, including drug abuse. It wasn't like Bean had never used drugs before Robert. It just wasn't on as grand a scale. Before long, he was regularly freebasing with Robert, which they cooked in the basement of Bean's mother's home. Months before Briana was born, though, Robert told Bean he was staying away from the drugs, and he wouldn't be coming around. Bean was caught off guard when, after declaring his loyalty to his newborn baby, Robert was pounding on his door.

"Let me in." Robert pushed past Bean, snorting like a bull in an arena.

"What happened?"

"She kicked me out." Robert paced back and forth across the area rug. He stopped in front of Bean. "Give me a cigarette."

Bean handed him a cigarette from the pack on the coffee table and lit it for him.

Robert inhaled deeply.

For the next few minutes, Bean listened as Robert ranted about Lauren. He cursed her and went on about how she didn't respect him, how he was the breadwinner, and whatever he wanted to do with the money was his business.

It wasn't until the end of the tirade that Robert noticed the coke on the dining table. Since meeting Robert, Bean had become a dealer, drawn in by the lucrative possibilities of the illegal drug. But most of his stash went up his nose, or was morphed for freebasing, so he never earned enough money to move out of his mother's house.

Robert's mouth watered. He hadn't used since he went into Daytop. He looked at Bean, then back at the white powder.

Bean followed his eyes with embarrassment. "Sorry, Robert. I didn't know you were gonna come over." He moved toward the table. "Look, I know you quit using. I'll just—"

"No!"

Bean turned around to face Robert.

"Forget about it." He rubbed his nose. "I'll tell you what. Why don't you, um … break out the baking soda. We'll get to cookin."

PART IV

ANGELS
WITH NYPD
GUNS

05232944

TWENTY-SEVEN

March 1994
Age 39

H ey, Ma, you want your coffee on the patio?" Robert filled a single cup of the brew from the carafe.

As far back as he could remember, his mother always drank coffee, something for which he acquired a taste only after serving time in prison. He made it the way his mother liked it—sugar with enough cream to make it caramel-colored.

A few days after the blowout with Lauren, she contacted Robert, who had been on a constant high. The call wasn't one of reconciliation. She informed him that his father's health was declining rapidly. Lung cancer, coupled with emphysema, was bringing him to the end of his life, and Lauren recommended Robert go to Florida to visit him one last time. Robert's mother sent him money for the plane ticket to Florida, but he ended up using the money to purchase drugs. Instead of saying his final goodbye to his father, he chose to stay in New York and get high. His father passed a few days later, in September.

The funeral was held in New York. On the verge of crashing, Robert made a huge scene with manipulative weeping, hoping to draw sympathy for his "loss" and thereby generate some generous donations to his drug fund.

The next day, while the family was eating at a restaurant, Robert blacked out, and his face ended up in his plate of meatloaf, green beans, and mashed potatoes.

His binge continued, inducing periods of sleep deprivation that lasted for weeks. He was arrested a couple of times in the following months, once on Halloween, and another in the early part of February 1994. Both times he was arrested for possession of crack.

Even though he danced freely with his addiction, his sobered thoughts focused on Lauren and Briana. He missed them and wished to be part of their lives, but his lust for crack was extremely powerful. He knew he had to make a life change to kick it.

With them in mind, he took advantage of an offer to fly down to Coral Springs, Florida, and live with his mother, now widowed for almost half a year. Years prior, she moved there to honor a promise she made to her dying granddaughter, Lisa. Ever since she was a baby, Lisa suffered from a heart condition that caused many other medical problems. At age eighteen, Lisa passed away, but not before Robert's mother promised to take care of Betty, who had multiple sclerosis. They rented the condominium owned by Betty and her husband, who then bought a nearby villa.

The condo was small but accommodating. The front door opened into a short hallway. On the left was a bedroom and bath. On the right was a good-sized kitchen. At the end of the hallway, a living/dining room combo opened to a small patch of concrete used as a patio. The community swimming pool was accessible through the back yard. Just off the living room was the master bedroom.

Robert's mother emerged, tying the sash on her cotton housecoat. "Why would I want to go out there, just so I can get all clammy? I'll take it in here." She sat at the dining table, one of the few pieces of furniture she brought from New York. It had been in her family since her grandmother purchased it from Sears and Roebuck when she was a little girl.

Robert set the doctored cup of coffee in front her. "There you go." He pulled out a chair across from her. With the glass of orange juice he poured for himself, he sat down. The old oak chair creaked. "I just stepped out. I didn't notice a lot of humidity."

"You're gonna hate it here," she said, ignoring his remark. She took her first sip of coffee. "They all brag about how good the weather is. I'm telling you, the humidity is just too much." Her accent was chiseled by a Brooklynite heritage. "Every day at four o'clock, you'd better have an umbrella, because without a doubt, it's gonna rain. You can count on it."

"I'll keep that in mind," Robert said with a chuckle, "just in case I need to set my watch."

"You laugh, but try being a sixty-six-year-old woman walking a half mile home from work in the pouring rain."

"Ma, you could take a taxi."

"To drive me half a mile? That's silly and expensive."

Robert took a big gulp of his orange juice. "I think you're missing New York."

She sighed, and then gave a little nod. "I never wanted to come here. I left all my friends, the rest of my family. But your sister needs me, so"—she sipped her coffee to fight off the sadness—"you going in for that job interview today, right?"

"Yeah. At eleven."

"Good. Get a good job. Keep your nose clean. That's what you need to do. Stay away from drugs and the gambling. Those two things got you into the mess you're in right now."

"You're right, Ma. That's why I'm here."

"That baby needs you. She needs her father. And those drugs are keeping you from doing that."

Robert examined his finger, where he had just clipped off a hangnail with his teeth. "I know."

"You're not a boy anymore. You're a family man now. You need to act like one. All that life'll get you is more prison time or an early death."

Robert studied the face of the woman who had stood in the gap for him for many years. Her hair was noticeably gray and reflected the fact that it had been a while since she had pampered herself at a salon. Her face was wrinkled more prominently under her cheeks than her mouth, but the fire still burned in her eyes, despite a pronounced weariness.

He smiled at her. "You're very wise, Ma." He kissed her on the forehead as he took his empty glass to the kitchen sink.

TWENTY-EIGHT

October 1994
Age 39

T he phone rang twice as Robert unlocked the front door. He ran to the kitchen and picked up the handset. "Hello?"

"Did I interrupt you in the middle of exercising or something? You sound like a choo-choo train." It was the voice of Anthony Ruggiano.

"No, I just … What's going on?"

"Listen, Nicky wanted me to get in touch with you. He's gonna be down there for a few days and wants to see you."

"Where's he gonna be? I'll come see him."

"He's staying at Fountain Blue Hotel. Meet him in the restaurant at noon."

~~~~~

Robert was a few minutes early to the meeting with Nicky and got a table for two. While waiting, he ordered a soda water for himself and looked over the menu.

Despite being out of the inner circle of the Mafia for a few years, Robert kept tabs of what was going on. Nicky and Lenny had become very wealthy men, with their hands in the tills of various operations and schemes. After John Gotti was locked up in 1992, both men were promoted to capos and became part of a ruling board that ran the Gambino family while Johnnie was in prison. Nicky was a very smart man. With the right moves, he could easily make it to the top.

During the summer, Robert had found a job as a commercial cleaning supervisor and was doing fairly well. He had also renewed his commitment to attending AA meetings. He knew the routine. He'd get sobered up, things would be going well, and then a lucrative but illegal opportunity would arise. Soon, he was making lots of money, and that soon led to loose living, which included gambling and drugs. Once he was at the bottom, he'd get sober, and the pattern started all over again. The thought of falling into that pattern made him apprehensive.

But this was Nicky, the man who took him in and treated him like a son. This was the one person who gave him reason to believe he could actually amount to something and be somebody. Unlike other made men, Nicky overlooked Robert's major blunders, such as playing the horses with the $12,000 craps bank. Something like that could have easily gotten him killed. Nicky not only overlooked it, but he covered the debt until Robert could pay it back. In Robert's eyes, Nicky was a good man.

"Robert, you look like a million bucks."

Robert stood and embraced Nicky. "You don't look so bad yourself."

"Yeah?" He examined his waist. "My wife has me on a diet. I guess it's working."

The two men sat opposite each other, and the waiter took Nicky's drink order.

"How's the baby? It's Briana, right?"

"Yeah. She's doing great. I just got to see her and Lauren a couple of months ago. They came and visited me."

"That's great. And you've got a steady job?"

"Yeah. I'm a supervisor at a commercial cleaning company. I make sure all the bums are doing their jobs."

Nicky chuckled. "Speaking of clean, I heard you've sobered up."

"Seven months now."

Nicky nodded. "Sounds like you're doing good."

The two men ordered medium-rare T-bone steaks and continued to talk about family.

When both steaks were gone, Nicky wiped his mouth with his napkin and took a sip of his tea. "I got an offer for you. Are you interested?"

Robert was prepared to answer such a question, if it were to arise, knowing Nicky would evaluate his commitment by the response. Without hesitation he said, "Sure."

Nicky patted Robert on the arm. "You're looking at some good money. Maybe you'll be able to move your baby and Lauren down here."

A sense of pride and acceptance filled Robert. That Nicky offered him work—especially after all the times he'd blown it—verified what he had hoped all along; Nicky truly held a special fatherly love for him.

Nicky pulled cash from his wallet and laid it on top of the check. "Syd'll call you tomorrow."

Nicky smiled as the two men stood. He hugged Robert again. "It's really good to see you. Be sure to say hello to your mother for me."

~~~~~

That night, Robert's sleep was sporadic. He finally got up and went out to the patio to light up a cigarette. His mother didn't allow smoking in the house ever since she quit many years back and became its number one enemy. She was especially critical lately, since she just lost her husband to lung cancer. So Robert smoked out-of-sight from his mother to avoid a venomous lecture about how it would send him to an early grave like his father. Even though she was already gone to work, Robert knew that if he were to smoke inside the house, she would still detect it, many hours later. He honored her order and smoked for the first few minutes of waking, while taking in the view of the bulbous clouds looming over Coral Springs.

After the last drag, he put out the cigarette in the ashtray on the patio table, blew out the smoke lingering in his lungs, and went back inside for a glass of orange juice. He started to open the refrigerator door when he noticed the small magnetic placard, which he read out loud. "The happiest people don't necessarily have the best of everything. They make the best of everything." He smirked as he placed the placard back on the fridge door and removed the orange juice from the top shelf. "Make the best of everything." He poured his breakfast into a tall, clear glass.

Over the course of the morning, Robert decided to work for Nicky but not give up his job as a cleaning supervisor. That weekend, he went back to the Blue Fountain Hotel, where he spent the next couple of days on the Miami beaches, hanging out with Nicky.

TWENTY-NINE

May 1996
Age 41

I t was two in the afternoon when Robert and his old friend Angelo, who had come to Florida for a visit, were sitting at the bar in the Blue Fountain Hotel lounge.

"And so," Robert said, "I go over to Syd's cousin's print shop, climb on the roof, and douse it with gasoline." He took a sip of the Scotch he had been nurturing between his hands. "I get down off the roof with the bright idea that I would use a Molotov cocktail to set the building on fire. I pour some gasoline into the bottle, put a rag in it, and lit it. My intention is to make the bottle land on the roof, but the building's taller than I'm thinking, and it hits the side instead, which just happens to be right where all the electrical stuff comes out of the building. The fire didn't last long, and all it really did was burn up all the wires."

"Why didn't you just throw another Molotov cocktail onto the roof?"

Robert slapped the bar top. "That's a brilliant idea! Except I didn't think to bring more than one bottle."

Angelo laughed.

"I call up Syd and tell him the job's done—knowing good and well that it ain't—and that I wanted the other half of my money. He had already paid me the first half up front." Robert waved his drink in the air, causing a little to slosh out. He took a thirsty mouthful. "Anyway, Syd said he needed to make a call and would get back to me. Well, I'm guessing he called the print shop and couldn't get through because the wires are all burned up. He calls me back and tells me to come get the money. I don't need to tell you, I get there as soon as I can. Syd gives me the money. I spend it before he had a chance to find out the truth. I tell ya, man, he was mad when he found out the building was still standing."

"Oh, man. I bet he was."

Robert finished off the drink and signaled the bartender for another one.

Angelo laughed. "I guess you officially fell off the wagon."

Robert's laughing subsided. "What do you mean by that?"

The barstool squeaked as Angelo adjusted himself. "I mean, I thought you quit drinking and were supposed to be going to AA meetings—"

"Are you my mother now?" Robert swore at him. "I don't need you babysitting me."

Angelo held up his hands defensively. "Sorry, man."

"Yeah, you're sorry."

The bartender set the next double in front of Robert, who downed it in one gulp while staring at Angelo. He slammed the glass in front of him. "Let's go."

As they were walking out the door, Robert put his finger in Angelo's face. "And if you go blabbing, sayin I 'fell off the wagon,' to anybody, I'll put a hole in your head. Got it?"

~~~~~

After being out all night and into the early morning hours, Robert walked into his mother's condo to the sound of a solemn voice broadcasting from the TV. His mother was in her chair with a tissue in one hand and her rosary in the other. He looked at the TV and saw a large plume of dark, menacing smoke rolling skyward in what looked like a swampy surrounding. The source of the smoke was unseen. The caption at the bottom of the screen read Valujet Flight 592 Crashes in Everglades.

"What happened?" Robert sat on the couch.

"An airplane crashed." She wiped her runny nose. "It's not far from us. Just in the next county over."

"I mean, why are you crying?"

She was weeping so hard her shoulders shook.

"Ma!" Robert knelt beside her and took her hand. "I never knew you to be so sentimental about these things."

"I'm not. It's just …" She blew her nose, threw the tissue in the trashcan next to her chair, and got a fresh tissue from the box on the end table. After dabbing away tears from both cheeks, she looked at her son. Her eyes were tired. "You gotta leave."

"What? Why?"

"I can't take it anymore."

"Take what?"

"Watching you destroy yourself."

"What are you talking about?"

She yanked her hand away from his. "Oh, Robert, don't act like I don't know. Do you think I'm blind? Do you think I can't tell when you're hopped up on drugs? Do you think I wouldn't notice the microwave was gone?"

Robert looked silently at his scuffed shoes.

"When you first came here, I warned you that you needed to keep your nose clean. But you got right back into it the first chance you had, didn't you?"

Still, Robert didn't say anything. There was no sense in denying her accusations or the self-proclaimed prophesy he made the day he met with Nicky over a year ago. He knew the cycle well and still charged into the same territory that had gotten him into trouble so many times. As he was told, the money he made through Nicky's shylocking business was sizable and gave him the means to buy a new car—a 1994 red Acura Integra—and lots of nice clothing.

For a while, he continued to attend the AA meetings, at the same time beating up men who were late on their payments to Nicky, who was content, knowing that Robert had a new motivation for staying straight—his family.

But Robert wasn't a man in possession of a long attention span. The money, none of which ever went to his mother, reawakened his craving for the fast-and-furious lifestyle. Mixed with an opportunity to impress a girl he met at AA, the craving opened up the doors to alcohol and cocaine. Once again, Robert allowed the drug into the driver's seat.

His mother lifted Robert's chin so he was forced to look directly into her swollen eyes. "Now, Lauren and the baby won't be coming to see me. I don't get to see my grandchild." She let go of his chin and sobbed.

Robert got up from the floor. "Sorry, Ma."

Silence squeezed a break in the conversation. Robert hoped a little pause and his sincere remorse would cause his mother to reconsider.

Even before she spoke, the uprightness of her head, no eye contact, and one last sniffle conveyed her final decision. "You can stay to the end of the week. Then you gotta go."

~~~~~

On Friday, Robert was on a plane headed for New York and another stay at the Daytop Rehabilitation Center. He called Lauren, who hadn't been answering his calls for a while. He left a message that he would be moving back. He also told her that he wanted to go back to Daytop to clean up. That was the hook that got her to return his call. She agreed that rehab was what he needed and told him she would pick him up at the airport.

While reclining in the coach seat of the Boeing 737, thoughts of his friends in Brooklyn, who would be more than happy to accommodate his addiction, kept popping up in his mind. When facing his demon, he fought back images of his daughter, almost three years old. He visualized the two of them running on the beaches of Florida, her little feet moving twice as fast as his, just to keep up. He saw himself swinging her to make up the distance between them. He saw the pictures Lauren had sent him. His favorite was the photo taken of her in a Dalmatian puppy costume.

The serene thoughts were suddenly interrupted by an appealing idea. Since he was headed for rehabilitation from his drug habit, why not have one last hoorah before going straight? He had a little cash on him. He could make more by playing the

Joker Poker machine at Vito's, and maybe afterward, he would get high just one more time.

There was a major kink in his plans. Lauren was going to meet him at the airport, pick him up, and take him straight to Daytop. That was the deal he made with her. If he was going to be a part of her and Briana's lives, he would have to go through the entire six-month program.

He thought to avoid her altogether. He could call up ... who could he call? He couldn't think of anyone, much less a phone number. He'd have to take a taxi. Of course, that would make Lauren mad and possibly create a larger fracture in their fragile relationship, if not altogether destroy it. But he was good with making up excuses, and he was sure he could come up with one that would salve over any damage caused by leaving her hanging at the airport.

Just the thought of another line of cocaine made him tremble.

Robert swore as he opened his eyes, annoyed at himself for entertaining destructive thoughts. He forgot he was sitting between two passengers. "Oh. Sorry," he said to the elderly woman on his left, whose eyes were wide with surprise. "I was just ... dreaming."

THIRTY

October 1996
Age 41

obert never made it to Daytop that day. Instead, he landed at Rocky's after calling Lauren and telling her he'd meet her there. While at the deli, he sidled up to his favorite source of gambling—the Joker Poker machine—and dropped quarters, four or five dollars' worth at a time. He won about a hundred bucks, but it wasn't long before that was being smoked in a crack pipe.

He never met up with Lauren.

Early the next morning, he found his way to his young friend Bean's basement apartment, penniless and wanting to stay on a high. Bean was more than happy to accommodate Robert and enjoy the ride with him.

For the next few weeks, Robert and Bean followed a routine. They sold coke and bought crack, since it was cheaper to buy it than make it. Then they partied, with and without friends, staying on a constant high with barely any sleep.

It wasn't long, though, until Robert found himself on the streets after an incident occurred in Bean's basement, which caused Bean's mom to kick Robert out. A tremendous commotion was happening in Robert's room. It was so loud, Bean's mom and sister heard it from the first and second floors. At first, they thought a burglar might be breaking in through the basement window. Bean went down and checked the door. It was locked, and he couldn't get Robert to open it. The noise finally died down, just as Bean busted open the door. Robert lay on the floor, naked and unconscious. Later, he recounted the story as an incident in which he was dying and fighting the devil, who he said was trying to claim his soul. Nevertheless, Bean's mom had enough of Robert and ordered him to leave.

In June 1996, Robert made the mistake of selling cocaine to an undercover police officer and was locked up. He stayed in jail for a week before Nicky posted the required $10,000 bail. Apparently, Nicky spoke with Robert's sister Anna and found out he was locked up. As a favor to her, he got Robert out.

Robert was in and out of court several times, with a lawyer who kept asking for payment, which Robert never made. By August, he discovered that the Feds knew he was back in New York and wanted him for crimes he committed in Florida, including the firebombing of the print shop. He never returned to court, afraid he would be arrested. Instead, to avoid his mounting problems, he went into hiding, jumping from crack house to crack house, staying on a constant high with his nameless and sometimes faceless "friends."

When on crack, Robert was a different person. Instead of being the tough guy who had earned a reputation as an up-and-coming star in the Mafia, he was withdrawn and paranoid. He became suspicious of everyone and was never found without a gun. He even took showers with a revolver, pointing the gun toward the bathroom door, ready to shoot anyone who dared to open it.

Because of his paranoia, he established a network of friends who shared the same interest of getting high in peace. He was at the house of one of these friends when someone came knocking at the door, looking for him. It was Lauren. Despite all that Robert had put her through, she still cared for him and knew it was important for him to be part of Briana's life.

Robert tried to hide, telling his friend to say he wasn't there.

"Robert, I know you're in there," Lauren yelled from outside the front door. "I came here to help you. You need to come with me."

Instead of going with Lauren, Robert slipped out the back door, just as she came in.

"Robert!" Lauren followed a shoeless Robert out the back and found him trying to hide behind a tree that was much thinner than he was. She couldn't help but laugh. "Robert, come on. I can see you. Just come with me, will you?"

"You're gonna take me to jail. Or rehab."

"No, I'm not. I just want to get you home so you can get cleaned up. I promise I won't take you to the cops."

"I don't believe you."

"Don't you want to see Briana?"

Robert was quiet for a moment. "Yes."

With that, Lauren convinced Robert to come with her, back to her mother's place. During the car ride, he fidgeted and talked to himself, from time to time looking suspiciously at Lauren.

"Geez, you smell something awful." Lauren waved her hand in front of her nose. "When was the last time you took a shower?"

"Why do you want to know?"

"Because you stink. And where are your shoes?"

Robert stared at his feet, unaware of what she was talking about.

"You still have some of your clothes at Mom's. We can throw these away. Better yet, we might ought to burn them."

"You're not gonna burn my clothes." Robert clutched his shirt.

"I'm just joking."

After Robert got out of the shower, Lauren put him to bed. The crash coming off the crack could not have been timed better. He slept for the next couple of days.

THIRTY-ONE

January 23, 1997
Age 42

H is last day of freedom proved to be much warmer and clearer in New York than it had been a few days earlier, when the high temperature never made it to the twenty-degree range. Inside the grayish-blue house on 89th Street, a sleeping Robert was not aware of the nicer weather, nor was he conscious of what was happening outside the front door, where two "angels with guns" awaited entry.

A month prior to that midwinter day, he found out that Nicky, who had managed to fly below the radar all these years, had been arrested for his shylocking business in Florida.

Once again, this sent Robert out of Lauren and Briana's lives and into the shadows of crack houses and brothels, avoiding his usual hangouts as much as possible. This afforded him the luxury of an incessant high, above the problems with the law, above the neglect of family.

Time was no longer a concern. Sometime before the twenty-third, Robert's charm, unhampered by his filthy clothing and foul smell, found the company of a strung-out prostitute and a friend with a basement apartment. Both were willing to share their crack cocaine. All three sat around the guy's apartment, smoking the crack pipe until their supply diminished. The prostitute left to score a trick or two to earn more money for crack. At 7:00 in the morning Robert grew antsy, on the verge of crashing. He went outside to make a call to a bar where he'd bought coke before, not thinking it was way too early for anyone to be there. When no one answered, he went back to the apartment, where he fell asleep on the couch. His friend left to find more crack.

His sleep was deep, the result of staying high for days without coming down, and therefore he never heard the door to the apartment unlock and open. But he did feel a nudging at his feet, which were propped up on the arm of the couch. He opened his eyes enough to see the source of the annoyance—a semi-automatic pistol.

Robert always knew he was most vulnerable when he was high. That's why he never committed a robbery or any other crime while on drugs, and he always kept a gun close by. He tried to be where most people would not know where he was. He knew of associates and made men who lost their lives because of their drug habits. When he was getting high, hardly anyone knew where to find him.

A few months ago, Little Joe died after his heart exploded from a drug overdose. Rumors said his drug usage brought shame to his former Mafia brothers, and money he was collecting was not making it to his bosses. So he was silenced.

Since Nicky was under the watchful eye of the federal government, Robert felt he was in the same situation. Any loose ends—like Robert—could put him away for the rest of his life. Staring at the blurred image of the handgun tapping his foot, he wondered if this was how it would end—with a bullet in his head, just after waking up enough to know what was happening to him.

For the first time, he didn't have a gun. He had pawned it to buy crack. This was it. At age 42, Robert, the former up-and-coming Mafia star, aka Robert the Crackhead, would no longer exist. He just hoped his mom would know what happened to him.

He heard his name called.

"Yeah, that's me."

"NYPD. You're under arrest. Get on your knees and put your hands on your head. Now!"

Robert's vision was still a little blurry, but he saw images of two plainclothes officers with their guns drawn, waiting for him to comply with their commands. Behind them was his friend, the key to the apartment dangling from his hand.

"Sorry, Robert. I—"

"Get up." An officer helped Robert stand, now in handcuffs. Escorted from the apartment, he entered the warmth of the sun's rays. A sense of relief surprised him. Trying to stay on a constant high had become a burden. With the arrest, that burden, along with the heaviness of depression and self-loathing, was disappearing.

He remembered a conversation with his mother a few months earlier. She said a federal agent had been to her house in Florida, looking for him. She didn't tell him Robert was in New York or anything else that might lead them to him. As the agent left, he gave her his business card.

Robert had little concern with the agent, content that his plan to hide in crack houses would safeguard him from the law. His only concern was the need for more money. As he had done many times, he asked his mom for financial assistance, claiming he needed money to get his clothes from the laundromat when he planned to use it to buy more drugs. As with any mother wanting to give her son the chance to do what was right, she agreed. But something strange happened at the end of the conversation. Without provocation, he said, "Ma, everything's gonna be okay." Despite his current condition as a homeless drug addict, regardless of his list of repeated offenses, without thought of his continuing dance with Death, he spoke words so improbable that even he knew they came from a source other than himself.

Apparently, his mother did too. "I know," she said. "Robert, I know."

While heading to central booking, Robert thought about that conversation. A smile without ulterior motives found its way to his face. *Everything's gonna be okay*, he thought, as he looked at the two officers in the front seat, men he would later call his "angels with guns."

"You will not change until the pain of staying where you are becomes greater than the pain of change."

– from *Soaring Higher* by Pat Mesiti

PART V

THE
DEATH
OF
ROBERT
ENGEL

THIRTY-TWO

April 1997
Age 42

Robert was stooped over, his sweat forming small puddles on the floor in front of him. As he caught his breath, his confidence soared, assured that he was about to score the winning point of a friendly game of handball with his friend "Six," a tough Latino who got his nickname after having four of his fingers blown off with a shotgun. Robert was about to put the small rubber ball into play.

"Robert Borelli!" His name boomed from the large gray speaker mounted high on the cinder block wall of the long, narrow common area of Cell Block A. "You have a visitor," the distorted voice said.

"Right now?" he said, as if the gray speaker could hear him. He shook his head and handed the ball to Six. "When I get back, I'm gonna finish you off. So don't disappear."

Six chuckled. "In your dreams, man."

Rikers is an island of detention facilities in New York City. The complex is solely dedicated to housing criminals with various ethnicities and backgrounds, with as many as 15,000 criminals on any given day. It was Robert's home from January to July 1997 as he waited for his case to come to trial.

He followed his prison-guard escort down the corridor to the visitor's area, where he got out of his street clothes, the standard wear for inmates awaiting trial and presented himself for a strip search. He then changed into red prison jumpers and entered the large room with many metal tables. A baby's cry chimed above the low-level chatter echoing off the concrete walls as wives, parents, and children visited the inmates. He wrinkled his nose as he mentally catalogued the plethora of odors: strong women's perfume, a diaper that needed changing, and various body odors. He was taken to a table where two young men were sitting, guys who worked for Nicky.

Their chairs screeched across the floor as they promptly stood and greeted Robert. The chubby one said in a low voice, "Nicky sent us. Wanted to see how you were doing."

Robert glanced around the perimeter of the room. Guards were standing every thirty feet or so. He and the two young men sat down. "I'm all right, for an old Italian white guy. Not many of us here. The Latin Kings? They got my back."

"That's good."

"I do need some money for commissary."

"Just dropped a hundred bucks into your account."

Robert nodded. "Good. How is Nicky?"

Chubby, apparently the spokesman of the two, shrugged. "Still locked up at MDC waiting for trial, just like you. Nicky and Lenny both."

"Yeah. This no-bail business stinks. Does he got his nephew working the case?" Robert was referring to Joseph, Jo Jo's son.

"Yeah."

"Any chance he might get out soon?"

"I don't know. What about you? Who's your lawyer?"

"Tony Lombardino."

"How's it goin with him?"

"It ain't."

"Why's that?"

"He needs money."

They talked about the case, and they updated Robert on what was going on in the neighborhood. When they left, they agreed to tell Nicky about Robert's situation with his lawyer. They said they'd keep the commissary money coming.

THIRTY-THREE

May 1997
Age 42

While at Riker's Island, one of the few highlights for Robert was his phone conversations with his daughter. Several times, he had enjoyed visits from Lauren, but despite his pleadings, she refused to bring Briana to the prison, not wanting to expose her to such a harsh environment.

Briana's fourth birthday was nearing, and a sobered-up, drug-free Robert was feeling the pain of separation from the child who owned a piece of his heart. He often thought about his daughter and how he would be a better daddy to her, once he was free.

As he walked down the corridor of Cell Block A to the bank of phone booths, he considered what type of gift a four-year old girl would want—even though her birthday was still a couple of months away. If he wasn't out by then, how could he get it to her?

As with any day, the lines to the phones were long. Fights often broke out among waiting inmates. Sometimes, stabbings occurred. Since Robert was generous with his commissary goods to the Latin Kings, his friend Six and some of his buddies assured him a place at the front of the line without any confrontation. When his turn came, Robert walked up to a phone and dialed "0" for the operator. After requesting a collect call to Lauren, he waited. Three rings filled the space of time. Lauren finally answered and accepted the charges. As they chatted, he sensed something was different. Her visits had become fewer and farther apart.

Robert was concerned.

"I'm just tired and frustrated, that's all." Lauren explained that her car had broken down. That was why she hadn't come to see him. After they had talked for a while, she said, "Here. Talk to your daddy."

Loud rustling was followed by Briana's munchkin-like voice. "Hello?"

"Hey, Briana."

"Hi, Daddy."

"How you doin?" He plugged his other ear with his finger.

"I'm okay. Where are you?"

Robert fidgeted. "I'm somewhere far away. So what's my little Briana been up to?"

"I just got out of the bath."

"Getting ready for bed?"

"Yeah, but I'm not sleepy."

The conversation went on about that day's adventures at the park and how she was excited about going to McDonald's tomorrow. Before long, her sentences became broken, and Robert heard distress in her voice. Soon she was crying.

"What's wrong, Baby?" He turned his back to the other inmates using the phones. He waited patiently as she sobbed for a moment without saying anything.

Finally, she settled down enough to speak. "My friend Ashley? Her daddy eats lunch with her every Tuesday." She sniffled. "Mallory's daddy is the soccer coach. Kenneth—he's not my friend. He said I didn't have a daddy. I told him I did. He said I didn't, so I hit him, and I got in trouble." The crying started again.

Reality rushed toward Robert like a freight train, but he could do nothing to change the course already directed by his selfishness and lack of concern for anyone but himself. He breathed deeply, looking over his shoulder at the other inmates. "Briana …"

"Daddy, why don't you come see me?"

The words were powerful enough to break through the cold steel that had encased his heart for many years and crush it.

"Briana, I … I …" His throat tightened as he tried to swallow without success. "Your Daddy is …" Realizing he was about to expose his emotions to the other inmates, he hung up without giving Briana words of comfort or saying goodbye. He ran back to his cell, thankful he didn't have to share his feelings with another inmate. He dropped to his knees at the side of his bed, completely broken.

A month prior to the heart-wrenching conversation with Briana, he had started attending mass, hoping to find favor with a God he didn't know much about. He prayed the rosary like he'd seen his mother do for years. Like many of his Latin friends, he knelt on the side of his bed every evening, rosary in hand, before going to sleep.

This time, as he knelt next to his bed, a few words formed in his mind that didn't conform to the rote prayers he'd been taught in Catholic school. Nevertheless, he had to get them off his chest. With the image of his daughter in his mind and her words still burning in his heart, he bowed his head while tears flowed down his cheeks. "God … if you're real, then change me. Or have someone kill me … because I can't stay like this. I'm not man enough to kill myself."

These were challenging words, but Robert didn't care. At that moment, he realized the path he had chosen was one that ended with an eternal incarceration in a place much worse than any he'd ever experienced, and that scared him. He also knew that God was the One who would be the final judge of that decision. The second option was never really an option in his mind but a statement that expressed the gravity of his despair.

His plea was simple but powerful words that had an immediate effect. The brokenness that had sent him running to his cell and falling to his knees in desperation was dissipating, and a tiny seed of hope was planted where his heart lay crushed.

For the next hour, Robert prayed in his jail cell. As he did so, he recalled a recent conversation with Angelo. After he realized that the mob wasn't going to help him, he had called his friends, looking for financial assistance. After several failed attempts, he called Angelo.

Angelo listened to Robert complain about the lack of help he had with his case and suggested he read the Bible. At the time, Robert thought the remark was simply another brush-off.

But now, Robert's desire to have more of God in his life led to a desire to read the Bible. He was already an avid reader, spending much of his time in his cell reading Robert Ludlum's tales of espionage and Stephen King's horror stories. Starting with about fifteen minutes, he read a Bible offered to inmates by a group of Christians who ministered regularly at Rikers Island. He learned that the Bible was actually a collection of books and was advised to first read the books of John and Proverbs.

The more he read the Bible, the more he learned about the God he'd asked to change his life, which he figured was the option God chose, since he was still alive. Slowly, his time reading the Bible increased as he became disinterested in the novels. Before long, the Bible was the only book in his cell.

THIRTY-FOUR

June 1997
Age 42

While at Rikers Island, Robert never received a visit from his lawyer, and he never heard from any of his mob associates. Several times, he was taken to the courthouse, where he sat in the bullpen for hours, waiting for a lawyer who never arrived. This increased Robert's anxiety, because the time he was spending incarcerated would not be counted toward the federal case pending in Florida. In essence, the longer he went without a lawyer, the more time he would spend in prison.

When Robert talked with Attorney Joseph Corrozo, Nicky's nephew, his frustration worsened. Of all things, Joseph advised him to get legal aide. Knowing the men Joseph represented had millions of dollars to spend on their legal cases and his lawyer only wanted $3,000, Robert felt betrayed. To add insult to injury, he read in the newspaper that additional charges were brought against Nicky and Lenny for bribing a guard into bringing outside food into the prison.

Because of his drug use, Robert knew he was no longer in good standing with the mob. They weren't supposed to be affiliated with him. But they were co-defendants in a federal case, and he reasoned that he should be taken care of, just like they were. The idea of wanting extra food in prison so badly that they would bribe a prison guard struck Robert the wrong way, especially since they weren't willing to provide him with a few dollars to be used at the commissary.

In early summer, Robert was transferred from Rikers Island to Metropolitan Detention Center in Brooklyn and was placed on the same floor as Lenny.

Sitting on his bed in the dorm-style room, Lenny was playing cards with another inmate. "Robert. What a surprise," he said as Robert was escorted to a neatly made vacant bed.

After laying down his clothes, Robert went to where Lenny was and hugged him.

Lenny introduced him to his card partner. "You were at Rikers, right?"

"Yeah, Rikers." Robert was miffed that Lenny wasn't sure where he was.

"They treat you well at Rikers?"

"You could say that. I just kept my head down and mouth shut."

Lenny laughed. "That must have been difficult for you, huh? "Have a seat."

Robert sat next to him.

"So why they send you here?"

Robert shrugged, trying to keep his nervousness from showing. "You know those corrections people, always playing a shell game with us prisoners. You ever see Nicky?"

"Yeah, I see him all the time."

"How's he holding up?"

Lenny huffed. "It takes more than MDC to shake him up. So what can I do you for? You got cigarettes? You need commissary? I can set you up for whatever you need."

If only you'd been so generous sooner, Robert thought.

Six weeks earlier, the thought of missing out on making memories with Briana had become too much to bear. After receiving no help, he called his mother and asked for the name and number of the federal agent who left his business card with her. The phone call to the agent started the ball rolling toward an agreement to cooperate with the federal government for a reduced sentence.

Not long afterward, he was in the custody of the U.S. Marshal and on his way to Florida. But for whatever reason, he had to make a layover at MDC. As he sat next to Lenny, a person he just might have to testify against, he wondered if the correctional department had just made a big mistake.

Robert did his best to play it cool. He took the cigarette Lenny offered but didn't light it. "Look, Lenny, I don't need any commissary," he said, tinged by a small amount of guilt. "But what I do need is a lawyer."

Lenny laid down the king of hearts. "I thought you would have had you one by now."

"I sent word that my lawyer needed three grand. He never got it, and I never heard from him. I've been in and out of the bullpen four or five times already, without an attorney."

"Oh. Well, I'll see if I can do something about that tomorrow."

"I'll be shipping out tomorrow. It'll be too late."

Lenny stared at him. "What? Nobody leaves outta here the next day." He turned back to his cards and considered playing the ace of spades.

"I'm telling you, I'm due out tomorrow. If you can do something for me, that'd be great."

That night, Robert had a hard time falling asleep, wondering if Lenny had caught on to what was happening. In that setting, where there were no individual cells, someone could easily take Robert out in his sleep.

Five o'clock a.m. came, and Robert was awakened. The corrections officer led him to the showers, where he got cleaned up. Afterward, he was put on a bus and driven to an airport somewhere upstate. From there, he was flown to a detention facility in Oklahoma City, a hub for federal prisoners. For his two weeks there, he had no commissary money and had no calls from Lauren, who had stopped answering his calls. After two more flights, he landed in Miami, where he was bussed to the Miami-Dade County jail. The next day two FBI agents signed Robert out, handcuffed him, and drove him in a white, unmarked van to the federal building in downtown Miami. Concealed by the cover of an underground parking garage, the marshals took him in a private elevator to the Assistant U. S. Attorney's office, several stories up.

One of the agents told the receptionist who Robert was. She immediately got up and escorted them to an empty conference room, where Robert took a seat at one end of a long, wooden table. The agents flanked his side. Within a few minutes two men in suit and tie walked in, both carrying accordion files.

"You can leave," the blond-headed one with a red tie said to the agents. He looked at Robert's handcuffs. "Oh. Take those off first." The agents left, and the other man closed the door.

The blond extended his hand to Robert. "I'm Brian McCormick, Assistant U.S. Attorney. This is Assistant U.S. Attorney Kevin March."

Robert shook their hands.

McCormick sat in the chair to Robert's right, and March sat next him on the same side. For a while, they talked about everything but the case—sports, family, weather—and Robert's experience in the penal system. As usual with people, they laughed at a couple of his jokes.

McCormick went silent as he opened the accordion file and removed one of the folders. He flipped through a few pages. "So from what I understand, you're willing to help us out. Is that right?"

Robert shrugged. "Yeah. That's why I'm here, right? You want me to testify."

"Of course." McCormick shut the folder. "What's in it for you? What do you expect in return for your testimony?"

"I don't want to do any time."

"You'll have to do some time." McCormick tapped the folder with his pen. "There are federal guidelines we have to go by. But if your information helps us put these guys away, I could accept a plea for the minimum sentence. We'll get to that later. First, I need to know what you know."

McCormick and March grilled Robert for the next two hours, asking about Nicky and Lenny and other defendants in the case.

They asked about his involvement in crimes he committed while working for Nicky, a purging of past sins from Robert's life.

Confessing his crimes to prosecutors felt strange. For as long as he could remember, they had been the enemy, the ones who barricaded the road that he thought would lead to happiness. How was he to trust them now? As far as he knew, they could take his information and slap him with a hefty sentence. Or worse, they could put him back into the general population, assuring that his life would soon be over.

Still, he had nowhere else to turn. With a different type of spirit guiding him now—the Spirit of Truth—he was determined to trust the prompting in his heart to do the right thing.

When finished, McCormick jotted a few notes on a legal pad from the accordion file. "All right. I'm going to shoot straight with you." He laid his pen on the pad. "Up to this point, our case hasn't been that strong. In fact, we've gotten some bad publicity that isn't helping. A federal agent handling the case was caught stealing money confiscated from your boss's operation. Right now, it's a big mess. With that said, it appears you might have some vital information we could use. The FBI takes over from here. They'll be visiting you at Miami-Dade to get more details. But let me warn you now"—he leaned toward Robert—"after we compile all the info, we'll administer a polygraph to make sure you've told the truth. If I find even one bit of information is a lie, all bets are off, and you serve the maximum penalty for your crimes. Am I clear?"

Robert nodded. "Yeah. Loud and clear. No lies."

~~~~~

After the meeting, the agents handcuffed Robert and loaded him into the van. Instead of going to Miami-Dade County jail, he was transported to Metro West Detention Center, a small correctional facility operated by the Miami-Dade County Corrections and Rehabilitation Department on the west side of Miami. He was placed in one of four solitary confinement cells, where he stayed all day except for one hour out in the yard.

He met daily with federal agents, who went over his testimony, sifting through the details, making sure everything was accurate and truthful. As he went from convicted criminal to government witness, he was also going through a more significant spiritual transformation. His desire grew to learn more about the One who was responsible for his change. He was already reading the Bible exclusively and praying more prayers from his heart, consistent with the one he prayed for the first time at Rikers Island. That not being enough, he absorbed the teachings of TV ministers who taught about the importance of a life that imitated that of Jesus Christ.

For three weeks, Robert kept the same routine: meeting with the agents who went over his testimony with a fine-toothed comb, spending hours reading the Bible and watching Christian programs, and breathing-in the one-hour of fresh South Florida air during his time in the yard.

During his walk from lock-up to the yard, he heard his name called. The trip to the yard led him by the cells of other inmates.

One of the inmates had a message for Robert. "I spoke with your buddy Anthony. He said don't do what you're about to do."

A week earlier, Robert had heard similar words from his nephew, who tried to convince him to recant his testimony. Robert explained that he had already passed the point of no return. His nephew knew testifying against the mob was enough for a death warrant to be issued. Robert was angry at whoever convinced his nephew to talk him out of testifying. If something happened to him, his nephew could bear the guilt of his death for the rest of his life.

Shaken by his whereabouts being discovered, he told the federal agents about the incident. In two days, he was transferred to a detention facility in Indian River.

~~~~~

During his previous incarcerations, Robert would never let his mother visit him. Now, he was back in Florida with a different perspective and was eager to see her.

Unlike Rikers Island, there was no open visitation with the prisoners. While sitting in a booth divided by a piece of glass three quarters of an inch thick, prisoner and visitor alike used phone handsets to talk to each other. Robert entered his side of the booth and sat across from his mother, who was already cradling the handset between her head and shoulder. She was wearing a blue dress, probably something she'd worn since the 1970s. Even though it had been only two years since he'd last seen her, she looked as if she'd aged a decade. She put her hand up to the glass, and Robert did likewise.

"Hello, Robert," she said with a compassionate smile. "You look so good."

"I feel great. Better than I can ever remember."

"I'm so glad." She spoke with a hint of skepticism in her tone, the result of seeing her son go back and forth from sobriety to strung-out so many times.

Robert noticed and accepted it. "Did you have any problem getting in?"

"Not really. I showed my I.D. They said I was on the list, so …" She smiled as she studied his face. "What is it?"

"What's what?"

Her brow furrowed. "You … look different."

Robert chuckled. "I'm changed, Ma."

"Changed?"

"Yeah. But this time, I can feel it inside me. Inside my heart." He lightly struck his chest with his fist. He told her what happened at Rikers Island and how, since then, he had a whole new perspective on life.

As he told his story, tears gathered in his mother's eyes and the tension in her face relaxed. "Oh, Robert. Thank God. I've been praying for you for so long." She produced a tissue to wipe her eyes.

As he looked at the woman who had endured all his hardships, he couldn't help but feel the load of guilt. Sitting across from him was the one person who'd proven to be his best friend—his mother. He'd taken advantage of her many times by taking her money, pawning her appliances, and robbing her of her emotional strength. The lines on her face and the weariness in her eyes were proof of that. Yes, at times she had enabled him to continue a lifestyle that caused her the grief. For that, she would take partial blame. Robert was culpable for the rest. For decades, he had been a grief to his mother, as well as a subject of her most fervent prayers. He thought about the many times she probably worried whether his latest binge would be his last, or if the next time she saw him would be in the city morgue, identifying his body. Sitting across from her in the booth helped him see the devastation his actions had on the one woman who never gave up on him. With that in mind, he joined her by shedding his own tears.

"Ma, I'm so sorry for everything. I—"

"Robert." She held up her hand. "I forgave you the moment it happened. Now you need to do the same."

As he thought about what he needed to say, Robert hesitated. "Ma, I gotta ask you something."

"If it's about pawning the microwave—"

"No, it's nothing like that. I—"

"What is it, Robert? You need money for commissary?"

Robert shook his head. "I think I still need a lawyer."

She nodded. "Okay."

"Nicky and Lenny wouldn't help me out."

"What are you trying to tell me?"

He took a deep breath, knowing his mother's stand on loyalty. "My lawyer needs $3,000."

"I thought the government was working a deal with you."

While in Oklahoma, Robert had told his family about his decision to work with the government. Everyone was upset with him. Most wouldn't talk with him anymore. His mother was among those who disagreed with his decision. She couldn't understand how Robert could turn against Nicky after all he had done for him. Of course, she was never aware of the specifics regarding what type of work Robert did for Nicky. Even though she knew Nicky was a mobster, in her eyes he was the lesser of two evils when compared to drugs. When Robert was with Nicky, he was cleaned up, working and with money. But unlike the others, his mother refused to cut the lines of communication with him. He was her son, and nothing could change that.

He bit his nail. "I'm a little afraid I'm gonna get railroaded."

"Robert! Stop that." She swatted at him on the other side of the glass.

Robert sheepishly pulled his finger away from his mouth.

"Now, tell me, what do you mean?"

"I've been givin these guys all this information without any kind of signed papers or nothin and … I don't know."

"You don't know what?"

"If I can trust them."

His mother leaned forward. "Son, listen to me. Don't worry. It'll all work out."

Reluctantly, Robert nodded.

She sighed. "Let's just see what happens."

THIRTY-FIVE

ndian River Correctional Institution was two and a half hours north of Miami, near Vero Beach—a slightly larger facility than the one in Miami-Dade County. Robert's cellblock was a double-decked, semi-circular room with tables and TV in the common area. For the most part, prisoners stayed in the common area, where their meals were delivered to them. At night they entered their cells to sleep.

Right after transferring there, Robert signed up for a Bible study group. Until then, he had contact with only a couple of other believers. The idea of participating in a Christian discussion group excited him. That evening, he went to the meeting, holding the Bible from Rikers Island. Four other inmates from his cellblock went as well. Two corrections officers escorted them to a long room with thick glass walls. The room had two columns of chairs with an aisle down the middle. As he and other inmates entered, a man in khaki slacks and plain white shirt greeted them.

Apparently, he had attended before. "Hello, my name is Maynard Sweigard." He shook Robert's hand.

Robert gestured toward himself. "I'm Robert."

"I haven't seen you before. This is your first time, isn't it?"

"Yeah, I just arrived. Thought I'd check youse guys out."

"Great. Well, thanks for coming. Feel free to take a seat anywhere you like."

A dozen or so inmates were already seated. Robert and the inmates from his cellblock sat on the second row. For the next few minutes, the group shared small talk while other prisoners were brought in.

An inmate said to Robert, "Your Mets are like nine games out right now. And they're on a losing streak." He was a young kid and quirky. "You think they have a chance to make the playoffs?"

Robert shrugged. "Hey, you never know."

"I bet you five bucks they don't."

"Hey!" Robert held up his hands. "You tryin to get an illegal gambling charge tacked on to what I already got?"

The other men laughed, but Robert knew it wasn't long ago that he would have taken the bet. For some, the wager would have been harmless. It was potentially dangerous for Robert, regardless of how small the amount.

Robert learned from others that Maynard was Indian River's chaplain. One man got a guitar out of its case and was tuning it. A second man was sitting on the front row, talking with two inmates behind him. These two were from one of the local churches. Their church and several others took turns hosting the meetings, which occurred twice a week.

The man with the guitar led the inmates in several songs. One song stood out for Robert above all the others. "I Am a New Creation" by David Ingles that said he was a new creation, a brand new man.

It was as if the song was written especially for him. The words moved him to tears. Unlike the day at Rikers Island, he wasn't afraid to show tears in front of the other men. Judging by their expressions, they were moved as well.

After the music, Chaplain Maynard guided the men in the study. Everyone was encouraged to participate. Outside of AA, Robert never had experienced a meeting where people were so open and genuine.

The study concluded, and the man who had been talking to the other inmates earlier approached Robert. He held out his hand. "The name's Delco. Just like the battery."

Robert shook his hand and introduced himself.

"I haven't seen you here before."

"This is my first time."

In his fifties, Delco had a kind face. He talked with Robert for a few minutes, mostly about the prison ministry and prison conditions. When the correctional officers returned to take Robert and the rest of the inmates back to their cellblocks, he said, "Say, would you mind if I came to visit you in a day or two? I'd like to continue our conversation, if you don't mind."

Robert was surprised. Just a few minutes ago, Delco was a complete stranger. Why would he take even more time out of his schedule to make a personal visit? "Sure," Robert said emphatically. "Beats hanging out with some of these knuckleheads I gotta bunk with."

Delco laughed, and the two men parted.

The next day, Robert met with Delco in a visiting room designated for contact visits. For two hours, Delco was kind and supportive as he listened to Robert air his grief about his current situation. He prayed with Robert right there and promised to keep praying. The visit boosted Robert's spiritual growth.

At the end of the next meeting, Chaplain Maynard announced that a baptismal service would be held next month. Due to time constraints, there would be time for only six inmates to be baptized. This was something Robert desperately wanted to do, but by the time he added his name to the list, seven other inmates had their names above his.

"Put your name down anyway," the man with the yellow pad said. "Sometimes guys back out at the last moment."

The Bible study meetings helped fulfill a hunger that began the day Robert's daughter cried out to him at Rikers Island. Every Tuesday and Thursday he was one of the first at the gate, carrying his Bible, ready to head down the corridor to the meeting room. There, he learned more about the life of Christ and what it meant to be one of His followers. Jesus gave the example of giving and not taking, a concept foreign to Robert's former lifestyle. He was taught to love his enemies, when before, he believed enemies must be eliminated to get ahead. He understood the principle of sacrificing his life, although he wasn't too keen on the idea. But he learned that Jesus was willing to die for everyone, and he did.

As Robert entered the meeting room the day of the baptisms, he learned that two of the seven men didn't make it, so he would be baptized that evening. He was elated.

During the past month, he'd thought deeply about how his physical situation correlated to his spiritual. He was about to enter the Witness Protection Program, where he would receive a completely new identity. His name, where he lived, and the way he earned a living would all change. The same applied for him spiritually. He now had a new name as a child of God—as well as a new final destination.

As the pastors prayed with the men, Robert sobbed more than ever before. Even when they were explaining the procedures of baptism—holding his nose, the cue to go into the water, bending at the knees—he never stopped crying, for he realized the baptism symbolized the death of the old Robert and the rebirth of a new one, made whole through a man who died in his place, some 2,000 years ago. As he entered the baptistery—a large tub on a rolling platform—the reality of the situation was more than he could bear. Robert Engel—Mafia tough guy, crackhead, and deadbeat father—was about to die. In his place would arise a new Robert, serving as a witness to his own death and a pallbearer at his own funeral.

~~~~~

On December twenty-fourth, Chaplain Maynard and the prison ministry volunteers hosted a Christmas party that included the inmates. They brought in snacks and candy, and served punch. There were prison rules that didn't allow merchandise, so no gifts were exchanged.

That Christmas Eve was memorable for Robert. It wasn't the typical partying to which he was accustomed. Except for when he was a kid, he had no memories of Christmas. It had become just another day to get high, with loud music and louder drunks.

Now, these people had taken time away from their families to be with him and the other inmates to celebrate the real reason for

Christmas—the birth of Jesus Christ. Even if they had only stayed thirty minutes or so as Robert figured, it would have meant a lot to him. They ended up staying for hours, singing carols and rejoicing over the Savior of the World. Once again, Robert was brought to tears over the demonstration of God's love for society's outcasts.

THIRTY-SIX

February 1998
Age 43

obert was shipped out of Indian River, headed for a state facility in Fort Lauderdale. Leaving his new family was difficult, especially since he'd flourished spiritually among them.

He was sent to Fort Lauderdale so he would be available for his sentencing. The details had already been worked out. He would serve a reduced two-year stint in a federal prison in exchange for his testimony. This meant his sentence would be over in a year, since he had already served a year awaiting trial.

When Robert arrived at the Broward County Jail, in error he was placed in the general inmate population. When it came to light that he was involved in a case where his testimony was needed, he was moved to solitary confinement for protection.

Like some other facilities, the cellblock was set up like a dorm, with tables, benches, and a TV. Eight cells were around the perimeter. As it turned out, Robert was the only prisoner in the entire cellblock. This was both good and bad. It was good that he could watch anything he wanted on TV, which amounted to Christian shows. It was bad because he had no one to talk to. Time seemed to drag.

The evening after he arrived, just before dinner, Robert emerged from his cell wearing only a T-shirt.

"Hey!"

Startled, Robert looked toward the gate that led into the cellblock and saw the correction officer staring at him, hands on her hips. She wasn't a large woman, but her bark would have competed with the best of drill sergeants.

"Can you read?"

"Can I read?"

"Did I stutter?"

Robert held out his hands. "Yeah, what of it? Do you need me to read something for you?"

She pointed to a wall near his cell. "You need to read the rules—after you put a shirt on."

"Why do I need to put a shirt on? I'm the only one here."

"It's a rule. All inmates must comply. Get a shirt on and read the rules."

Shaking his head, Robert went to his cell and put on a shirt over his T-shirt, trying his best not to curse the woman. As he emerged from his cell, he looked toward the gate. She wasn't there. Instead of reading the rules, he stretched out on the bench to watch TV.

"If you had read the rules"—the booming voice nearly caused Robert to roll off the bench—"you would have known that each prisoner must make room for other prisoners on the bench."

"Are you kidding me?" He looked around. "There's nobody to share the bench with."

"You can't do that. You must comply with the rules. You are not special."

Resentfully, Robert sat up.

For the next couple of days, the same prison guard tortured Robert with her hardcore ways during her shift. The more she drilled him, the more sarcastic his tone toward her became.

Robert continued his habit of morning prayer, but he found his heart was full of resentment toward the female guard. During one of his prayers, he remembered reading in the Bible about something Jesus said about praying for those who persecute you. He shook his head at the thought of praying for the woman in charge of his keep. But instead of resisting, he got down on his knees, next to his bed.

"Lord, I really don't want to be doing this, but this girl … I think she's being ridiculous. She's being mean to me. I don't think I deserve the way she's treating me. But Your Word says I should pray for her. I don't feel like it. I don't want to, but I'm gonna do it, because that's what Your Word says."

A couple of days after Robert started praying for her, she brought his dinner. "Don't know how you're gonna get full on that." She placed the tray down on the table.

"Hey, they gotta make budget cuts somewhere, don't they?"

The woman laughed. "As long as it ain't my salary."

"You got that right."

"Hey, I bet I can get you a sandwich to go along with …" She looked down at the tray. "I don't even know what you'd call that."

They both laughed.

"Yeah, that'd be great."

As the corrections officer left the cellblock, Robert stared at the gate in astonishment, then looked skyward. He mouthed the words, *Thank you, Lord.*

The corrections officer catered to Robert the rest of the week.

After his sentencing, he was sent to the federal prison in Sandstone, Minnesota to serve out the rest of his time behind bars.

THIRTY-SEVEN

March 1998
Age 43

A sprinkling of snow was dusting the tarmac as Robert's flight landed at the Minneapolis airport. He battled the blistery wind as he tucked his chin into his shirt as best as possible. "Geez, fellas. You could have told me to dress a little warmer."

The marshals loaded him into the back of a black sedan and then got into the front seat. During the ride, the vehicle was void of conversation.

When they made it to Sandstone Federal Correctional Institute, the marshals took Robert into the processing area and released him to the custody of the correctional officers. After exchanging his personal clothing for prison garb, he was photographed and taken to the area he would call home for the next year. The facility was separate from all the others, especially suited for those being proposed into the Witness Protection Program. He was fortunate to find several other WITSEC prisoners who were followers of Jesus. Every week, they attended two Bible studies and one worship service together. They also prayed together every evening, an event that became vitally important for Robert.

About a month after being admitted into Sandstone, Robert learned that his mother had been diagnosed with cancer, only a year after having heart surgery. The news was devastating enough that Robert considered abandoning his plan to enroll in the

Witness Protection Program. He didn't care that he would be putting his life in danger. His mother had always been there for him. Now it was his turn to be there for her. While reading his Bible in his cell, Robert prayed about his situation. While praying, he fell asleep. When he woke up, Genesis Chapter 12 was on his mind. He wasn't familiar with the different Bible stories yet, so he began to read how Abraham left his family to go to the land of Canaan. God blessed him for his obedience. Robert saw that as possible confirmation that God wanted him to continue, but he was still uncertain. He felt he needed more confirmation, so he called his mother to propose the idea of coming home.

"Don't worry about me. You just need to take care of yourself," she said.

This was the proof he needed.

Six months into his sentence, the federal marshals interviewed him for the Witness Protection Program. They drilled him with a battery of questions to discourage him from wanting to be in the program. He went through psychological testing as well as a polygraph. He was told to pick three places where he would like to live. Thinking more like his old self, Robert's top two picks were Hawaii and California. His third pick was Pennsylvania. That way he'd be close to home.

~~~~~

Robert's release date of March 7, 1999, was fast approaching. With it came anxiety. He was living the way God wanted. Besides his regular Bible study, he had signed up for correspondence courses through Set Free Ministries and accumulated thirty-two college credits. But the words "jailhouse conversion" were floating among some of his fellow inmates, who were trying to convince him that after he was released, he'd go back to doing drugs.

Two months before he was released, Robert feared that what they were saying was true. In his cell at his regular morning quiet time, he felt a fervent need to take the issue to God in prayer. He got down on the floor, opened his Bible, and placed his face against its pages. "God," he prayed, "let Your Word get into my mind so I never forget it." He adjusted his position so his heart was directly over the Bible. "God, let Your Word penetrate my heart. Let it live in my heart." This became part of his routine from that day to the day of his release.

March seventh fell on a Sunday. Since prisoners were not processed out on weekends, his release date was moved back to Friday, March fifth. It was against the law to hold a prisoner past his release date. This was both good and bad. Robert got out two days early, but the two marshals in charge of him said they were unable to book a flight out until Monday. Robert was out, but it would be a couple of days before he left Sandstone.

They drove him to a hotel, where he was set up in a room. With the low temperatures in the single digit range, Robert convinced them to set him up with warmer clothes, including a jacket. They told him he was free to go where he wanted but recommended that he not wander off too far. His situation required that all ties to his past life—including his driver's license and Social Security card—be severed. Therefore, he had no I.D. If for some reason, he was asked to produce some, he would be in a precarious situation.

Robert took their advice. Except for a visit to a local church on Sunday, he settled into his room, where he ate, prayed, and waited.

On Monday morning, the marshals returned. The drive to the Minneapolis airport from Sandstone was a bit unsettling. His mind entertained wild thoughts. No one except the government—his former enemy—knew where he was. It would be nothing for him to disappear into the frozen forests of Minnesota, or into the deep waters of one of its many lakes. These guys could shoot him dead and say he was trying to escape. All the men indicted on the case involving him took pleas, so he was no longer needed to testify. As far as he knew, there were no other cases for which his testimony would be used. Since he had already served his purpose, it would be a lot cheaper for the government to get rid of him than to keep him.

All sorts of scenarios played in Robert's mind, all ending with him on the short end of the stick. As the van finally arrived at the airport after an intense two-hour drive, his anxiety eased.

Like clockwork, two more marshals received him at the Minneapolis-St. Paul International Airport and whisked him onto a jet, which flew them to an undisclosed location. When they landed, Robert was greeted by two more marshals, who put him in a windowless van. They drove for a while and then stopped. When they opened the back of the van, Robert got out into a tunnel next to a concrete staircase.

The marshals took him up the stairs and brought him to a suite with a patio. One of them said, "This is where you'll stay for the next few days." He looked at the black plastic bag Robert was carrying. "What's that?"

Robert held it up. "This? Pictures of my mom and daughter and some certificates for college courses."

"I'll need to take that from you. You can't have anything in your possession that relates to your past."

Reluctantly, Robert handed him the bag.

"If you need anything, just let us know."

"All right, I'll do that."

"Are you hungry?"

"Not yet."

"We'll get you whatever you want to eat, within reason. There are snacks in the mini fridge."

Robert saw the small refrigerator to his left. "That's great. So like, what's gonna happen next?"

"You'll be informed soon."

"Do you know where I'm gonna live? Can you tell me that much?"

"No."

"Boy, youse guys are full of information."

The marshal smiled. "You've come a long way in the process. Just be patient a little while longer."

"Yeah, okay. Thanks."

After the marshals left, Robert opened the sliding door out to the patio. The top of the walls around the perimeter were two stories high and solid.

Wow! These guys really don't want me to know where I am.

He closed the patio door, went to the front room, and sat down. He chuckled as the thought of how, only a few nights ago, he was sleeping inside a prison cell, eating whatever was put before him. Now, he was in a nice suite, being treated like a V.I.P.

The thought of his mother prompted a search for a telephone. He didn't find one. The last time he'd spoken with her, she wasn't doing well. He wanted to see if she had made any improvements. He hated that he didn't ask the marshal about it while he had the chance, but it would be at the top of the list when he saw him again.

The next morning, Robert awoke to a knock at the door. He got up, stumbled to the door, and opened it.

The marshal said, "You've got twenty minutes to get dressed. Then I'll bring you breakfast. What would you like?"

Robert scratched his head. "I'm not really much of a breakfast person. Just bring me a cup of coffee and a glass of orange juice."

After he showered and shaved, the marshal returned with the coffee and juice.

"Thanks. Hey, listen. Is there any way I can check on my mom? She's been fighting cancer, and I'd like to know how she's doing."

The marshal shook his head. "I'm sorry."

He gave Robert a few minutes to enjoy his liquid breakfast, which was difficult to do, considering the marshal's answer.

The marshal took him to a room down the hall, where three more marshals introduced themselves. They began a battery of questions and tests similar to the ones Robert took at Sandstone. This went on all day, breaking only for lunch. When evening finally rolled around, he was told by one of the marshals that his "homework" was to come up with a new last name.

The following day was the same routine, except Robert started out with a more substantial breakfast. "I came up with a couple of names," he said. "How about Gotti, or Capone?" He laughed, but the marshals didn't join in. "Okay, I guess that's a no. Seriously, I thought about Russo, or maybe Baducci. Those are good Italian names."

A marshal jotted down the names and left. When he returned, he shook his head. "No, you'll need to try again."

The next day Robert had several more names, but none of them worked. That evening while eating dinner, he was watching an old episode of M.A.S.H., with a visiting doctor with the last name Borelli, a famous heart surgeon. This name struck him as one most appropriate. This doctor saved the lives of his patients, and Robert wanted to be a minister who saved souls. The next morning, he gave the name to the marshals, and it was accepted. From now on, he would be known as Robert Borelli.

When the marshals finished processing Robert, he asked where he would be living.

"For security purposes, we can't tell you right now. We will tell you on the way to the airport."

Instead of a van, the marshals put Robert into the back seat of a car to drive him to the airport.

"Okay, so now can you tell me where I'm going?"

The marshal in the front passenger seat turned around. Robert didn't like the grin on his face.

"San Antonio."

"Really?"

The marshal nodded, obviously amused.

"San Antonio, Texas? Like with cowboys, and horses and buggies?"

The marshal laughed.

"Boy, youse guys really know how to pick em. I shouldn't have any problem blending in there."

THIRTY-EIGHT

March 11, 1999
Age 44

R obert flew to Texas. When he arrived at the San Antonio airport, he met two more marshals.

"This is Marshal Lewis," the older one said, motioning toward the other man, "and I'm Marshal Martinez."

Since Robert had only the clothes on his back, there was no need for the baggage claim area. They went straight to the unmarked car in the parking lot and to a hotel in downtown San Antonio.

"You'll be holed up here for a while," Marshal Martinez said. Even though Marshal Martinez was of Hispanic descent, his Texas drawl overrode any ethnic accent he might have had. "We'll be getting you some I.D. under your new name before we can get you an apartment or job. Do you have a high school diploma?"

"No, I never finished school," Robert said. "I did get a G.E.D. when I was at the Danbury prison."

"Under your old name?"

"Yes."

"That's not gonna work. We'll need to get you a G.E.D. with your new name." He gave Robert the key card. "Feel free to get out and stretch your legs. There are plenty of bars around, lots of sites to see."

Robert was taken back by the marshal's suggestion. He figured they would know he had a drug and alcohol problem and wouldn't suggest such a thing. Robert realized he would have to depend upon God, as well as himself, to avoid that pitfall.

"You have a per diem of $40 to live on."

Robert furrowed his brow. "Per diem?"

"Per day. You get $40 for food, drink, travel, and incidentals." Marshal Lewis sounded like he was reading from a manual.

Forty dollars wasn't a lot of money. Robert would have to rethink the way he spent. "What about clothes? All I got is what I'm wearing."

"We don't have a fund for clothing. You'll have to buy clothes with your per diem."

Robert laughed. "I'm barely gonna eat with that money. Listen, I just think it's gonna look kinda funny that I'm walking around this hotel every day with the same clothes, that's all."

The two marshals conferred with each other.

"I'll see what I can do," Marshal Martinez said.

Over the next two weeks, Robert was involved in the process of his transformation. Two days after arriving in San Antonio, he was given funds to go shopping for clothes and shoes. A few days later, they flew to an undisclosed location, where Robert received a new Social Security number. He was taken to the Department of Motor Vehicles to get his Texas driver's license. He was supposed to have two forms of identification and proof of insurance, but somehow the marshals got him past that requirement with just a thumbprint. After taking the test and passing, he got his driver's license.

As Marshal Martinez drove up to the front of Robert's hotel, he said, "You'll be taking the G.E.D. test tomorrow."

"What? I thought I'd have some time to study."

"Don't worry, I'm sure it'll all come back to you."

The test intimidated Robert. The last nine months of his incarceration were spent studying the courses offered to him by Set Free Prison Ministries. He had done well on them, but his education in basic essentials was limited to eighth grade. Even with that, he didn't remember much. Looking back, he saw that all the time he spent clowning around or in detention or suspension were wasted years.

That night, he prayed that the Lord would help him with the test. The next day, his prayer was answered when he received word that he had passed. Whether the marshal had anything to do with it, he didn't know. He did know that God had something to do with it.

Robert was now ready for the next two stages: finding employment and a place to live. But before he could continue his quest for a new life, he had to deal with a personal tragedy.

THIRTY-NINE

March 1999
Age 44

One of Robert's requirements was joining a support group such as Alcoholics Anonymous. The first week in San Antonio, he found a place not far from his hotel. This was important, since his only mode of transportation was his feet. He made at least one meeting a day, usually at that location, which was held in the afternoon.

He also attended a meeting on weekends, ten miles away, so he took the bus. The large building was somewhat run down and contained several rooms. At this meeting, Robert stood during share time and introduced himself. He told about the part of his life dealing with his addiction to drugs and alcohol, cautiously leaving out his involvement with the mob and the Witness Protection Program.

At the end of the meeting, a man in his late 60s approached Robert and held out his hand. "My name's Bill. I noticed your accent. What part of New York are you from?"

Robert shook his hand. "Brooklyn."

"Well, it's good to meet a fellow New Yorker. Could I buy you a coffee?"

Robert and Bill sat in the dining area, chatting about old times in New York.

Bill was co-owner of Guadalupe River Ranch in Boerne, a small community just northwest of San Antonio. "Listen, Robert. There's a get-together next month of people who used to live in the New York/New Jersey area. Since you are new in town, might you want to come meet some people?"

"Sure. That sounds great, because I don't think most of these Texans understand what I'm saying anyhow."

Bill laughed. "I know what you mean. If you can, I'd like for you to come out to the ranch for Easter weekend. We're going to have a big shindig. I think you'd like it."

"I shouldn't have a problem with that," Robert said, since he had no obligation to a job yet. "The only problem is, I don't have any wheels."

Bill thought for a moment. "I'm going out of town for a few weeks, but I'll be coming in right before Easter. How about I pick you up?"

"That works for me."

On April third, Bill picked up Robert in front of his hotel, and they made the forty-five-minute drive to Guadalupe River Ranch. The 370-acre resort/spa was on a bluff overlooking the Guadalupe River Valley. The main house once belonged to the actress Olivia de Havilland and accommodated forty-five guests. Along with being a working ranch, the resort also had a petting zoo for the kids and offered kayaking down the Guadalupe.

On two acres near the back of the ranch, Bill had built his own home. He put Robert up in one of the rooms at the resort so he could enjoy the full benefits of the place.

Robert was thankful for the opportunity to get out and get away from the stress of building a new life, although he felt guilty about not paying for it. Bill was someone he barely knew, which made him feel like he was taking advantage of him. Bill insisted that Robert just enjoy it.

Despite the downtime at the ranch, Robert's mother was constantly on his mind. Using a calling card to be sure his phone number wouldn't be traced, he was making regular calls to Florida. Through talking to her and his brother Richard, he was aware of her failing health as she struggled to survive the cancer.

On Sunday, April fourth, he tried calling his siblings to check on his mother's condition, but no one answered. Finally, he got in touch with Richard.

"Mom's gone," Richard said, his voice shaken.

Robert felt his chest tighten. "When?"

"Saturday before Easter. How about that?"

"Seems fitting."

After the conversation, Robert slowly descended the stairs to where Bill and his wife Ellie were and told them the news.

"We're so sorry," Ellie said, gently touching his arm. "Is there something we can do?"

Robert shook his head.

"Are you going to go back home?" Bill said.

"I can't."

"Why? Is it money? If it is, we can help you with that." Bill was unaware of Robert's situation.

"It's not money. It's just ..." Robert was tempted to tell them about what was going on. They had been so kind to him, and the burden of the secret was difficult to bear. "It's just the way things are right now. I can't go back."

"Okay. If that changes and you need help, just let us know."

Over the next few days, Robert went through a gamut of emotions. He was frustrated at his situation. Not only was he not there when she died, but he couldn't attend her funeral. He felt despair because his best friend, his biggest supporter in the world, was gone. Most of all, he was angry with God. His mother had gone through decades of hell, dealing with Robert—his addictions, his involvement with the Mafia, his selfish mentality. Now that he was a new person, he wanted most to share that change with her. She was gone, but the guilt of what he'd put her through remained.

~~~~~

The following weekend was the New York/New Jersey get-together Bill had mentioned to Robert, weeks earlier. At first, Robert wasn't interested in going. The grief over his mother's death had kept him holed up in the hotel room.

Bill didn't give him an option. "Be ready in twenty minutes," he said. "Ellie and I are on our way. We'll pick you up at your hotel."

Robert forced himself to get ready and left with Bill and Ellie. The meeting was at an Italian restaurant, not far from where Robert was staying. As he entered the private room inside the restaurant, he immediately heard voices from his part of the country, talking loudly and erupting in laughter.

He nudged Bill. "This reminds me of home."

Bill nodded and smiled.

After everyone introduced themselves, a group of ladies invited Robert over to their table.

"Go on. Mingle," Bill said. "Stay away from the bar."

"Don't worry about that."

"You'd better worry about that."

Bill was right. When he thought he had his alcohol addiction kicked was when he was most vulnerable. He headed to the table and reintroduced himself.

The oldest woman smiled. "Hello, Robert. My name is Sharon, and this is my daughter Melissa." She gestured toward the woman on her left, then looked right. "My daughter Kerry." She pointed across the table. "And my friend Bernice."

"It's nice to meet you, ladies. Did I hear one of you say you're a church group?"

"Yes," Sharon said. "From Evers Road Christian Church. Melissa's husband—my son-in-law—is one of the pastors there."

"Oh, really?"

The church was on Interstate 410—about ten miles away. Kerry headed up the church's nursing home ministry.

After the evening ended, Bill and Ellie dropped Robert at the hotel. "I know this is a tough time for you," Bill said, "and the temptations are going to be there. I'll be out of town for a while, but I want you to call me if you need to talk. You've got my mobile phone number."

"Thanks, I will." Robert patted Bill on the arm. "Thanks for making me go tonight. I just might have found a church home."

~~~~~

Government witnesses receive funds to live a normal life for up to two years, but it's not an exorbitant amount. Robert found this out with the first per diem he was allotted for food and travel. When he went car shopping, his budget was a mere $4,000. He bought a 1984 BMW. Despite being an older car with well over 100,000 miles, the BMW far exceeded walking everywhere. For that, Robert was grateful.

The car also meant he could get to Evers Road Christian Church without needing a ride. The first Sunday he had the chance, he drove there to worship with his new friends. He met Senior Pastor Phillip, who was kind and receptive to Robert. He also got to meet Melissa's husband, Brent, who was also a pastor there. Since Melissa's family was from back East, he felt comfortable with them. Soon, they were inviting him to go out to eat and to visit them at their home.

Robert built friendships with Pastor Phillip and Brent by visiting them every morning at the church office, bringing donuts and making coffee. He was hungry not only for their friendship but also the brotherhood found among Christian men, which fed his desire to become closer to God.

He began to visit the elderly residents at a nearby nursing home. Kerry, who headed up the ministry, asked Robert to come with them some Saturday morning, right after the men's prayer breakfast. At first, he wasn't interested and avoided attending by leaving the men's prayer breakfast before the women arrived. He was still dealing with his bitterness toward God for taking his mother before the new Robert had a chance to love her. But as he was leaving one morning, he felt a strong urge to take Kerry up on her offer.

"Robert, you're gonna love these people," Kerry said as Robert drove them to the nursing home. "They have so much gratitude."

"What exactly do I need to do?"

"Just be yourself. Show them love."

It was Robert's first time in a nursing home, so he was nearly floored when the stench of urine burned his nostrils.

As they walked down the hallway, Kerry noticed his response. "It's common among the elderly to be unable to control their bladder. You can imagine how humiliating and embarrassing that must be."

Robert nodded. He was glad that was never an issue for his mother.

Kerry pointed to one of the rooms on the left. "There are a couple of women in this room that I'd like you to meet—Martha and Mary. But be careful of Mary. She's a feisty one."

As Kerry and Robert entered, the two women with them went down the hallway to visit another senior. The drab gray walls of Mary and Martha's room were colorfully decorated with family photos, greeting cards, and children's drawings. A blaring TV was in the middle of the back wall. Two twin-sized beds were on opposite sidewalls. A frail woman in her eighties was on the left, wearing a knitted shawl and sitting on the edge of her bed. She was struggling to get her slippers on. Her roommate was slightly younger, sitting in a chair at the end of the bed.

"Hello, ladies." Kerry turned down the TV sound.

The woman on the left slowly stretched out her arms.

Kerry hugged her. "Hello, Martha. How are you?" She squatted next to her.

Martha said something to Kerry, but Robert couldn't distinguish what it was.

Kerry nodded as she listened intently.

The woman's eyes then made their way to Robert.

"This is Robert," Kerry said.

Robert took Martha's hand. "It's good to meet you, Martha," he said in a loud voice.

Martha smiled, then whispered something to Kerry, who then laughed.

"What'd she say?"

"She wants to know if you will marry her."

"I don't know about that, Martha," Robert said. "I just might get accused of robbing the cradle."

The three of them laughed.

Kerry continued her conversation with Martha as Robert stepped back.

"Hey!" It was the woman in the chair calling him. She waved him over.

Robert looked back at Kerry, who was enthralled in whatever Martha was telling her.

He turned back to the woman in the chair, assuming she must be Mary, still waving for him. He walked to within three feet of her.

"Come down here," she said.

Robert squatted to eye level with her. "You must be Mary."

Without warning, the woman slapped him with all the might a woman her age could muster.

Robert was shocked as he quickly got to his feet.

"That's what you get for two-timing me." Mary shook her fist at him.

"Ms. Mary!" Kerry said as she stood next to Robert. "You can't do that."

"But she's right," Robert said, chuckling. "I shouldn't have been two-timing her. I deserved it."

By the time Robert and the ladies involved in the nursing home ministry left that day, he had two more proposals for marriage. Fortunately, there were no more slaps.

As they arrived back at the church, Kerry stayed in the car while the other women left. "You were pretty quiet on the trip back," she said. "What did you think?"

Robert gathered his thoughts. "I know what it's like to be trapped inside a prison cell. But I knew when I was going to get out—that my time there was limited. Even with that, I can't imagine what it's like being trapped inside your own body, unable to feed yourself, unable to speak, unable to use the bathroom on your own. Jail was easy compared to what these people are going through."

Kerry nodded with a smile. "You get it."

As he was praying before bedtime, Robert thanked God that his mother never had to suffer through what he saw at the nursing home. He never missed another Saturday visit to the nursing homes, and he was no longer plagued with bitterness for God taking his mother. She had been saved from a far worse fate, and there were plenty of senior adults with whom he could share the love that he wasn't able to share with his mother.

FORTY

June 1999
Age 44

The next order of business was getting a place to live. The problem was, from 1999 and earlier, Robert Borelli had no credit history. This caused confusion for apartment managers, not to mention wariness. He approached Marshal Martinez with his situation.

"Well," Martinez said, "we can help you. But we'll have to let the apartment manager know your circumstances. Otherwise, it could fall back on us."

"I don't like that at all," Robert said. "The idea that someone in the apartment complex knows who I am? That doesn't seem too smart."

Robert had to come up with something on his own. He talked to his friend Bill about it, and Bill allowed Robert to use him as a reference. That opened the door to get his apartment. Marshal Martinez got permission from his supervising officer, and Robert moved into his new apartment in Boerne.

He was also able to buy furniture—a bed, a dining table and chairs, a sofa, and a TV, along with a few kitchen utensils. They didn't give him a lump sum of money. Instead, he had to purchase the item and present a receipt for reimbursement.

Employment was to be another difficult area. One test he took was used to evaluate what vocation he would likely be successful in. According to the results, cosmetology was the best fit for him. He checked out some nearby schools and presented the information to the marshals, who forwarded his request for funds to their superiors. His request was rejected, so he started work on the night shift at H.E.B. supermarket as a stocker. He soon became frustrated with the job. He wasn't good at stocking shelves, and the hours of midnight to 8:00 a.m. were not appealing. He expressed his frustration with Marshal Martinez. Between the two, no ideas emerged.

At church, Robert asked that his job be an issue of prayer for his Sunday school class. Afterward, Pastor Brent—Melissa's husband—suggested he get his real estate license. Before Brent became one of the pastors at Evers Road Christian Church, he had sold homes. If Robert obtained his license, they could partner through the same real estate company.

"You've got the personality," Pastor Brent said, "and the market's great right now. You have a chance to make good money."

In June, Robert enrolled in a real estate class. By September, he was wheeling and dealing in the real estate market.

Within six months of being released from Sandstone, his life had dramatically improved. He had his own place and a reputable job. Every day, he went to the church, bringing donuts and coffee and hanging out with the pastors. His church attendance was regular, and he was actively involved in the nursing home ministry. Above all, his relationship with God was growing exponentially. As a result, the memory of his past addictions were fading.

FORTY-ONE

August 2000
Age 45

O ver the next year, Robert filled his time with church activities and calls to his friends in New York, using a calling card to avoid disclosing his location. Still, he was lonely and missed home. His conversations with his friends were helpful, especially from those who were Christian and understood his hardship. It was suggested he start dating. At first, he thought dating would be a good thing. So he began a relationship with a woman he met at church. Before his life changed, Robert's ideas about sex were very loose. But since becoming a Christian, his eyes were opened to the tragic results often associated with that way of thinking. He hoped this would keep the relationship from becoming physical, but the opposite proved to be true. Before long, he and the woman were sleeping together, even though something inside him kept telling him not to. One evening while he and his girlfriend were alone in his apartment, the message came across loud and clear. The plaque on his wall said, *As for me and my house, we will serve the Lord.* With those powerful words, he knew he had to dissolve the relationship.

Robert never intended to permanently sever his ties with his family—especially his daughter Briana. After he'd fulfilled his obligation, he wanted the government to help him establish a new life and then cautiously rebuild the ties that were broken upon entering the Witness Protection Program. What he didn't count on was the reaction from Lauren, who totally cut off communications between Briana and her father, fearing her daughter's life might be at stake because of their connection. His family also distanced themselves from him, not understanding how he could turn on his friends and become a "rat" for the government.

Nevertheless, his sister Betty provided updates on Briana. "She's getting really big," Betty said. "But boy, does she have a cocky attitude."

By then, his daughter was seven years old.

Robert laughed. "She gets that from her mom, not me."

"We both know that's a lie."

Outside of his sister, he also stayed in contact with his old friend Angelo, who had also miraculously surrendered his life to Christ. They spent a lot of time on the phone, talking about old times and old friends. He told Angelo that he was lonely and asked that he join him in praying about a soul mate.

Sometime later, Angelo had a dream that he relayed to Robert. The dream centered on Abraham finding a wife for Isaac. The key point was that the woman—Rebekah—had to leave her family and go to the land where Isaac was. With that in mind, he felt Robert should meet Patricia.

Patricia was from Howard Beach, working in the school district as a bus driver for the disabled. She had been married and divorced twice. The first marriage was to a man who beat her, and the second man cheated on her. Two years after marrying her second husband, she became a believer in Christ. It had been four years since her last divorce, and recently she had started praying for God to send a godly man into her life. With her permission, Angelo gave her phone number to Robert.

"Great," Robert said. "I still don't know how that could work out. I mean, how can you date someone who lives 2,000 miles away?"

"Forget about it. Just talk to the woman. She's got a heart for God. You've got a heart for God. Let Him work out the details."

"Did you tell her about my situation?"

"I told her you were in a situation, but I didn't elaborate. I told her she could never call you."

"How did that go over?"

"She didn't ask. She just said I could give you her number."

That night, Robert called Patricia, once again using his calling card. The conversation began with accolades for their mutual friend and progressed into questions about their churches and how Christ came into their lives.

After an hour, Patricia brought the conversation to an end. "I've gotta get up early in the morning to drive my bus," she explained.

"Will it be okay if I call you again?"

Patricia hesitated. "Yeah, sure."

Robert didn't call her back until the next week. He was already nervous about the whole idea of a long-distance relationship, and when he asked if he could call her back, she hesitated. Her response made him think she might not be interested in him.

Still, he really enjoyed talking with her, sensing he had met someone who loved God like he did. This wasn't what he was accustomed to. Sometimes sponsors of the AA meetings in downtown San Antonio would host events such as dances and invited members to come. Robert always attended the dances and had no problem finding a dance partner. He did have a problem keeping them. His love for God was so deep that he had no inhibitions telling others about Him.

"This isn't a religious organization," one woman said.

"Yeah," Robert said, "but we're all the time talking about this Higher Power. I thought I would go into a little more detail about who that is."

The responses were always disdainful and ended in curt goodbyes. This made his chats with Patricia all the more pleasant, since they shared a common love for God.

Over the next few months, Robert and Patricia had many conversations. At first, Robert called her once a week, but eventually, they were talking every day. Sometimes Robert called her from work at the real estate office so he could use the 800 number to keep his location a secret. Most of the time, he used the calling card at home. He called at night, and they talked for hours, like two teenagers.

During these chats, Patricia realized who Robert was. She knew his old girlfriend Cookie. She and the people she ran around with talked about a "Robert who's always in and out of jail." Still, she didn't know he was a government witness tucked away in Texas Hill Country.

In the first part of December 2000, Robert asked Patricia to visit him. He promised to pay for her flight, and Pastor Brent would open his home to her while she visited.

"I'd love to visit," she said. "I just don't know where to tell everyone I'm going."

"You can't tell anyone," Robert said. "It's got to be a secret. I will tell you that Christmas where I live is a lot different from New York."

On December 20, Patricia flew to San Antonio. As she entered the waiting area, Robert was standing with Pastor Brent's wife, Melissa. Robert recognized Patricia from her photo and waved her down as he ended the conversation on his newly acquired cell phone.

He held out his hand. "I'm Robert." He turned to Melissa. "Patricia, this is Melissa. Melissa, Patricia."

Melissa and Patricia hugged as if they were sisters. "It's so good to meet you, Patricia."

"It's good to meet you too. Thank you for letting me stay at your house."

"You're more than welcome. We wouldn't have it any other way."

Patricia looked at the overhead signage. "I need to get my luggage."

They walked to the baggage claim area.

"You stand over there." Robert walked up to the baggage carousel. He grunted as he loaded a cart with her luggage. "Holy moley," he said, struggling to lift the largest bag. "What? Do you got a dead body in there or somethin?"

Melissa looked at Patricia. Her smile was thin, and her eyes were slightly widened.

After loading the baggage into the car and getting on the road, Robert talked to Melissa more than Patricia as he whipped in and out of traffic.

Over the next few days, Robert and Patricia spent most of their time trying to get to know each other, but nothing was clicking. On the third day, while heading to Brent and Melissa's after eating dinner, Patricia said, "You look disappointed. Are you disappointed?"

Robert looked over at her. "Do you really want to know the truth?"

Patricia hesitated. "Yes."

Robert cleared his throat. "Well, you look older than you do in your picture, and you're taller than I anticipated."

Patricia sat there for a moment, dumbstruck, shedding tears hidden from Robert, who'd gone back to watching the road.

The next morning Brent called Robert.

"What's wrong with you?" he asked.

"What?"

"You're treating Patricia like dirt."

"What do you mean?"

"Ordering her around, making comments about how old and tall she is. You don't even talk to her."

"I talk to her."

"No, you don't. You may say something to her, but it's not nice. You need to treat her right."

"That's just the way we do things in New York. She knows that."

"I think she expects more out of you. Trust me on this."

Two days before she was supposed to return to New York, Patricia took Robert out for his birthday at a local restaurant.

Near the end of the meal, Robert took a deep breath. "Will you marry me?"

At first, Patricia was unable to say anything. "Are you kidding me?" she whispered. "Just a week ago, you were saying how disappointed you were—how I was too tall and too old. You haven't said one kind word to me. And now you have the audacity to ask me to marry you?"

Robert bowed his head, his eyes flitting from left to right.

Patricia dabbed her cheeks with her napkin. "You do realize you're just as much short as I am tall, right?" More tears came. "You need to know something." She tried to regain her composure. "When we first talked over the phone, I had no interest in you. I had made a list of what I wanted in a man, and one thing was he needed to be over six feet tall. When I saw the picture of you next to your car, I could tell you didn't even come close to six feet. I talked with you that night, not expecting more than a friendly conversation and that's it. But the more I talked with you, the more I saw a person who was totally in love with God. That was at the top of my list because it was the most important. Without a doubt, you met that requirement." She sniffled. "Robert, I fell in love with you, not because of your looks or your height, but because you loved God so much. And that's why I agreed to come here. But now that I've met you in person, and you've treated me this way ... you still got this mobster mentality."

Robert felt guilt flush his face. "I grew up with the idea that you just don't go out with a girl taller than you, and they had to be younger. And you're right, it is a mob thing. You're a beautiful woman, and I've had that rolling around in my head the whole time you've been here. I'm sorry."

Patricia gave a slight nod.

"I was praying this morning," Robert said, "talking to God. I asked Him what I should say to you. I mean, your visit has been a catastrophe, and I take all the blame for that. I said to Him, *What am I gonna tell her? She's gonna expect me to say something, like will I ever see you again, or should I call anymore?* And He said, *You need to ask her to marry you.* Of course, my first thought was, *That doesn't make no sense.* I was wondering whether it was really God talking to me or someone else."

Patricia laughed.

"Then I heard Him say, *You'll never find anyone that'll love you the way she loves you.*" Robert took Patricia's hand. "That's what I've wanted all my life—someone to love me, not for my looks or that I'm a Mafia tough guy or that I buy gifts. I need someone to love me because of what's in here." He pointed to his heart. "Apparently, that someone is you."

For a moment, they sat in silence.

Then Robert said, "You need to answer me."

She shook her head, but the smile on her face told another story. "This is scary. That means I've got to pull up roots from New York. Leave my family. I've got a daughter there, you know."

Robert nodded. "I've been with the same prayer group for the past six years. They've been praying for me the entire time that I've been here."

Patricia sighed. "Yes."

Robert furrowed his brow. "Yes?"

"Yes."

"Yes, you'll marry me?"

"Wasn't that the question?"

"Yeah. I mean, okay then."

PART VI

THE
PATHWAY
BACK

FORTY-TWO

March 2001
Age 46

o I have to listen to you again?" The shaky scream came
from across the hall and echoed throughout the lounging
area of the nursing home.

Robert was teaching from the Bible to a group of
seniors. Apparently, the man had heard enough of Robert. Only a
couple of seniors participating in the study group responded by
looking up from their handouts and adjusting their hearing aids.

After getting married in February and returning from their
honeymoon, Robert and Patricia jumped right into ministry work.
Ever since Kerry relinquished her role as head of the nursing
home ministry to Robert, he and Patricia had been visiting every
week. Incorporated with the friendly visits were Bible lessons, for
which he enjoyed a good response.

The disturbing outburst vented toward the green pastor caught
him off guard. "You talkin to me?" he said, borrowing the
famous line from Robert DeNiro's character in the movie *Taxi*.

"Robert!" Patricia scolded him with a furrowed brow.

"What? I was just joking," he said with a cowered expression.
Some of the seniors understood the joke and laughed.

"You shut your mouth," the angry voice screamed again.

Glenda, the nursing home's activities director, excused herself
from the group and went to the room across the hall. "Now Mr.
Anderson, you can't be shouting out like that."

Robert cleared his throat. "Now where were we? Oh yes. Paul was explaining to the people of Corinth that they were going to have new bodies in Heaven, not the same old worn-out bodies we have on Earth. And that's what I'm telling you. If you commit your life to Christ, he promises a new life, not only here but in Heaven too. In Heaven, you're not taking this body you got on Earth. You're gonna have a brand spankin new body with nothing worn-out. No arthritis. No bone degeneration. No loss of memory. You know how you can barely get around right now? In Heaven, you'll be dancing. You'll run after your grandchildren and great grandchildren—after they make it there. Isn't that great?"

Smiles grew on the faces in the room—except for Caroline, who was sitting quietly in her wheelchair, weeping. She was a diabetes victim. Part of her leg had been amputated from the knee down.

Robert thought he might have said something that offended her. After the lesson, he sat in the chair beside her. "Caroline, I saw you were crying. I'm sorry if I said something that hurt you."

Caroline patted Robert on the hand. "Oh no, not at all. I just got to thinking about what you said about dancing, how I'll be ..." She subconsciously brushed down the blanket that covered her legs as she choked back more tears. "It's just good to know that someday I'll be able to dance again." She gave Robert a huge smile. "I so love to dance."

Robert struggled to contain his own tears. "That'll be somethin, won't it?"

~~~~~

After Robert took over ministering to the senior adults, he cultivated ideas of how the church could further advance its outreach to them. The Senior Adult Ministry arose from meetings with the pastors at Evers Road, Patricia, and a few others. The ministry encompassed not only regular weekly visits to the nursing home but also gave Robert the opportunity to teach. Coordinating with the activities director, he pulled together a good-sized core group of seniors interested in the Bible study.

Along with the weekday meetings, the ministry also incorporated Saturday events geared toward providing a little variety in residents' lives. Sometimes the ministry hosted a movie, complete with popcorn and soda. They might have an ice cream social. Sometimes, the ministry members treated seniors with manicures and pedicures. The ministry was very successful.

The nursing home administrators were pleased. They welcomed Robert and Patricia as fellow workers concerned about the residents' quality of life during their twilight years.

The San Antonio years were a vital part of Robert's growth, of which Patricia and the Senior Adult Ministry were instrumental. Except for a couple of hiccups, his life in Texas had been a fairly smooth ride, for which he thanked God.

But it is through trial by fire that a person's relationship with God is really tested, and Robert and Patricia were about to feel the flames.

FORTY-THREE

May 2001
Age 46

R obert was scrounging through the papers on the kitchen countertop. "Patty Ann, where are my reading glasses?" He patted his chest to see if they were in one of the breast pockets of his jacket. "I know I just had them." He went into the living area and searched between the cushions of the couch.

Patricia emerged from the bedroom. "Over there, on top of the TV." She adjusted her belt. "Did you call your sister?"

Betty had been sick the last couple of weeks, and Robert had intended to call to check on her. "Oh, shoot!" He walked over to the TV. "I'll call her now." He stuck the glasses into his pocket.

On the third ring, his sister answered. "Hello?"

"Betty, how're you doing?"

"I'm fine Robert, but you may not be."

"Why?"

"They know where you are."

It only took a second for Robert to understand who Betty was referring to and what it meant for them to know where he was.

"How?"

"I don't know. My guess would be because of you and Patricia getting married. They just put two and two together."

Patricia moved closer to Robert. "What's going on?"

Robert held up a finger. "Okay. Thanks, Betty."

Betty said, "Robert what are you gonna do?"

"I don't know. I need to talk to Patricia. I'll call you later."

"What's wrong?" Patricia looked concerned.

"People back home know where we live."

"How do you know?"

"My sister just told me." Robert looked out through the blinds.

"Don't be so paranoid."

"You obviously don't understand what these guys are capable of. Believe me, I know. I used to be one of them." He retreated from the window and picked up the phone.

"Who you gonna call?"

"Marshal Martinez." He punched in the numbers.

"This is Martinez."

"Good morning, Marshal. Listen, I got some bad news."

"What is it, Robert?"

"The people back home." Robert glanced at Patricia. "Seems they know my whereabouts."

The marshal paused. "Then that's it. You're out of the program." With that he hung up.

Robert held the phone out in front of him.

"What did he say?"

Robert looked up at Patricia. "He said I'm out of the program. And then he hung up."

"What?"

Robert pressed the redial.

"Marshal Martinez."

"What am I to do if these guys come after me?"

"Call 9-1-1." Again, the marshal hung up.

"I can't believe this."

~~~~~

After church services, Robert and Patricia met with Brent and Melissa in his office and told them about the phone call. Robert had yet to tell them the entirety of his story, since he was obligated by his agreement not to tell anyone about being in the Witness Protection Program.

"This is very disturbing," Brent said.

"Tell me about it."

Brent looked at his watch. "Let's talk about this later. We have to feed the kids some lunch. I'll call you."

When Robert and Patricia drove through the parking lot of their apartment complex, he scanned the area for rental cars.

Patricia said, "What are you doing?"

"Looking for uninvited guests. Guests you probably invited."

"Me? I got nothing to do with this."

"Yeah." Robert kept looking around.

"Stop the car," Patricia said. "Right now!"

Robert brought the car to an abrupt halt, and Patricia got out.

"What are you doing?"

"I'm walking the rest of the way home." She slammed the car door.

By the time Robert parked the car and got up to the apartment, Patricia had already packed one bag.

"Now what are you doing?"

"I can't stand being with you anymore." She crammed another piece of luggage with clothing from the dresser drawer.

"Oh, great. You let the mob know where I am and then leave. I see how it is."

"You're a difficult man who still has a lot of issues," she said.

"Where you gonna go?"

"Back home. At least I know I'm loved there."

"So now you say I don't love you?"

"If you do, you have a weird way of showing it."

With those words, Patricia slammed the bedroom door.

Robert retreated to the couch. For the next two hours, he sat in front of the TV, watching *The Sopranos.*

The phone rang. "Hey, Robert. It's me, Brent."

"Oh. Hey listen, I'm sorry about all this. It's just that—"

"I know, you didn't have a choice. We can respect that. I hope you can respect what I'm about to tell you."

"What?"

"Melissa and I have been talking and praying, and—"

"What is it?"

"You know we share the same website through real estate ... people associate us ... well, I think it would be best, for the protection of my family, that we do our business separately."

Robert felt like he got kicked in the stomach. He couldn't say anything.

"We love you two, and we believe God has a great life for you. It's just that ... it's just too risky."

"Brent, I don't know if it's that risky."

"Robert, I can't take that chance. What if they want to get to you through us? Do you think they'd care whether they hurt us? I just can't risk my family. I hope you can respect that."

Robert sighed. "I do, Brent. I really do."

Within a day, the new world of Robert Borelli crumbled. His new bride of only three months had locked herself in the bedroom, threatening to leave him. His business partner could no longer associate with him. And the government that had sworn to protect him had abandoned him.

He clutched at his stomach. "Why are you doing this to me, God? I thought I was doing what you wanted me to do."

At first, he sat on the couch, drowning in self-pity. After finding no comfort in that, he thought about what others had told him. Both Brent and Melissa saw how he treated Patricia and called him out on it. Patricia said he still had the *mobster mentality*. Was that true? He watched that old Robert guy die at his baptism. Was it possible that he still hung on to portions of the old guy?

With that, he examined himself. He felt like a big shot when the marshals were escorting him around from airport to airport, acting as his personal bodyguards. He was proud of how he was able to buy his wardrobe at the government's expense. Only a BMW was good enough for him to drive. After all, he was the one who put his life on the line to help the government put away guys far deeper into the Mafia life than he was.

Sure, he wasn't the same man he was before Christ. Instead of a habitual liar, he was completely honest—even at the expense of hurting his wife's feelings. Instead of spending hours at the horse races, he spent time in God's Word—and letting everyone know it. Instead of filling his body with destructive drugs, he invited the

Holy Spirit to dwell in him—while badmouthing the junkie on the corner, begging for change. Yes, instead of thinking about himself all the time, he was pouring himself into the lives of the elderly—while basking in the admiration.

Those thoughts were eye-opening, for they revealed one particular sin in his life that was generating a lot of his hardship—pride.

Without hesitation, Robert dropped to his knees. With tears of remorse, he begged God for forgiveness, that God would give him the grace to love his wife as God loved her.

He heard a faint click, and the bedroom door opened.

Patricia stepped out. "Robert?"

Robert got up walked over to Patricia. "Are you staying?"

"You want me to leave?" she said with a grin.

"No, not at all. I just thought you would have booked a flight by now and would be headed out."

She pointed to the empty luggage on the bed.

Robert said, "What've you been doing all this time?"

She shrugged. "I cried. I punched the pillow. Then I decided to talk with Pastor Phillip."

"Yeah? What did he have to say?"

"He told me divorce wasn't an option. I just thought, *It is in this girl's book.*" She laughed, but Robert didn't. "It's a joke." She ignored his raised brow and smirk. "Anyway, he convinced me that I needed to stay and work things out, that I need to be in this marriage for the long haul."

Robert nodded. "God's been showing me how I've been a jerk to you. I got pride issues. I'm really sorry for that."

Patricia smiled. "I forgive you." She wrapped her arms around his neck and kissed him. "I also talked with my sister. It seems that our marriage was the culprit. People just put it all together and figured out that we're here."

"Well … that makes sense." He paused. "Tomorrow, I'll see about getting permission to move somewhere else."

"What about our friends? And the senior adults?"

Robert picked up the luggage. "Dead, I'm not gonna be good to anybody. Anyway, I just talked with Brent, and he seems to think that, business wise, we should go our separate ways. Said it was too risky for his family. I don't blame him."

"Oh no. How's that gonna work out? I mean, with church?"

"I don't know. I guess we'll have to play along as we go."

"What about us? Do you think we're in danger?"

"Yeah. I told the government everything I know. A lot of men out there could go to prison because of me."

"So you think we should move?"

"I don't know. It's all depending on whether my supervisor/release officer will let me."

FORTY-FOUR

September 2001
Age 46

A few months passed, and the tension from being left without government protection faded. Robert and Patricia still attended Evers Road Christian Church and even continued their relationship with Brent and Melissa, although Robert was no longer on Brent's real-estate website. Pastor Phillip was understanding of Robert and Patricia's situation and told them they were always welcome.

The Senior Adult Ministry continued its success. Added to the already extensive outreach was a once-a-month Senior Sunday. The staff from the nursing home shuttled seniors to the church so they could enjoy worshipping with the people from Evers Road Christian Church. At times, as many as a dozen attended.

One of those seniors was Caroline. In spite of being weakened by her ongoing battle with diabetes, she came regularly. She and Robert grew in their relationship, and she took advantage of any chance she had to be involved with the ministry.

One Senior Sunday, the seniors arrived a few minutes after the singing had started. A man Robert didn't recognize was pushing Caroline's wheelchair. He and the woman walking next to him sat in the pew alongside Caroline.

After the service, Robert made a point to introduce himself to them as they entered the foyer.

Caroline said with labored breath, "Robert, I want you to meet my son and daughter-in-law."

"I'm Matt, and this is my wife, Suzanne." Matt shook Robert's hand. "We've heard a lot about you and wanted to let you know how much we appreciate what you're doing for my mother."

"Are you kidding? The pleasure's all mine. Your mother's a real sweetheart. She makes it easy to love her."

"Oh, Robert," Caroline said, inciting chuckles. "You're gonna make me blush."

"Suzanne," Matt said, "would you take Mom to the bus? I'll catch up with you in a second."

As Suzanne pushed the wheelchair, Caroline said, "Don't forget to tell him … what I said."

"I won't, Mom." Matt's smile disappeared as he turned back toward Robert. "Mom's not doing so well."

"Yeah, I can see she's weak. What does the doctor say?"

"He doesn't know how much time she's got, but it's probably not very long."

Robert shook his head. "I'm so sorry."

"She wanted me to ask if you would say something at her funeral."

"Me?"

"Yes, she wants to have the service at your church. I know, it's kind of strange that a woman who considered herself Catholic all her life would want a protestant preacher over a Catholic priest. But that just shows the effect you've had on her."

Robert's throat tightened. "Tell her I would be honored."

~~~~~

The following week, Robert rushed to the hospice where Caroline had been admitted. Matt had called Robert, telling him that Caroline didn't have long to live. She requested he come.

As he entered Caroline's room, he saw her sunken into the white bed linens, which were drawn all the way up to her shoulders. Her left hand protruded from the covers and held onto the hand of Matt, who sat in a chair next to her. Suzanne hovered over his shoulder.

Matt leaned closer to his mother. "Robert's here, Mom."

Caroline's head movement was slight at first. But then she turned her eyes to Robert, who was now standing at her right side. "Robert." Her voice was barely above a whisper.

"I'm right here, Caroline." He took her other hand. "You look like an angel."

A small smile flowed across her face, and then she said something indistinguishable.

Robert leaned closer to hear.

Mustering her meager energy, she said, "I'm about to dance."

Robert's own smile appeared. "Yes, you are."

Robert stayed for a while. He said a prayer for Caroline and her family and sat next to her as he read comforting scriptures from the Bible.

The next day, Caroline died.

Three days later, amid tears of sorrow for his lost friend, Robert said some final words at her funeral service, as promised.

The following Sunday, he was pleasantly surprised to see Matt and Suzanne attending the morning worship. Soon after that, they prayed with Pastor Phillip to receive Christ and committed their lives to His service.

"I can't think of a better outcome of death than someone getting saved," Robert said to Patricia as they drove home from a dinner date.

"What a sweet lady she was," Patricia said. "You know she's ecstatic, knowing her son and daughter-in-law are going to reunite with her one day."

Robert's cell phone rang. "Hello?"

"Can I speak with Robert Borelli?"

"Who's asking?"

"This is Agent Grover from the FBI field office in Florida."

~~~~~

"Are you kidding me?" Patricia said as she and Robert walked into their apartment. "After they kicked you out of the program, they have the audacity to ask for your help? That just takes the cake."

"It wasn't them who kicked me out of the program, Patricia. It was the marshals."

"Still, here we are with our lives on the line, and they want us to help them."

"It's what I agreed to. I have an obligation, whether the marshals protect me or not."

Patricia threw her purse onto the kitchen table and opened the refrigerator to fetch a bottle of water. "That's just not right. They should help us out some way."

"I think they'll help us relocate. That way we don't have to keep looking over our shoulders."

"No kidding." Patricia put the bottle on the bar. "When is the trial?"

"They didn't say." Robert took off his jacket.

"Who will you be testifying against?"

"I can't say."

"Why not? I'm your wife. You should be able to tell me everything."

"It could compromise their case."

"Great. This is just great."

"Hey, I told you before we were married there'd be times like this."

"Yeah, but that was when you had protection. Now we're just a couple of sitting ducks."

"I know. It's bad enough for us that I was used against Nicky. Now, if the guys back home see that I'll be used against them on a regular basis ... that's probably not gonna sit too well with them, because I know some of the things they did."

Patricia shook her head and walked toward the bedroom.

"Where you going?" Robert said.

"I'm gonna take a nap."

FORTY-FIVE

December 2001
Age 46

Anthony "Tony Pep" Trentacosta was one of the wiseguys from the old neighborhood in Brooklyn. He was friends with Alberto Devacio and would frequent his club next to the candy store, where Robert worked as a teenager. Years later, when Robert was in Florida working for Nicky, Robert had reconnected with Tony Pep.

In early December 2001, while the United States was still grieving from the Al Qaeda attack on September 11, Robert flew to Florida to testify against Tony Pep. He and two other men— Frederick "Fat Freddy" Massaro and Ariel Hernandez—were accused of conspiring to murder an exotic dancer, who they believed was a government informant.

As he walked through the gate at the Fort Lauderdale-Hollywood International Airport, Robert was thankful to have his feet back on the ground.

Two men in slacks and blazers discreetly approached him. "Mr. Borelli?"

Robert recognized one of the agents from when he first started cooperating with the government.

"I'm Agent Grover."

"Yeah, we've met before."

"Right. This is Agent Cruz."

After claiming his baggage, the agents escorted Robert to their car and drove him to a secure location, where he slept and ate during the entirety of his time in Florida.

The following day, Grover and Cruz picked up Robert and brought him to the same federal building he had visited years earlier, when he made the decision to become a federal witness. This time, he had no handcuffs. He went into the office of Assistant U.S. Attorney Lawrence La Vecchio, who stood from behind his desk.

After introducing himself and shaking Robert's hand, La Vecchio said, "We've got a lot of work to do, so let's get started." He sat down and opened a manila folder with a white label. "I've gone through your statements and read what you said about Mr. Trentacosta."

"Oh yeah? Well, what did I say?" Robert was half-joking.

"I can't tell you that. I can't coerce you to say something, even a reminder of what you said."

"Why not, if I already said it?"

"It could compromise our case. All I need you to do when you testify tomorrow is be completely honest. I'll ask you questions about Mr. Trentacosta, and you answer them. The defense attorney will get up and ask you questions too. You answer them truthfully. That's all."

Robert shrugged. "Okay. I have no problem with that."

"We appreciate your cooperation, Mr. Borelli. I know you're putting yourself out there by doing this, but we have a chance to see justice done for a woman who was brutally murdered."

"But I don't know anything about a murder Tony Pep committed."

"We know you don't, and we don't expect you to say anything like that. Again, honesty all the way down the line. Whenever I ask you a question, just answer me to the best of your knowledge."

~~~~~

The following morning, all eyes were on Robert as he was summoned into a full courtroom. He went through the gate and straight to the witness stand, where the bailiff had him place his hand on the Bible and lift his right hand.

"Do you swear to tell the truth, the whole truth and nothing but the truth, so help you God?"

A flash of what Robert said to Patricia the night before went through his head. He was nervous about his upcoming testimony, so they prayed together over the phone, asking God to give him the strength to not only be a witness for the government, but also be a witness for God.

"I do."

"State your name for the court."

"Robert Engel," he said, careful to use his old last name.

The bailiff gestured toward the witness stand.

Robert stepped in and sat down.

La Vecchio approached him. His line of questioning revolved around Robert's stay in Florida, when he was living with his mother and working for Nicky. At the time, Tony Pep was in charge of the Gambino family's operations in Florida. A meeting took place that Nicky, Robert, and Tony Pep attended. Robert testified that, during the meeting, Tony Pep referred to Fat Freddy as "being with him," meaning he was part of Tony Pep's crew. With this connection, the federal government tied Tony Pep to the murder of the dancer, even though it was Fat Freddy who gave the order for her execution.

"Thank you, Mr. Engel." La Vecchio turned toward the defense's table. "Your witness."

For the first time, Robert looked at Tony Pep. Fat Freddy was being tried simultaneously with his boss. Their expressions were tame and unthreatening, but Robert sensed the hatred they had for him. He was one of them at one time, and he knew the workings of a twisted mind as well as the next guy. There was no fear, although being in a courtroom was not his idea of a tranquil setting. Instead, he felt sorry for the men, even though he didn't have a personal connection to them as he did others. Like him, they were products of a delusion.

Trentacosta and Massaro's attorney approached Robert. "Mr. Engel, you've been in the Witness Protection Program for what? Two years now?"

"Yes, I have been cooperating with the government." He skated around the fact that he was no longer in the program.

"The U.S. Attorney's office promised to protect you while you were in the program. Is that right?"

"Yes, it is."

"They promised you a new identity, a new place to live, and living expenses. Is that also right, Mr. Engel?"

"Yes, it is."

"They promised you this expenses-paid new life in exchange for your testimony against certain individuals, right?"

"They helped me settle into a new place and get my life started. That's all."

"In exchange for your testimony against men you used to associate with."

Robert felt his heart pounding hard against his chest. "They asked me to testify, yes."

"And this isn't the first time you've testified against someone, is it?"

"Actually, it is."

"What happened on the last case where you were supposed to testify?"

"I believe they took a plea."

The case the attorney was talking about involved Nicky and Lenny, who were currently serving time in a federal penitentiary.

"So you really didn't have to do much of anything." The attorney turned to face the jury. "Basically, the government pays you to live a leisurely life, and all you have to do is *testify* for them."

Robert couldn't believe the attorney's audacity. *To insinuate that I would lie* ... "I told you, they don't pay me. And life in the Witness Protection Program ain't what it's made out to be. You're out there with no family, no friends. You live with a lot of uneasiness. You see a guy in the grocery store who looks out of place, and it makes you wonder if he was sent to whack you.

Sure, the government gives you a couple of bucks to get started, but after that you're on your own." Robert trembled. "So don't call it a leisurely life. And don't act like I'm gonna say anything just to get paid. That insults me. I've missed out on so much of my life. I haven't seen my daughter in years." A tear broke loose and trickled down his cheek. "I couldn't even go to my own mother's funeral."

Realizing his scheme to discredit Robert had backfired, the defense attorney returned to his table with no more questions.

~~~~~

Robert returned to San Antonio the next day.

Two weeks later, he learned that the jury found Tony Pep and Fat Freddy guilty of several charges, including racketeering and murder.

After several years, both men died in a federal prison while serving out their sentences.

FORTY-SIX

August 2002
Age 47

T hree months after the Trentacosta trial, Robert and Patricia relocated to Utah. The trial in Florida left Robert feeling that if he and Patricia were to stay in their apartment, their lives could be in jeopardy. His career in real estate also left him exposed, since much of the information about him and his new life was on the Internet. He had the information removed, essentially ending his career selling homes. He and Patricia stayed with one of the senior adults from their church, who knew of their circumstances and opened his home to them.

A week later, after the man's daughter found out about the situation, the man reluctantly asked Robert and Patricia to leave. They landed at the home of Pastor Phillip, where they stayed for three months until Robert's time under supervised release expired.

Bill came through for Robert on the financial end. He had a freeze-dried-goods business and needed a sales rep in Utah. He offered the position to Robert, who saw the opportunity as a way for them to get back on their feet, since he and Patricia had been out of work for three months.

In March 2002, Robert and Patricia moved to Park City.

All the while, Robert was dealing with a deep desire to be a pastor. The time he and Patricia spent ministering at the nursing home had kindled a fire to serve God, not only as a comforter to the elderly but also a leader. He expressed this desire to Bill, who talked with his friend Pat Robertson of *The 700 Club.*

"He told me to tell you," Bill said to Robert, "that even guys in the Mafia have a respect for the clergy. If you really want to be a pastor, you ought to apply at Christ For The Nations. They won't bother you there."

"I don't know about that," Robert said. "I lived with these guys for most of my life. Some of them are ruthless. Those kind don't care whether you're a pastor or a pimp. They'll gun you down just for the fun of it."

Still, Robert liked the idea of going back to school and getting an education based on theology. In May 2002, Bill made arrangements for Robert to visit the campus in Dallas, where they stayed at a hotel for a couple of days while checking out the school. When he returned to Utah, Robert filled out the application. Wanting to be up-front with them, he included the history of his past dealings with the Mafia and his relationship with the U.S. attorney's office as a witness. He sent it in the mail and waited for a reply.

Weeks went by with no response, so Robert took the initiative and called CFNI.

The Dean of Admissions said, "You have to understand, Mr. Borelli, that this is a situation we've never had to deal with. It's something we must earnestly pray about before we make a decision."

While waiting for the board's reply, Robert learned that selling dry foods in Utah was much different than selling stolen goods on the streets of New York. He had no connections, and since Y2K had come and gone without a food crisis, few were interested in what he was selling. He found out rather quickly that Mormons—the predominant part of the population—liked doing business with fellow Mormons. With that in mind, he tried to use a couple of Mormons as front men. Still, the business floundered.

In August 2002, the CFNI board's reply came in the mail.

"We feel that you would do well at our campus," Robert read from the letter to Patricia. "Our only concern is that if potential students and parents of students were to learn that a person with your situation were studying at our campus, it might deter them from attending. With this in mind, we accept your application to attend CFNI, but only under the condition that you are never to share your testimony concerning your past involvement with the Mafia or your current relationship as a witness for the U.S. Attorney."

"Yes!" Patricia wrapped her arms around Robert in a celebration hug. "I'll start packing now."

Robert laughed. "Don't you think there's a few more things we need to do before we pack? Like, find jobs?"

Patricia joined him in his laughter. "I say we just go."

"But what about jobs? We need to have jobs to pay for schooling, food—"

"I say we depend on God for the jobs."

Robert shrugged. "Okay. Let's do it."

~~~~~

Within a few months, Robert and Patricia were on the campus of Christ For The Nations. They were immediately able to move into an apartment complex, which once was a motor inn. The apartment had two rooms, and despite having to share it with a growing family of cockroaches, they were grateful for the place.

Patricia found a job with a shipping company.

Robert felt his exposure in real estate was too risky, so he finally landed a job valeting at a restaurant.

For the next three years, Robert concentrated on his education—the first two at CFNI, where he received his associates degree, and then Criswell College. While at CFNI, he reunited with the senior adults ministry on campus and eventually became its leader. He patterned the ministry after the one he headed in San Antonio, with not only a variety of social activities but also Sunday morning preaching.

The Evangelism teacher at CFNI, Scott Camp, asked Robert to join the staff at Fellowship of Joy, the local church he pastored. He needed someone to minister to the seniors of his congregation and the community. He felt Robert was the right man for the job. Pastor Scott also had ties to Go Tell Ministries, an evangelistic outreach that went into public schools and prisons. This gave Robert the opportunity to minister to at-risk kids—something Robert had wanted to do since he first gave his life to Christ when in prison.

After moving away from Dallas, he and Patricia started a home church, from which they ministered to two area nursing homes. They proceeded in much the same way as they had in the past, but Robert felt there was something more God wanted him to do. In his mind, seniors were no longer getting the respect, nor the honor, they had painstakingly earned.

In the fall of 2007, the first annual Senior Adults Appreciation Banquet was held to honor all the elderly, not only in the nursing homes but also in the entire community. It was held at a local park so the seniors could have a day away from the nursing home, enjoy the warm sun, and have the pleasure of watching the children at play.

Robert, Patricia, and the other volunteers were busy filling plates with barbeque brisket, potato salad, and baked beans—then shuttling them to the guests waiting at the decorated tables shaded by a large pavilion. For entertainment, three men from the church were playing guitars and singing in one of the corners of the pavilion.

Robert wrapped his arm around Patricia's waist. "How do you think it's going?"

"They seem pretty happy. The food is really good. Have you had any yet?"

"I grabbed a slice of the brisket." He pointed to a shuttle bus where volunteers were unloading more seniors. "Looks like we have more coming."

As volunteers pushed wheelchair-laden senior adults up to the pavilion, Robert noticed that the dress of one attendee was not properly covering her.

"It appears Ms. Lipinski needs a little help," he whispered to Patricia.

She saw what Robert was referring to and went to the woman's aid. Patricia tried to help by unhooking the dress from the wheelchair and pulling it down over her knees.

The woman looked in horror as Patricia said something to her, after which she slapped Patricia on the hand and scolded her.

By the time Patricia returned to Robert, she had a tear in her eye. "All I was trying to do was help her," she said, soothing her hand.

"What did she say to you?"

"She said my husband needs to quit looking up her skirt."

Both Robert and Patricia turned away so no one would see them laughing.

The first Senior Adult Appreciation Banquet was considered a success by the church and the nursing home staff, who were appreciative for the effort to make the day special for their residents.

As successful as Robert's ministry was going, there was still one area of his life that bothered him—the absence of a relationship with his daughter. Soon, Robert would witness God's amazing power to restore even the most hopeless of relationships.

FORTY-SEVEN

January 2010
Age 55

C ome on, you lousy bums!" Robert was intense as he watched the Arizona Cardinals and the Philadelphia Eagles face off in the NFC championship. It was the fourth quarter, and the Eagles had just scored on a sixty-five-yard pass from Donovan McNabb to DeSean Jackson, putting the Eagles in front by a score of 25 to 24.

"Robert, come in here," Patricia said from the study.

Robert looked toward Patricia, then at the TV. "I'm in the middle of a game here. Can't it wait?"

"No! Come now."

Robert paused the game, thankful for the technology that allowed him to watch later, and scurried to the study. "What was so important—"

"Look."

Patricia was sitting at the desk in front of their computer, which showed a window with the Facebook logo at the top. The profile picture was a teenage girl with long, dark hair and sunglasses. "It's your Briana, isn't it?"

Robert did his best to see the girl's name next to the photo. He felt the butterflies battling in his stomach. "Yeah, I think so."

"It has to be. She's got your old last name, and she's from New York."

"Yeah, that looks just like I remember her ... except older, of course."

"Do you want me to contact her?"

It had been thirteen years since that life-changing conversation with her while he was at Rikers Island—the conversation that began his transformation. After he went into the Witness Protection Program, he tried to talk with her, but Lauren was afraid he could jeopardize Briana's safety if the wrong people wanted to use her to get to him.

When Patricia asked him the question, Lauren's reasoning still lingered in the back of his mind. "Let's pray about it first. I don't want to cause any problems for her."

Six weeks later, Robert gave Patricia the go-ahead to establish contact with Briana. While he was still in the shower, Patricia burst in. "She sent you her phone number."

Robert felt his legs get weak. As he got out of the shower and dried off, he cried uncontrollably, reminiscent of the time when the three-year-old version of his daughter asked why he didn't come see her. It took several minutes to regain his composure. Finally, he went to the study and dialed the phone number.

"Hello?"

"Briana?" Robert's voice was shaking.

"Hi."

Sniffles, tears, and tissues filled the next hour as Robert explained his absence with as little detail as possible, intent on letting his daughter know that she was always on his heart and mind. The separation between Robert and Briana had been way too long. As the conversation progressed, Robert promised he would do whatever he could to visit her.

Robert hung up the phone and went back to the office, where Patricia was sitting in front of the computer. He remembered what God had told him at the end of her visit to San Antonio, just before she was about to return to New York: *You'll never find anyone who will love you the way she loves you.* Over the years, Patricia had proven the prophetic words, leaving behind her family in New York, working side-by-side in ministry, which included cooking many Italian meals, and bouncing from place to place.

Now, the initiative she took to reconnect Robert to his estranged daughter was one more sign of her strong love for him.

He placed his hands on her shoulders and planted a gentle kiss on the top of her head.

She turned and faced him. "How'd it go?"

"It went well. I'm gonna try and hook up with her."

Patricia smiled. "Good."

Robert knelt next to her. "Thank you."

Patricia caressed his face. "You're welcome. I love you."

Robert's eyes watered. "I know. And I love you too."

~~~~~

An ever-present danger existed for both Robert and Briana if he resurfaced in New York. So he contacted his FBI liaison and told him the situation. He was given permission to visit, but only under certain conditions.

Two months later, Robert landed at LaGuardia Airport amid the wintry cold and went to a hotel restaurant in Long Island, where he had arranged to meet Briana. He arrived fifteen minutes early and secured a table but was too nervous to sit. The anxiousness of not knowing how he would be received made his stomach unsettled.

Even though the two of them had talked over the phone, and conversations were at least amicable, he was still plagued by the guilt stemming from his absence in her life, which generated feelings of unworthiness. Instead of waiting at the table, he stood near the front door, hoping to glimpse familiar faces through the glass panes. Within minutes, Lauren, her sister Linda, Briana, and another girl who appeared to be about the same age were walking up to the restaurant, wrapped in coats to fight off the windy chill.

Robert opened the door for them, which was a struggle as if it were a sail caught in a gale. All four made it inside before Robert let the door slam shut. "Wow!" he said as he greeted Lauren and Linda with hugs. "Feels like a hurricane blew in." He looked down at his daughter, whose eyes were flittering from one place to another, never settling on him. "Briana," he said, trying his best to maintain his composure while understanding the discomfort she was experiencing by being in his presence.

"Hi." She stepped up and hugged him.

A sense of warmth rushed through him, gently sweeping away the butterflies in his stomach.

"This is Rachel. She's my best friend."

Robert shook Rachel's hand. "Nice to meet you, Rachel. Any friend of Briana's is a friend of mine." He directed them to his table, where he helped them with their coats.

Initially, the conversation went from Briana's performance in school to memories of when she was a little girl to Robert's explanation of where he had been the last thirteen years of her life. As he explained, Robert felt the awkwardness grow between him and his daughter. Eventually, the conversation was split.

The adults talked about old times and friends while the teen girls ventured into a private discussion.

The entire meeting and dinner lasted three hours.

After bundling up in their coats, scarves and gloves, Briana and her entourage said their goodbyes. As she hugged Robert, his heart once again warmed from the contact, and he didn't want to let go.

He sensed the uneasiness and released her, holding her at arm's length. "You get those grades up, you hear me?" he said sternly, trying to hold back his tears.

Briana turned her eyes to the side with a smile. "Okay."

"Good." He kissed her on top of the head and gently urged her to catch up with her mother and the others, who had already gathered outside.

As the door blew shut behind him, he watched Briana through the window as they walked away, imagining what it would have been like if he had steered clear of the drugs that tore him away. Without a doubt, God had used the government to save his life through the Witness Protection Program. The meeting with his nephew while incarcerated in Florida was proof enough that he was a dead man, just for considering the idea of becoming a government witness. Silently, he thanked God for this moment.

He now had a good anchor point for his relationship with Briana. It would take time to win her trust. But it would be well worth the difficulties he would encounter with her, knowing he didn't deserve the second chance she was giving him.

After seeing Briana, Lauren, Linda, and Rachel get in their car, he turned back to his table to retrieve his coat. He sucked in a short breath when he saw two men standing directly behind him. The younger one was tall, dark, and lean, wearing black slacks under a black wool overcoat. His dark eyes roamed throughout the restaurant from left to right.

The other man, husky and with salt-and-pepper hair, had his eyes trained on Robert. He wore an overcoat as well, a gray twill that matched his hair color. Across his left arm was Robert's coat. "You'll need this." He handed Robert the coat. "A little jumpy?"

"A little?" Robert took the coat and worked his arms into the sleeves. "Wouldn't you be if you were me?"

The man didn't answer but motioned with his head. "Follow me."

The younger man right behind them, Robert followed him through the restaurant and hotel, his eyes still probing the area the entire way. They went through a gauntlet of staff as they eased through the kitchen and out the back door. As they headed for the employee parking area, a familiar car approached from his right. Lauren with the rest of the girls were headed for the exit, looking surprised, not from seeing him but that he had company. Except for a small smile, he made no effort to acknowledge them. He and the men waited for them to drive by.

The older man grabbed Robert's arm. "Let's go."

They continued the trek to the back of the parking lot, where the older man opened the rear passenger door to a blue sedan and motioned for Robert to get in. The man then took the front passenger seat.

The younger man went around to the other side. As he opened the driver's door, Robert saw the holstered gun hidden by the overcoat. They sped out of the parking lot and onto the street that ran in front of the hotel.

Robert turned to look through the back window, then turned to the men. "You know, there was a time when I wouldn't have been comfortable sitting in the back seat, taking a ride."

The older man laughed. "I can only imagine."

"Where are we headed?"

"Back to your hotel."

By New York standards, the traffic was light, and they soon arrived at the hotel. Both men got out, and Robert followed them to the elevators and to his room. The younger man entered first. Robert watched from the hallway as he searched the room. "It's clear."

The older man said, "You'll need to be packed and ready to leave in the morning. We'll pick you up at 6:30. Until then, stay in your room. Keep the door bolted. Don't answer to nobody except me."

"Okay." Robert walked the two men to the door. "Hey, Terry. Thanks … for making this happen."

Terry smiled. "That's what I'm here for." He started to walk away but then turned around. "By the way, how did it go?"

"Good. It's a start."

"Great." Terry moved quickly to catch up with the other man, who was holding the elevator door.

~~~~~

Boarding the plane the next morning was uneventful. Robert was grateful. After finishing a conversation with Patricia over the phone, updating her on the evening's turnout, he found sleep evasive. Memories and thoughts of how his decisions affected Briana bombarded him relentlessly. He finally forced himself out of the warmth of the covers and onto his knees next to the bed, where he prayed for his daughter and her healing. When his burden appropriately passed, he climbed back under the sheets and drifted off to sleep. He was pleased the next morning when Terry arrived with a large cup of coffee, already creamed, and a bagel, which he ate on the way to the airport.

Settled into a window seat, he felt at peace as the airplane ascended, destined for his adopted homeland. As the plane banked left, he peered outside at the Statue of Liberty. After the attack on New York, public access inside the statue was discontinued from 2001 to 2009. Now, people milled around its base like a bunch of ants.

In all the years Robert lived in New York, he never visited Liberty Island or its famous statue, nor did he ever care to. The old Robert was disconnected from anything that had no immediate bearing on him, and something like Lady Liberty, the World Trade Center, or any of the other famous landmarks of his home state were simply tourist attractions that brought in annoying outsiders.

Now, the new Robert had a different perspective. This was especially so for the statue as he flew high above her, barely able to make out the chains and shackles at Lady Liberty's feet—one of the few things he remembered from school at Our Lady of Lourdes. They once were his chains, binding him to his addictions, but not anymore. As with Lady Liberty, his shackles lay at his feet, broken loose the day he accepted that Jesus alone could fill the void in his life. He looked to the apex of the statue—its torch—and remembered the light that appeared to him through his daughter as she cried out for a daddy who never came to see her. That light broke through the shroud of corrupt power and evil wealth that was a delusion meant to distract him from what is most important in life.

As the airplane rose into the clouds, a tired but relaxed Robert continued to stare out the window, unable to take his eyes off the shrinking monument. In the midst of the chaos and turmoil of testimonies and trials, of clandestine meetings, of moving from one place to another, he was at peace with himself, knowing he had made the right decision to become a witness—not just for the government, but more importantly for the Savior who orchestrated his freedom. As the clouds thickened, his eyes became heavy, and the Statue of Liberty disappeared from sight.

~~~~~

Thank you so much for reading *The Witness*. If you enjoyed it, would you please take a moment to leave a review at your favorite online book retailer? Your support is greatly appreciated.

Robert

The Witness as a Novel

For three years, Robert and I spent hundreds of hours poring over his story, viewing it from many different angles—reevaluating, and rewriting. It has been quite a challenge for Robert, who had to trudge back to a time and place he had left so many years ago. With a new perspective on life, he found that many of his actions that once were badges of pride were now needles of shame.

Throughout the project, Robert emphasized the importance of revealing the power of God's ability to restore, more so than the sensationalism of his crimes. In fact, when talking about his crimes, he never had an air of braggadocio and often used a disconnected tone and words, evidence of remorse associated with his past life. Yet telling his story was what God wanted him to do, and because of this, God saw to it that Robert had the mental and emotional strength to persist.

For the most part, every event mentioned in this book actually took place. As they are revealed, it will become apparent that adding elements of sensationalism for the sake of beefing up the story was not needed. As the saying goes, "Life is stranger than fiction." However, we write Robert's story as a true-to-life novel for several reasons:

- Verbatim conversations from decades past and exact locations and times are sometimes impossible to replicate or remember.
- We didn't want Robert's story to be a grocery list of events in his life.
- Some people involved in Robert's story did not want their names used. Out of respect for this request, some names were changed.
- There were many people who played a part in Robert's life. We wanted to include them without cluttering the story stream with too many characters. So on more than one

occasion, I combined two or more real persons into one character.

Because of these additions and changes, we found it was appropriate to label the story a true-to-life novel rather than a memoir.

No matter the format through which the story is presented, our desire is that you, the reader, see that God has no limit to His grace, and that the same grace extended to Robert is available to all of us, no matter how little or great our grievances.

Scott

ACKNOWLEDGEMENTS

From Robert:

With a sincere heart, I want to thank the following:

- My mother, who I wish could've read this story. She never gave up and continued praying for me, even when she couldn't see any results.
- My daughter, Briana, who is such a big part of this story and why I wrote it.
- Evers Road Christian Church for loving and adopting me as one of their family at a time when I was missing my family.
- Scott and his lovely wife, Stacey, for putting up with my New York attitude over the last three and a half years, for their hard work, diligence, and extreme love for the Lord. Without them, this book would never have been possible.
- My great friends, Kelly and Toni. "Youse guys" have been a backbone of support for many years, not only for me but the ministry as well.
- My beautiful wife, Patricia, who God gave to me. You had to make so many sacrifices when we married, and you never stopped encouraging me to share my story with others. Thank you, Patty Ann, for staying with me and never giving up when times got really tough for us.

There are so many other people who have played such a big part of my life in writing this book, but I would have to write another book in order to thank them all.

From Scott:

- To my beautiful, tenacious wife, Stace. Over and over again, you've proven that you are "all in." Thank you for your sacrifice, encouragement, and staying power. Above all, thank you for putting God first in your life and letting me do the same. I love you so much.
- To my mother, Dolores. No one could have asked for a better mother than you. Your considerate heart has taught me the importance of compassion and the need to sometimes bite my tongue. Thank you for being the example of Jesus that you are.
- To Robert and Patricia. Many thanks for opening your home to us and introducing us to real Italian food. Most importantly, thank you for being a ray of God's light in a hope-deprived world.

We both would like to thank:

- Pastor Stan. If it weren't for you acting on a thought, we would not have been brought together for this project.
- Nancy, Julie, and the rest of the crew at Lovell-Fairchild Communications. Your input has been invaluable, and we greatly appreciate it.

May God bless every one of you in ways that extend beyond anything our minds can fathom.

Above all, we thank our Lord and Savior Jesus Christ for bringing His light into a world full of darkness, giving us hope when everything seemed so hopeless, and comforting us when we felt all alone. Without Him, there would be no story.

m o b s t e r - t u r n e d - m i n i s t e r

ROBERT BORELLI

| Rescue | Redeem | Restore |

Here's what others are saying about Robert:

Robert is a trophy of God's grace...His testimony of God's transforming power will thrill the hearts of your people and draw the lost to Christ. I urge you to use him; the Spirit certainly is!

— Dr. Scott Camp
President
Scott Camp Ministries

An anointed, God-inspired story...[Robert's] testimony transcends cultural, racial and denominational differences. Call him. Book him. He will bless you and your people.

— David Fogarty
Pastor

For information on booking Robert for your next event,
visit his website at

www.robertborelli.com

Made in the USA
Middletown, DE
18 June 2023

32309343R00163